Postal carrier and amateur surfer, Samantha Diaz, lives an uncomplicated life. Well, other than helping her sister with childcare, crushing on her unavailable customer, Lauren Brennan, and catching as many waves as possible before hurricane season begins. Suffice to say, she isn't looking for much more, but when Lauren invites her to a monthly game night at her house, Sam happily agrees.

When Sam sets out on an early morning surf, the last thing she expects to do is die, but a sudden thunderstorm thrashes offshore, creating a riptide that steals Sam's life. She awakens to a snarky woman named Margo speaking cryptic nonsense. Not only does she claim to be one of the many Grim Reapers, or Grims, in the world, Margo makes Sam an offer: she'll bring Sam back from the dead, as long as she becomes Margo's temporary assistant. Sam accepts but soon realizes the deal was too good to be true, and the consequences she faces may be worse than the death she dodged.

THE GRIM ASSISTANT

Tales from the Grim, Book One

Jodi Hutchins

A NineStar Press Publication

Published by NineStar Press
P.O. Box 91792,
Albuquerque, New Mexico, 87199 USA.
www.ninestarpress.com

The Grim Assistant

Printed in the USA
First Edition
August, 2019

Print ISBN: 978-1-951057-19-0

Also available in eBook, ISBN: 978-1-951057-18-3

Warning: This book contains sexually explicit content, which may only be suitable for mature readers, references to death and dying, mentions of cancer and other terminal illnesses, cheating, drowning, PTSD, and bullying.

To Grandma (8/1/51—6/11/19), who always encouraged my hunger for a good book.

Chapter One

THE PLANKS OF the boardwalk were hot against Samantha Diaz's feet as she bounded up the stairs, surfboard tucked beneath her arm, water trickling over her shoulders. The calm waters and equally serene beach left her with only the early morning anglers standing out at the ocean's edge, casting their lines along the jetty.

"Same time on Friday?" her best friend, Josh Keller, asked as he ambled up the stairs after her, his bushy blond hair stuck to his face and neck. A trill from a bicycle bell filled the air, coalescing with the call of a flock of seagulls harassing a group of teens munching on breakfast. The oily aroma of freshly fried doughnuts mixed with the scent of crisp saltwater as Sam took a deep breath.

She smiled broadly. "Absolutely." Beads of seawater dripped down her dark brows, and she swept her hand across her forehead in a feeble attempt to dry it. The pair crossed the boardwalk, heading down the long ramp to the parking lot.

Reaching her Jeep, Sam tossed her board in the back and grabbed a towel, drying her face and ruffling her unruly crop of black hair. People flooded the tall staircase, beach tags fastened to their large bags overflowing with colorful shovels and towels. She grabbed a dry shirt, pulling it over her head to cover her bikini top before putting her wallet in the damp pocket of her board shorts. Josh stood staring at her. "Damn, what I would do to get a tan like yours," he mumbled sheepishly.

Sam chuckled, noting the red tinge forming along his pale, freckled shoulders, and then glanced at her own tanned skin. "I don't know, man, I'll always be jealous of your freckles," she joked, elbowing him in the arm. "You want to grab some breakfast?"

"Sure, why not?"

Sam and Josh followed the influx of people. She was determined she would get herself a fresh bagel before heading home for a shower and babysitting her nephew. Cyclists pedaled down the bicycle lane on the wood, and early morning joggers were swiftly being replaced by excited children heading to the beach or the waterpark. The tiny hole-in-the-wall bagel shop Sam frequented was set back beside one of two amusement parks on the boardwalk, and she stepped into the short line. Depending on what time she had to be in to work, Sam's summer mornings always started the same if Josh was available. She didn't surf without him by her side unless there were lifeguards present. The last thing she wanted was to get caught in a riptide and end up miles offshore.

The two moved into the queue of people, and Josh turned to her. "How's it going with Katie?"

Sam's stomach sank at the mention of her older sister, and she shrugged. "I don't know. The divorce is official, but now it's all parenting plan crap and custody issues. She's stressed out."

Josh gave her a sympathetic grimace, causing her to wonder if he regretted asking her the question. "Yikes."

"Yeah. They had a meeting with her ex's lawyer, and I don't know how it went yet."

"Hey, Sam," a voice called from behind her. Sam whipped around as her friend, Lauren Brennan, stepped into the line where Sam was already standing in wait. Lauren's long chestnut hair hung over her shoulders, her wide smile reaching her vibrant green eyes.

"Lauren." Sam's tone came out a lot more breathless than she intended. Josh must've noted the change in her demeanor, so he nudged her in the back with his elbow.

"They have the best pork roll egg and cheese sandwiches," Lauren said, curling her lips upward, a delicate dimple surfacing as she smiled.

Sam nearly sighed with longing, her heart rate quickening, and she swallowed back her feelings. The blue sundress Lauren wore hugged her body, the color accentuating her lovely summer tan. *She's off limits.*

"They sure do. Order anything good lately?" Sam agreed.

Nodding enthusiastically, Lauren said, "Actually, I did! I ordered this new lesson kit online and a few other things for the classroom." Sam had been delivering Lauren's mail since the science teacher moved to Ocean City from New Brunswick two years prior. "And a few new books. Speaking of books, how'd you like the one you borrowed?"

"I absolutely loved it. Is it just me or is my taste in books rubbing off on you?" Sam said. Josh sighed indignantly. Sam held in a retort while she waited for Lauren to reply. Lauren blushed, and the sight had Sam nearly swooning. "I have to say your taste has rubbed off on me. My true love will always be gritty literary fiction, but you've got me hooked on those dark fantasies now."

"Hey, I forgot about that thing I have to do," Josh interjected. When Sam gave him a puzzled smile, he continued, "You know, the thing? I'll see you Friday."

"Oh, all right. Aren't you going to get breakfast?" Sam asked. He shook his head and waggled his eyebrows, head jerking toward Lauren. His gesture wasn't as discreet as Sam preferred, but she didn't believe Lauren noticed. She knew he was leaving because of her interaction with Lauren. Before she could say more, Josh moved out of the line and hurried toward the ramp leading to the sidewalk.

She moved forward in line, ordering her food and stepping aside while Lauren ordered hers. While they waited, Sam leaned against the railing. "I've got a new one I know you'd love," she said.

"A dark fantasy? You'd better bring it by the next time you work. I ordered a bunch of stuff, so I should be seeing you sometime next week," Lauren added, pulling her purse strap over her shoulder.

"Okay, I will. Maybe Boo will let me pet her this time," Sam chuckled, referring to Lauren's skittish cat. In the last two years, the cat only let Sam touch her four or five times.

"Don't take it personally because she doesn't even let Bethany pet her." Yep, there was the pesky reminder of her unavailability. Sam laughed regardless of her feelings toward Lauren's girlfriend. It wasn't as though she didn't like her for the sole reason of being with Lauren; Bethany and Sam had known each other in high school and the memories were anything but fond.

"Boo's such a cutie. Maybe I'll start bringing some cat treats again," Sam offered. The young man behind the counter caught Sam's attention and handed her the pork roll she ordered. "Thanks." She grinned at Lauren, continuing their conversation. "That's how I got Boo to let me close at first."

"School starts on Wednesday, but you should come by one night and have a drink with us, maybe play some cards. I always try to plan a game night once a month, especially when school is back in session." Lauren took her food from the man, then faced Sam as they moved out of the way of other customers.

"I'd love to," Sam said honestly. Sam enjoyed Lauren's friendship, despite having to tolerate Bethany in small doses. She and Bethany may have had their differences, but they were adults now.

"What about, say, next Saturday night? I'm heading to Newark this weekend for a family barbeque, but I'll be home Tuesday."

"Yeah, sounds perfect."

They stood staring at each other for longer than etiquette warranted, triggering Sam to wonder if Lauren felt the same attraction as she did. She hastily dispelled the fleeting thought and smiled. *She's simply a friend and can't be more.* "Well, I'll let you get on with your day. I've got babysitting duty with my nephew, anyway."

"I'll see you later this week, I'm sure. Don't forget the book," Lauren said. She turned, heading down the boardwalk. Lauren left, the sway of her hips causing her skirt to swish back and forth with each step, and once Lauren disappeared in the flowing crowd, Sam headed to her Jeep.

The drive back to her house was quick and she was fortunate she missed the tourist traffic. Although Ocean City, New Jersey, was a busy tourist spot during the summer, Sam couldn't see herself living anywhere else. The tiny seaside town was home to her and her sister, the beach and the community far too important to leave behind and live in a larger city.

She parked her car on the side of the road, finding a spot relatively close to her sister's little condo, and she ambled up the stairs, leaving her surfboard in the back of her Jeep. The steps leading to the porch creaked beneath her feet, the white paint peeling off the railing and the stucco face of the home. The three-bedroom condo was large enough for her sister and nephew to live in comfortably. Sam had been staying with Katie for a few weeks at a time to help with her nephew and to covertly keep an eye out for her sister's mental health. The divorce was taking its toll on Katie, but Sam knew her sister would never ask for help.

"I'm glad you're here. I've got to run and get gas before I head over to work," Katie said as she bustled around the living room, grabbing a laundry basket full of clothing from the couch and tossing it on the kitchen counter. Already clad in blue scrubs, her black hair pulled back in a tight ponytail, Sam figured Katie must've been anxiously waiting for her to get there.

"Sorry. I stopped to grab some breakfast. Is the little man awake yet?"

Without glancing up from her task, Katie shook her head. Sam stopped, placing her keys on the island in the kitchen leading off the living room, and she really took in her sister's appearance: red-rimmed eyes, wrinkled scrubs, head lowered.

"Katie." Her sister finally met her gaze. "How'd the hearing go yesterday?"

Katie drew a breath and straightened. "Like crap. I don't think we're ever going to work out a parenting plan."

"He didn't agree to your terms?"

Katie scoffed, and her shoulders visibly slumped. "No. His lawyer told us he wanted more time on different days. Evidently, his schedule doesn't work with what I offered," she said, shaking her head and touching her fingers to her forehead. "At this rate, it's going to go on into the new year."

"He's lucky you don't fight for full custody, the fucking asshat." Sam loathed her ex-brother-in-law for how he treated his sister and wasn't shy about speaking her feelings toward him now the divorce was official.

Her sister shot her a reproachful glance before she headed to the refrigerator. Katie's voice was low when she said, "Just because he and I didn't work out doesn't mean he's a bad father. Ben has every right to know him and I don't want to take his father away from him because John was unfaithful." She threw a yogurt into her purse along with a package of granola before grabbing her keys from the counter. "I'll see you tonight," she said as she stepped out the front door.

Sam lounged on the couch, kicking her feet up on the coffee table as she closed her eyes. Her muscles were sore from surfing, and all she wanted was to rest her head before her nephew woke.

"Auntie Sam, Mama gone?" a little voice cut off her thoughts. Her five-year-old nephew came wandering down the hall, his little stuffed animal pig tucked under his arm, his free hand rubbing his face.

"Yeah, Mama had to go off to work. Do you want some breakfast?" Sam asked.

Ben eagerly bobbed his head.

LAUREN BRENNAN FIDDLED with the wrapper around a soy sauce bottle in her hands, grumbling when the plastic wouldn't budge. "Here, let me help," Bethany said, taking the container from her and removing the cap with ease.

"You did that way too easily," Lauren remarked, turning away from her girlfriend as she poured the contents into a measuring cup. "My grandma wants us to bring those little chocolate wafers, so we can make the cake you brought last time we went together."

"I forgot to tell you I won't be able to make this weekend," Bethany said.

She whipped around. "What do you mean? I already told them you were coming." She scrunched her eyebrows as she shook the sauté pan, garlic-scented steam wafting into her face as she peered at Bethany. Bethany shrugged, a sheepish smile on her lips.

"I'm sorry, babe. I promised James I'd get the research for this case done over the weekend."

For the second time in a row, Bethany was backing out of a planned visit to Lauren's grandparents' house. "But you said the same thing last time."

Bethany rose from her perch at the small kitchen table, her blue eyes glimmering in the bright lights of the kitchen as she crossed the room. The closer she got to Lauren, the broader her smile became, and the more her blonde locks dangled into her face. "I swear I'll make it up to you," she said, placing a palm on the counter as she sidled up beside Lauren. The aroma of her cologne swirled around Lauren. As charming and beautiful as she found her girlfriend, Lauren was seeing a pattern, one which started two months before.

"You can't take a little time off?"

Bethany sighed as she retreated from the counter, easing herself into a barstool at the high end of the island. "I wouldn't be very good company if I did because I'd still be working the whole weekend." Since Lauren had told Bethany she loved her during a weekend getaway two months prior, her avoidance was becoming the new normal for their relationship. The silent response Lauren received the evening she spoke those three words hung over them like a dense fog, periodically stoking Lauren's insecurities. The situation was exacerbated further by her grandmother's insistence on asking Bethany an inventory of questions each time they visited her.

Lauren gently stirred the contents of the pan then turned with purpose, knitting her brows in concern. "I know my grandparents can be a little overbearing and I'm sorry."

"Lauren, don't apologize," Bethany began, shaking her head. "I have to prove myself to James, and that's all this is about. If it weren't for trying to squirm my way up the ladder, I wouldn't have to stay behind."

"Okay. I know you're trying to get in his good graces, but he seems like he's pushing you a lot lately."

Bethany chuckled. "Well, of course, he is. He's trying to see how far he can push me until I crack, but I'm not going to." As if on cue, Bethany's business phone began to ring, the noise cutting into their conversation as it did frequently. Bethany glanced at the phone in her hand, grimacing. "Why don't you take Jackie with you? I'm sure she'd be better company than me, anyway." Bethany's work phone continued to ring.

"She's got her monthly art class she does for free in Philly this weekend, or I would," Lauren exsplained. Her best friend would join her if she'd asked, but Lauren wanted Bethany to go with her. She wanted to feel the semblance of the normalcy they had before the night things shifted dramatically when a swift disconnect insinuated itself between them.

"I've got to take this. I won't be long," Bethany said as she answered the call. She rushed through the kitchen to the back door, her voice raising an octave as she began in what sounded like a heated argument.

Lauren sighed, turning away from where she could see Bethany's form. The soft drone of Bethany's voice drifted in from the backyard through the open window facing the alleyway. A buzzing across the dining room table caught Lauren's attention. She peered over the kitchen counter and her cell phone glowed from beneath a sheet of paper. Lauren crossed the room and grabbed it, swiping her finger over the screen to open the device. When a keypad opened for Lauren to put a password in, she realized with horror the device wasn't her phone but Bethany's. On the lock screen, a confusing text appeared.

We're still on for this weekend, right? I can't wait to see you again.

A kissing face sat beside the words on the screen.

Lauren chewed her lip and reread the text message once again before the screen dimmed. Bethany reentered the kitchen from outside, causing Lauren to put the phone back where it was. Lauren's heart pounded in her chest as Bethany came in, sighing and tossing her work phone on the table. "Everything okay?" Lauren ventured, trying to reign in her anxiety with a smile. What did the text message mean, and who was Mistie?

Bethany shrugged. "Yes, and no. I'm sorry but I have to run to the office." She sifted through the papers on the table, gathering them into a pile before grabbing her personal cell phone where Lauren stuck it.

"Right now?" Lauren asked incredulously. Bethany nodded, gathering her bag along with her cell phone from the table.

"I'm sorry."

Lauren touched Bethany's shoulder. "It's okay, I understand."

Bethany leaned forward and kissed Lauren softly on her lips. "I probably won't be home until late," she whispered.

"Okay."

All alone, Lauren dished herself some of the stir-fry she had cooked for them and sank onto the couch. Her thoughts went to the text message. Lauren had gone into the relationship with Bethany knowing full well she didn't intend to partake in commitment. However, the closer they became, the stronger Lauren's aversion to sharing became. After six months of dating, they became exclusive, with Lauren finally disclosing her painful past and subsequent trust issues. They were reaching their year and a half mark, and Lauren trusted her.

Lauren placed the plate of food on the coffee table, barren of any appetite as she recalled the text message. Was Mistie another lawyer, or was she something else entirely? Lauren didn't want to fathom Bethany cheating on her after knowing Lauren's history. *There's no way she'd cheat on me. Mistie is probably a coworker.* But if this woman was another lawyer, why hadn't she contacted Bethany through her business phone rather than her personal one? Lauren crossed the room, located her phone on the table where she'd left it, and sent her best friend a text message.

I just made some stir-fry. Want to come over?

Hell, yeah, was the swift reply.

Twenty minutes later, Lauren's best friend and colleague, Jackie Hayes, walked through the front door without knocking. "Holy crap, dinner smells good," she said as she strolled into the kitchen. She immediately snagged a bowl from the cabinet without looking at Lauren. Her long black dreadlocks were tugged together in a hair tie, the strands running down her back, cascading over her shoulders.

"Nice to see you, too, Jackie." Lauren laughed as she stood to reheat her food. Her friend turned with a large grin, and Lauren noted with amusement that splotches of paint were scattered over Jackie's loose-fitting T-shirt.

"Excited for school to start?" Jackie leaned her hip against the counter before digging into her bowl.

Lauren placed her plate in the microwave and pressed the start button before replying, "I *am*, actually. I hope the kids haven't lost much knowledge over the summer from too much junk food and television."

Nodding in agreement, Jackie shoveled more food in her mouth. After finishing her bite, she said, "Well, I for one always love the start of a fresh year. The first day makes me feel so invigorated and ready to get things done. Some of the kids are easier, but you can't win them all."

They chatted about school for a few minutes, both finishing their food before moving to the living room, where they sat on opposite couches. Jackie peered around. "Where's Bethany?"

"At the office," Lauren said without making eye contact.

"Hm, I swear she doesn't stop working for anything. I thought she'd lighten up a bit after she moved in, but I bet even if the zombie apocalypse hit us, she'd be too busy working on a case to notice."

"Yeah." Lauren had the same notion when Bethany first moved in four months prior, but if anything, she worked more after the move, as she was much closer to her office. Bethany's old condo was located on the mainland, which made for a fifty-minute commute, and when her lease came to an end, Lauren invited her to move in.

Lauren lifted the remote control, flipping through channels as she debated with herself about the text message. Though she held strong trust in her friend's judgment, Lauren didn't want to make it seem a bigger deal than it was. On the same level, she also didn't want her friend confirming her suspicions, Jackie having helped pick up the pieces after her last abysmal breakup.

"How're things going between you two?" Jackie asked after a bout of silence. A few months before, Lauren had been hesitant whether to tell Jackie about the night she professed her love to Bethany. The evening had been embarrassing, and the rejection nearly kept her from disclosing the incident to her best friend. At first, Jackie neglected to shield her irritation with Bethany, however, she convinced Lauren the lack of a response didn't mark the end of their relationship. *Maybe you scared her*, Jackie had suggested.

Lauren tensed. "Things could be better."

Jackie sat forward. "Okay, what's up with you?"

"Nothing," Lauren lied. Jackie pursed her lips, lifting a dark eyebrow almost to her hairline. "I guess you could say I came across something that made me a little uncomfortable, and I don't know if I should be worried about it or not."

"Keep going."

"You know how Bethany and I have similar phones?" When Jackie nodded, Lauren continued. "Hers vibrated with a text, and I thought it was mine. When I picked it up, I happened to see a text message from someone named Mistie."

Jackie held up her hand, halting Lauren's words. "Hold on, you looked at Bethany's phone behind her back? I know I don't date, so I really can't be handing out relationship advice, and I know you have trust issues, but you shouldn't have looked at her phone."

"I didn't look at her phone to pry, I thought it was mine. Anyway, the text said something along the lines of 'I can't wait to see you again' and making sure they were still on for this weekend with a little kissy face emoji. The thing is, Bethany bailed out on going with me to Newark for the weekend. She claims it's because of work." Her cheeks burned.

"Oh." For the first time in their six-year friendship, Jackie was speechless. Lauren waited for her to speak but the silence stretched on, her discomfort expanding. Jackie avoided her stare, apprehension clear on her face as she fingered the gem on her necklace, the purple stone glimmering in the sunlight filtering in through the window. Amethyst, Jackie called the crystal. To Lauren, the object was just a pretty rock but to Jackie, the piece of jewelry was an appendage. Her best friend's faith in the otherworldly had never bothered her, though she wondered what she received from her beliefs. Would having faith in something help Lauren through her dismal bout of relationship busts?

"Say something," Lauren pleaded. Jackie glanced at the television. "Jackie?"

Jackie sighed, turning back to Lauren. "I don't know what to say. Did you ask her about the text?"

"No, I didn't really get a chance because she had to leave for the office. Please tell me I'm making a big deal over nothing."

Jackie's obsidian gaze peered up at the ceiling, and she pursed her lips, the actions sparking more doubt within Lauren. "You two live together now, and you need to talk, and I mean really talk. It's been two months since your trip to Cape May, and you two still haven't discussed what happened; am I right?"

Lauren nodded.

"This is a problem. You expressed your feelings, and she said nothing, not even a simple rejection. Anything is better than silence, Lauren. As for the text, for your sanity, you need to ask her."

Lauren shifted uncomfortably, wishing she hadn't accidentally picked up Bethany's phone in the first place.

Chapter Two

THE STREET WAS busier than usual, even for a Friday, and Sam was having trouble navigating her path. When another car let her merge, she pulled her little mail truck out into the crowded one-way street. On top of the traffic coming to a standstill, the weather was hot—far hotter than it should've been for September. Sam turned up the air conditioner, the mail in the plastic baskets fluttering in the breeze coming from the vents on the dashboard. It didn't give her much relief, but it was better than sitting in the stifling heat while she waited for the light to turn green.

The mail in her possession was dwindling, signaling the end of her day, but it was the Friday before Labor Day. The roads were packed with vehicles, tourists from Philadelphia, New York, and Delaware. Traffic crawled a few feet and she groaned, laying her forehead on the steering wheel. As she made it to the stoplight, the signal turned red. She would've rather stayed at the beach with Josh that morning after their surf session than trudge off to work, but, unfortunately, she couldn't live off the waves.

She stole a glance at her phone, seeing a flash as she received a text message. *Stuck at work. Can you pick Ben up from sitter?*

"Well, crap," she muttered aloud. She was already late running her route, and she still had two streets to do before she could head back to the post office and get her car. She replied, *I'm running late, but I can once I'm done.*

Her sister didn't need to worry while she was at work. Sam would ensure she got there even if she had to leave work early.

Sam tapped her fingers on the steering wheel as she pulled her mail truck forward, cursing the Labor Day traffic. Tourists bombarded the tiny coastal town during the summer months, and Sam was just getting excited for the cool fall weather and the scant traffic of autumn. Labor Day happened to be blessed with an unusual heat wave, much to the dismay of Sam and other Ocean City residents. The pleasant weather ushered in countless tourists. It was the last hoorah for the local economy, and she understood this, but it didn't mean she had to like it, especially when somebody cut her off for the sixth time.

She withheld from punching the horn as she slammed on her brakes, a little Prius with New York plates sliding right in front of her. "Could we keep moving?" she gritted through her teeth in a hushed tone. Finally, the traffic abated, and she continued her course. The last neighborhood on her route came into view and she pulled up to the first house, parking her little truck as she located the box she had to deliver. Neatly trimmed rhododendron bushes flanked the little bungalow, the grass cut away from the pebbled walkway leading to the porch. Her favorite customer.

The first time she saw Lauren two years before, her breath had literally caught in her chest. Lauren had just moved to the city, taking a position at the local high school as a science teacher. She was gorgeous, her wavy brown hair a light mahogany in the summer sun and her emerald gaze catching Sam's. Alas, before Sam made a move,

Lauren started a relationship with someone. Not just any someone, but the girl who endlessly taunted Sam during high school.

Nerves fluttered alive within Sam's gut as she made her way up the slanted pathway to Lauren's porch, her anticipation to see her friend irritatingly potent.

Sam held in a groan when Bethany Walters answered the door in lieu of Lauren. "Hey, Sam, what can I do for you?" Bethany stood much taller than Sam's five foot five, her short blonde hair tousled and rakish. The woman held a sense of affluence even when she wasn't dressed for work, her confidence and self-importance oozing from her.

"I've got a package for Lauren. Is she here?" Sam held out the package for Bethany's inspection.

Before Bethany could answer, a woman in a tank top and tiny shorts walked into the living room behind Bethany, combing her fingers through dark, luscious curls. "Is it finally the pizza, baby?"

Bethany's jaw tightened at the pet name, a shift stirring in the air. "No, just the mailman," Bethany called behind her before meeting Sam's gaze again. The woman walked through a doorway and disappeared. *Oh, shit*, Sam thought. "Can I sign for it? Lauren's in Newark visiting her family this weekend; you know, for the holiday," Bethany said, her tone quiet and tinged with sarcasm.

"Sure, sure, you can." Sam handed Bethany the clipboard and stared at her shoes before Bethany handed her back the pen and paper. "Thanks," she said, offering the box.

Just as she went to leave, Bethany cleared her throat. "Hey, Sam."

"Yeah?"

Her voice was quiet as she murmured, "Lauren doesn't need to know about this interaction, okay?" Sam knew Bethany meant the half-naked woman inside. In Lauren's house. Calling Bethany 'baby.' Who wasn't Lauren. *It's none of my business.*

"Right," Sam said before heading back to her tiny truck. Switching on the ignition, Sam drove away as fast as possible. What the hell? Traffic was thinning out toward downtown, offering Sam a shorter trip than she anticipated. Did Lauren know about the woman in her house with Bethany? She wanted to tell Lauren immediately, but sparking strife between the two women wasn't exactly what Sam had in mind.

"It's none of my business," Sam whispered under her breath as she climbed into her personal vehicle. When she started the car, she turned the music up to dispel the moral ambiguity of the situation.

Luckily, she was in time to pick Ben up from his babysitter's house, and her plight had settled to a low annoyance in the back of her mind. When Sam walked up the rocked path toward the small cottage, her nephew came bolting out of the house. "Auntie Sam!" he shouted, jumping onto her in a full run.

"Hey, buddy. Ready to go home?"

"Yes, please."

Sam chuckled at her nephew's politeness. She wrangled his booster seat into the back of her Jeep and helped him in. With a quick thank you to his babysitter, Sam got into the car.

Once they were on the road, Ben sighed loudly. "Auntie?"

"What's up, bud?" she asked, peering through the rearview mirror.

His little face was full of worry, and he was kicking his feet at the back of the passenger seat. "Why doesn't daddy live with us anymore?"

Sam drew a breath. Shit, she did not want to have this conversation with him. Not only was it not the place nor the time, but she also wouldn't explain the true reason nearly as age appropriately as her sister would. "I think you should ask Mama when she gets home from work. Now, what do you want for dinner? I'll let you pick whatever you want."

They promptly digressed from the topic. "Even chicken nuggets and French fries?"

Sam chuckled. "Yes, even chicken nuggets and French fries." If only everything was as easy as distracting a hungry little kid.

A WEEK WENT by without Sam seeing Lauren or Bethany. Every time she stopped by Lauren's house for mail delivery, the house was dark, empty due to the beginning of the school year. Each day, Sam fought with herself about whether she would talk to Lauren about the woman she saw in her house. She'd hoped to catch Lauren home to disclose what she witnessed but hadn't been given the opportunity. Texting her was an option, but she was disinclined to broach a subject in such a way.

Friday evening, Sam meandered around the backyard after work with her nephew. Ben scribbled an interesting depiction of a rainbow on the concrete slab with chalk. "Wow, I love it," Sam said, ruffling her nephew's hair before sitting on the ground beside him. He beamed at her and then went back to his task, his little hand swiftly transforming the white patio to a colorful design.

Her sister, Katie, was navigating the new normal that was her and Ben's life post-divorce with the help of Sam and a handful of sitters. Katie's ex-husband had yet to agree to a parenting plan and had rarely seen his son during the court proceedings, citing impromptu travel requirements due to work. The situation frustrated Sam because he was giving her sister such a hard time with the parenting plan, wanting more time when he was barely around as it was.

Sam's phone buzzed in her pocket and she leaned over to yank it from her shorts. *You feel like surfing tomorrow?* The text said. Sam chuckled.

Duh. Be there at sunrise. Don't dip out on me again.

During the summer, the two tried their best to surf together at least once a week, if not more. However, Josh was bailing on their routine as of late because of a serious relationship. Sam was happy her friend had found someone he wanted to keep around, but she also loved to mess with him, especially because he missed their scheduled surf earlier that day.

When are you going to ask the cutie from the bagel stand on a date?

Sam rolled her eyes, smiling at Josh's text. The comment was expected, and Sam had been wondering when he was going to tease her about Lauren.

Checking the time, Sam guessed Katie would be home in the next half an hour. She wasn't going to try to explain who Lauren was through text messages.

Want to go grab a beer?

His reply was almost instant. *Sure.*

"Why don't we go inside and get cleaned up," Sam said. Her nephew sighed noisily and brushed the chalk from his shorts before he stood. As she helped Ben find his step stool and position it at the kitchen sink, Sam thought about Lauren again. What would she say if she found out Bethany had another woman in her house? Bethany's secret rendezvous really wasn't any of Sam's business, and for all she knew, Lauren could be aware. She and Lauren may have considered themselves friends, but Sam didn't know how her and Bethany's relationship functioned, what was okay and what wasn't. *Lauren doesn't need to know about this,* Sam remembered Bethany saying. Why wouldn't Bethany want her to know if she wasn't guilty?

Katie barreled through the door, grocery bags over her arms. Sam jumped up to help her sister carry the groceries to the kitchen while her nephew ran to his mother and wrapped his arms around her. "Mama, you're home!" he exclaimed. Katie knelt and hugged him back, ruffling his dark hair and planting a kiss on his forehead.

"Hey, sweetheart. Did you have fun with Auntie Sam?"

He nodded enthusiastically, running back into the living room and retrieving the color page he had done. "We colored and sang some funny songs and ate grilled cheese!"

Katie smiled. "That's a great coloring job." She glanced up at Sam. "Was he good for you?" she asked under her breath as she opened the food packages.

"Yeah, he was awesome. I'm going to grab some dinner with Josh over the bridge." Sam dispersed the groceries into the fridge and cabinets as she spoke.

"Okay."

"Any word on the case?"

Katie shoved a box of cereal into the pantry before turning to face Sam. "My lawyer wants to have another meeting with John's, but—" She paused, grimacing before she continued. "—I don't know if I can afford this anymore."

"I'll help you."

"No," Katie said sternly. "You are not forking out money for my divorce attorney. You already do enough around here. You help with Ben, you do the dishes, do my laundry. No."

Katie reached for a can on the counter, but Sam grabbed her wrist. There was no way Sam would allow her sister to refuse her help this time. "Please, Katie. I can help you more than babysitting Ben. This is too important, for you and Ben."

Katie's forehead crinkled in hesitancy. "But, Sam—"

"No buts. I'll give you whatever you'll take on payday."

Blowing a sigh through her nose, Katie nodded. "Thank you so much, Sam."

As Ocean City itself was a dry town, Sam hopped into her Jeep and headed toward the long 9th Street bridge connecting the coastal town with Somers Point. There were abundant bars and other establishments lining the bay's edge, the nightlife endless to make up for the family-friendly island. As Sam waited in stalled traffic while a colorful schooner passed through the raised bridge, the evasive interaction with Bethany slipped into her mind again. Did she and Lauren have an open relationship? She wanted to say something to Lauren but didn't want to put herself where she didn't belong. Sam turned the volume on her stereo up as the bridge lowered and the cars ahead of her began to move.

The music did little to hinder her thoughts. Sam could recall the moment when she began to loathe

Bethany Walters. The two had gone through school together and Bethany's bullying began shortly after high school started. Bethany's taunting wasn't limited to Sam's lack of fashionable apparel but also lingered in discriminatory territory that only worsened once Katie graduated, leaving Sam unguarded the next year. Sam used every bit of money she'd earned from her summer job as a lifeguard to afford what she needed.

The bullying began far before her mother's death but was only intensified in Sam's distress following the traumatic loss. Part of Sam wanted the satisfaction of exposing Bethany's infidelity because of the resentment she held against her; however, Sam knew it wouldn't change the past.

Their relationship was none of Sam's business.

The internal conflict plagued her as she parked at the bar and grill she and Josh frequented. Josh was sitting at the bar, tipping a beer bottle as he tilted his head back until he captured every drop. Sam climbed onto the barstool beside him and ordered a beer for herself. "God, it took you long enough to get here."

She bumped his arm and chuckled. "Well, I was watching Ben for Katie, and at least I showed up."

"I'm just giving you crap. Yeah, my bad. So, who was the cutie at the boardwalk flirting with you a couple Fridays ago?" Josh asked, turning to Sam to wait for her reply.

The bartender brought her a beer and she took a swig before clearing her throat. "A customer on my route."

"A customer? Do you look at all of your customers like you're mentally tearing their clothes off?"

The uncouth comment was expected, and Sam shook her head as she laughed, nearly choking on the sip of beer she had in her mouth. "No, I can't say that I do."

Josh smirked at her. "'Oh, Sam, you have the best books in the world and the biggest. Gosh, I can't get enough of your big books,'" Josh said, his voice upped an octave. He fluttered his eyelashes, fanning himself with a napkin. Sam whacked his arm and he giggled, continuing in a deeper voice. "'Is my taste in books rubbing off on you?' Sam, really—just a customer?"

Sam pinched the bridge of her nose and chuckled. "Yeah, yeah, you caught me. Regardless of my obvious interest, she's taken and we're only friends."

Josh whistled, the bottom of his beer bottle hitting the bar loudly. "Shit. I bet she's straight too."

Turning her head, Sam met his eyes and grinned. "Nope, she's a lesbian, but that's not even the kicker. Guess who her girlfriend is?"

"Who?"

"Bethany Walters."

"Wasn't she the girl who outed you to the entire junior class? Tall, blonde, and handsome? God, she was such a bitch." Josh slapped the surface of the bar. "See? You should've let me deck her in the face when I had the chance. She's such an asshole."

Sam finished the rest of her beer before she spoke again. "She saw the error of her ways and apologized for her crappy behavior eventually." The awkward event hadn't been half-assed, and Sam often wondered what sparked Bethany's apology long after they graduated.

Josh shook his head, tipping the bottle to his mouth again. "I thought she moved away, to New York or something."

"She did, for college. Once she finished, she landed herself a good job with a local firm." Sam met his eyes, raising an eyebrow. "She's a civil attorney."

"Oh, now you've got yourself in some serious competition, Sam. A postal worker or a lawyer," Josh said, raising his hands as he mimicked a set of scales. "I love you, but I don't think you stand a chance." Bethany was attractive, and given her chosen field, was well paid, at least to Sam's standards. Sam wasn't expecting a miracle.

She rolled her eyes and finished off her beer. "I'm not interested anyway." The statement was a lie, but Josh was right—she really didn't have a shot, not that it was even a lingering possibility in her head. Okay, an elaborate fantasy, maybe.

A waiter came around and the two ordered their food. When they were alone again, Josh sighed. "You need to get yourself out there, maybe try Tinder or something. You can't live with your sister for the rest of your life and be a celibate little butch." Both Josh and Sam laughed raucously, and she punched him in the arm.

"Shut up. I'm taking a break from relationships anyway. I don't need the drama while I'm helping Katie through her own stuff. Plus, I'm not living with her. I just renewed the lease on my apartment." She'd been staying with Katie for a two-week stretch due to the inevitable stress revolving around the current court hearing, and Josh knew that. However, he couldn't miss the opportunity to give her crap.

"Whatever you say," Josh snorted.

"I'm serious. She's in a really bad spot with all this, and I know she's terrified he'll be granted fifty-fifty custody. If he does, it'll make things difficult because he travels for work so much." Poor Ben was stuck in the middle of an ugly adult situation he had no concept of. It pained Sam to see him hurting and for Katie to be at such a loss for explaining it to him. There weren't any good children's books on explaining the ugly truth of divorce.

Josh sighed, thoughtfully chewing a French fry. "I bet it is hard to see Katie all torn up like she is."

"That's the problem—she won't ask for help. She lets her vulnerability slip once in a while, but for the most part, she's quiet about it unless I push. She won't ask for a shoulder to cry on or help with her mortgage. She's all stoic and stubborn as hell, but I was finally able to get her to agree to take some money from me to help with the lawyer fees." Katie had to do what helped her get through the tough messes of her life, but Sam wished her sister would accept her assistance easier even if it was only an ear to listen. Katie had been the strong one when their mother passed, and Sam wanted to do what she could to return the love and stability Katie had provided her back then.

"She's always been a tough person though." Josh touched Sam's arm. "She'll get through this."

Sam needed a distraction, or her abysmal mood was only going to deepen. "What about you, how are you and Brad doing?"

Josh scratched his head, visibly uncomfortable about the question. "He wants me to move in with him."

"Is this a bad thing?" Sam asked. Josh grimaced as the waiter walked up with their food, placing it on the bar.

"No, it isn't really a bad thing, per se."

"But?"

Josh took a deep breath. "I don't know if I'm ready for that kind of commitment." Sam gave him a dubious gaze and he crumbled. "Okay, the real reason is I'm stuck in my stupid lease and I don't want to break it. Brad understands," Josh claimed. "We're getting a place together next January when my lease is up, and I'm pretty excited about it." The grin on his face showcased his excitement. She clasped an arm around his shoulders and gave him a side hug.

"I'm stoked for you."

He chuckled and hugged her back before they let go. "If you could find a girl who isn't taken, then we'd be getting somewhere."

Sam elbowed him in the ribs, and he chortled. "You better not bail on me again tomorrow."

"I'll be there."

Sam's phone buzzed, and she pulled it from her pocket. A text message from Lauren lit her screen.

I hope you like pizza because that's what we're having tomorrow. You're still coming, right?

They hadn't talked since she saw Lauren at the bagel shop because school was back in session, and Sam missed their conversations.

Yes, absolutely. Pizza is amazing. I can't wait to see what kind of games you guys have.

"Hey, Sam, do you hear me?"

Sam glanced up from her phone and caught Josh glaring at her. "Yeah, sorry."

"What're you doing?" Josh inquired as he peered over her shoulder. He laughed and pulled back. "Oh, pizza." From the look on his face, Josh knew her smile had nothing to do with pizza.

Chapter Three

LAUREN SIGHED AS she sifted through the pile of quizzes. Her students hated quizzes in general, but their hatred was heightened when it was the second day of school. Why start school on a Wednesday? Opening the school year with a quiz was the best way to gauge what the students remembered from the year before, and she would continue the practice until the day she retired, whenever that would be. She found them far too valuable to do away with just because of a few teenagers complaining. After grading a handful and becoming frustrated with the number of wrong answers, Lauren stood, and stretched her sore back.

She stepped into the kitchen, fishing around in the freezer to see what she had to cook. Late evening sun filtered in through the cracked window above her sink, dust particles hanging in the air. After a futile search, she pulled her phone from her pocket, planning on sending Bethany a text asking her to pick up some takeout. A new message from Jackie halted her progress.

Have you talked to Bethany yet?

Lauren sighed. Although she and Bethany saw each other in passing every morning and spent their nights together, Lauren hadn't brought up the suspicious text message yet. They'd both been busy, and Lauren didn't want to ruin a pleasant evening together with her girlfriend by starting the conversation.

No, I haven't really thought about it much. Maybe I'm being overdramatic?

She knew Jackie wouldn't let her get away with not confronting Bethany. After finally sending the message to Bethany about dinner, she debated on her excuse for Jackie. Ignoring the situation wasn't her end goal but Lauren wasn't eager to bring the topic up to Bethany. How was she supposed to slide something so serious into a normal conversation? *Hey, baby, I saw this possibly incriminating text. Are you cheating on me?* When she did, Lauren was also poised to confront Bethany's silence after the confession of her feelings, the elephant in the relationship that had been present since their getaway. She sent a text to Sam as a diversion.

I hope you like pizza because that's what we're having tomorrow.

Lauren let herself out the back door, her cat instantly greeting her. "Hey, girlie. What are you doing?" She knelt and scratched the scruffy Russian blue under her chin, earning herself a noisy purr from the cat. The sun still lightened the sky, so Lauren plopped herself into one of her patio chairs to soak up the lingering warmth.

Her phone buzzed, and she groaned when she read the text from Jackie, not Sam.

Bullshit, you need to ask her about the text and the other thing. Ease your mind. What's the worst that can happen?

She knew Jackie meant for the question to be rhetorical, but Lauren couldn't help imagining what the worst *could* be. Nonsense.

The current events reminded Lauren why she preferred realm of science. A vast majority of mysteries in the world could be explained to some level of understanding with aspects from scientific study. From basics such as the weather to the complexity of Einstein's theory of general relativity. This made sense to Lauren even when it didn't to others.

Not everything held a pristine explanation, but at the very least, one could come close to a semblance of reason. Emotions were an entirely different story, and this infuriated Lauren. Like lighting a match, reading a handful of words on Bethany's phone had ignited a flicker of doubt within her that she couldn't ignore.

The cat jumped into her lap and Lauren patted her head. Another text from Sam sparked a wide grin.

Yes, absolutely. Pizza is amazing. I can't wait to see what kind of games you guys have.

If she wanted things to progress further with Bethany, they needed to talk about the evening Lauren told Bethany she loved her. Lauren couldn't have known those words would be responsible for such a mountainous rift between them. Speaking of rift, she acknowledged she was going to have to ask Bethany about the text message or it was going to eat her alive. Lauren stood before heading back inside.

She gathered the quizzes from the coffee table and brought them to the kitchen counter, laying them out. With a satisfying click of her red pen, she began the tedious task once again. She was hoping that after a few weeks, memories of basic science would flutter to the forefront of their minds.

Bethany came through the front door moments later. "Hey, I got some dinner," she said, placing a paper bag filled with fast food on the counter.

"Thanks," Lauren said, taking Bethany's face in her hands, kissing her. "I forgot to tell you that Sam's going to come over tomorrow for game night."

If Lauren hadn't been paying close enough attention, she might not have noticed Bethany scrunch her nose at the mention of Sam's name. "Oh, okay. I'm going to take a quick shower before we eat, all right?" Bethany said, shrugging out of her suit jacket and hanging it on the back of a chair.

"Sure." Lauren placed the food under a towel to keep it warm as Bethany went off to the shower. Though Lauren once had a crush on Sam before she and Bethany began dating, Bethany was unaware of it, and the infatuation had seemingly passed once she and Bethany became a couple. Grabbing the basket full of clean laundry, Lauren began to fold the clothes, her mind on how she'd approach Bethany about the text message. As stupid as it was, Lauren could've let the text go if it hadn't been for the silly little kissy face. Why would a colleague send such a thing with a message about getting together? The text could've been an accident, although Lauren wasn't naïve enough to believe that was so. With the clothes folded, Lauren got up and meandered down the hall to her room.

The sound of running water filled her bedroom and she smiled to herself at the thought of Bethany in the shower. The bathroom door was slightly cracked, so Lauren contemplated slipping under the water with her girlfriend but dismissed the thought. If she followed her impulse, there would be no discussion about the text message. Lauren walked into the closet and began putting clothes away. A black garment peeked from beneath a pair of discarded jeans. Squinting, she bent to pick up a pair of panties. They weren't hers. Lauren swallowed back a gasp. Bethany wore boxers. How had she not seen them before? She dropped the panties, her heart hammering against her chest, hands clammy.

Lauren took a sharp breath and stepped back, fear gripping her. She shook her head, trying to banish the assumption Bethany was unfaithful while she was gone, backing up until she hit her bed, and then sinking on the soft surface of her bedspread. No. There was no way, right? She blinked, swallowing back the fear bubbling in her throat. Bethany wouldn't cheat on her after Lauren told her she loved her, would she? Not after she'd told her about Maribel, her last unfaithful girlfriend.

Her jaw clenched, a tear slipping down her face as Bethany stepped out of the bathroom already dressed, toweling her short hair. "Baby, what's wrong?"

Lauren's lower lip trembled as she tried to speak, her face damp as more tears fell from her eyes. "Who do those belong to?" she asked, finger pointing to the panties on the floor of her closet.

Bethany moved closer, tossing the towel in the laundry hamper as she leaned her head into the closet. Bethany's posture stiffened, and her mouth was slightly ajar when she turned back to Lauren. "I...um..."

It wasn't how she'd planned the confrontation, but Lauren continued, "And who's Mistie?"

Bethany blinked rapidly as she stood in the threshold of the closet, speechless. They stared at each other for what could've been an eternity. Bethany closed her eyes, letting out a long breath. "Lauren, I'm sorry."

Lauren sniffled, swiping her face as a sob tore through her, the apology admission enough. "You cheated on me?" Bethany came forward, arms outstretched as she took Lauren into an unwanted embrace. Lauren squirmed away.

"I'm not going to lie to you... I made a mistake when you were out of town," Bethany said as she took a few steps back, allowing Lauren the space she needed.

"How could you, Bethany?" Her voice full of venom, she fixed a teary scowl at her lover. Lauren clambered off the bed, her chest heaving.

Shame darkened Bethany's cheeks a deep red, and she stared at the floor, refusing to meet Lauren's gaze. "I'm sorry, Lauren."

Lauren chuckled without humor. "Really, a mistake? That's all you have to say?" An ache formed within her heart, the pain threatening to double her over as Bethany lifted her head to meet her gaze.

"I had a moment of weakness and there's no excuse."

"No, and you don't even have the right to try to make up an excuse." She wanted to say more, wanted to relay her hurt to Bethany somehow, but she knew it was impossible. Before the sobs took over, Lauren had to remove herself from Bethany. "You have five minutes to grab as much crap as you can. I don't care where you go but you can't stay here." She turned and hurried down the hall, teeth clamped on her lower lip to stifle the cry that threatened to escape her lips.

Retrieving her phone, Lauren headed out into the yard, her back facing the door. Noise emanated from within the house as Bethany gathered her belongings. Lauren couldn't catch her breath, but she would not allow herself to cry anymore in front of Bethany. Holding her lip between her teeth again, Lauren jumped as the back door opened. "I left my key on the kitchen counter. I'll come back for the rest of my stuff when you want me to." Lauren held her breath, feeling Bethany's eyes on her back, unmoving as if waiting for Lauren to say something. Silence fell over the yard, but just as Lauren readied herself to tell Bethany to leave, Bethany returned to the house. She waited until Bethany's car started and she drove off before Lauren let go of her lip.

A sob rattled Lauren and her head fell into her hands. How could she be so stupid? She stood, and went into the house. She let it go—the tears, the pain, the angst that followed her from her last two failed relationships.

She kicked a stray shoe in her way before throwing herself on the couch and clutching a throw pillow to her chest. How could Bethany not only cheat on her but in her own home when she was out of town? Through teary eyes, Lauren grabbed her phone and texted Jackie.

Bethany and I talked. It didn't go well. Can you come over to my place for a few?

Well, Lauren hadn't found out who Mistie was, but she gathered the mystery woman was presumably more than a friend.

Lauren fell back, lying on her side and bringing her knees to her chest. The pain was unbearable, and she needed to calm her breathing, or she was going to hyperventilate like a dramatic teenager. Sure, the broken trust hurt, but she didn't need to lose herself over it. Lauren took an uneven breath and then another, snatching a tissue from the coffee table to blow her nose.

Her phone vibrated, and she read the text from Jackie.

Be there in five.

Less than two minutes later, Jackie came through the front door. Lauren sat back up, blowing her nose again as Jackie took in the sight of her emotional state. "Oh, honey, what happened?" She came over and sat beside Lauren, placing an arm over her shoulders.

"I kicked her out," Lauren hiccupped. "She cheated on me and she didn't even try to deny it." Fresh tears trailed down her face and Jackie took her into a crushing hug as she sobbed. Jackie let her cry, rubbing Lauren's back while offering the occasional word of encouragement. When Lauren settled, she took a shaky breath and pulled away from her friend. "Thank you," she murmured.

Jackie brushed off her appreciation and stood, heading to the kitchen. "You want chamomile or green tea?" she asked as she placed a kettle on the stove.

"Chamomile sounds wonderful." The clatter of the kettle hitting the stove reverberated from the kitchen and Lauren relaxed. She should've known. How hadn't she come across the pair of underwear the entire week? If Bethany wanted to cheat on her, why did she move in with Lauren in the first place? "Here you go." Jackie handed Lauren her tea.

Hot cup in hand, Lauren leaned into the steam and closed her eyes, hoping the aroma of the tea would help her breathe easier and calm the turmoil thrashing within. "I'm here if you want to talk, and I'm also here if you just want quiet." Jackie put a gentle hand on Lauren's shoulder. She loved the kindness Jackie offered.

"Quiet company sounds nice. Or, maybe a horror movie."

Jackie chuckled, picking up the remote control and opening the menu for the movie channels. "Slasher flick and tea, it is."

Chapter Four

LONGBOARD TUCKED UNDER her arm, Sam took a deep, exhilarating breath of the salty air as she peered out at the water. Waves crashed against the black rocks of the jetty, white froth shooting into the sky. Dawn approached, the sun peeking over the horizon, splaying orange onto the surface of the ocean. Although the temperature was close to seventy degrees in the air, the water was sure to be chilly, and Sam preemptively wore her wet suit, the heavy fabric hugging her body as she took a deep breath. Josh was supposed to have already been there, and she was getting impatient. When they parted ways after their dinner at the bar, Sam reminded him again not to be late, yet, he was just that. Hopefully, he wasn't going to bail like he had the previous morning.

If she waited any longer for her surfing buddy, tourists would be swarming the area and she wouldn't be able to enjoy the calm the beach offered in the early hours. Seldom did she surf by herself, unless there were lifeguards present, due to the risk of getting caught by a riptide. However, the water didn't appear too bad, considering the time of year, and she wasn't going to waste any more time waiting for Josh. The sky was relatively clear, the scant clouds dotting the horizon taking on a pink hue as the sun crested. A jogger ran past, their sneakers hitting the planks of the boardwalk behind her with a soft slap each step they took. The wicked swell became a hollow barrel before Sam hurried down the wooden steps onto the cool sand of the beach ready to catch a wave.

She tucked her small backpack on the beach a few yards up from the water and grabbed her phone. A text from Josh filled her display and she chuckled.

Just woke up, on my way.

Low tide was coming in an hour or so, and she didn't have to worry about her bag getting swept up by the tide but was concerned she'd miss the waves. Enough waiting. Josh would be there soon.

Granted, the beach wasn't the best spot on the East Coast for surfing; she'd had better luck in Sea Isle City or when she took a vacation in Florida, but it was better than nothing. The water lapped at her feet and she threw her board in, pushing it out into the deeper shallows. She climbed on top, legs propelling her forward into the shifting water. She was excited for her plans with Lauren later that day, albeit mildly nervous to be in the same room as Bethany. Their previous interaction left her with a strange foreboding.

Water splashed over her, disrupting the discomforting memory. This was where she loved to be, in the water with her innermost thoughts, serendipity among the errant breezes, briny air and nostalgic sounds of slushing, sputtering waves. After getting some distance from the shore, she climbed fully upon her board, letting her legs dangle as she buoyed on the surface, tilting her head as the sun's warmth engulfed her. A laughing gull flew overhead before dipping into the water and mimicking her posture afloat on the drifting current. She paddled farther out into the ocean, the water splashing over her biceps and chest, and she noted how choppy the current was becoming. *There must be a storm brewing a few miles off shore*, she thought as she continued, increasing her speed as a wave began to form.

With a duck dive, Sam pushed herself and her board downward, beneath the powerful wave to avoid the swell from crashing over her. Unfortunately, she wasn't fast enough, and the wave fell over her, ripping her from the safety of her board before throwing her to the sea floor. Her head hit the bottom, dazing her temporarily before she pushed upward, thrusting herself to the surface. As her head bobbed above the water's edge, she gasped for air, taking in her surroundings. The water was churning all around her, the wind speed rapidly increasing.

Dark clouds threatened from above, obscuring the freshly risen sun. There hadn't been a touch of rain in the morning forecast, much less a thunderstorm, but Sam recognized the distinct mushroom-like appearance as the ominous cumulonimbus formation grew closer. Her board bumped into her arm, the leash tugging her ankle where it was attached. Sam clambered on, paddled her arms, and shot toward the shoreline. Where the hell had the storm come from? She hadn't been in the water longer than ten minutes and she hadn't noticed any indication of the swift weather change.

The wind whipped at her, causing her short hair to stick to the side of her face as she quickened her pace, the muscles in her arms straining from the movement. But she made no progress in her efforts to reach the shore. Through the echoes of waves crashing around her, she heard her name and spotted a form standing at the shore, waving their arms. Josh! He stood, the black of his wetsuit visible on the backdrop of beige. Battery acid filled her veins, making her arms sore from the excursion of paddling against the current. Yet, she pushed harder, straining her limbs to continue on the futile mission.

Risking a glance back, Sam turned her head and was met with a wave coming down on her, knocking her from her board and submerging her in the water once again. She avoided hitting her head this time, pushing herself back to the surface just to be yanked by a stray current again. Gasping for air, she clawed toward the surface, her heart racing. Darkness obscured the sun, the thick clouds rumbling overhead. Black rocks to her left jutted out of the rapidly shifting waves and fear gripped her. How the hell had she gotten so close to the jetty?

The current drove her nearer, yanking her board along with it, and she fought its strength. She was an experienced surfer; she shouldn't be fighting for her safety in the place she was most comfortable in, where she found her inner peace. Yet, as another wave crashed over her head, leaving her sputtering for oxygen; she was fighting for more than just her safety. Her board crashed into the rocks first, her feet too busy trying to propel her away from the same fate, leaving her unable to remove the leash around her ankle.

The rumbling of thunder overhead was muffled by the rush of waves throwing her into the rocks, and her body smacked the jagged surface. She cried out, reaching for somewhere to grab, her fingers clawing out at the roughness. Another swell pulled her away from the jetty and back again, this impact worse than the first. The leash connecting her surfboard to her ankle became snagged between two boulders, and she fought to stay afloat.

Her head hit the rocks, slamming her submerged body into the jetty, and her face went underwater. Breaking through the surface, Sam flailed as she struggled to remain afloat. Another wave crashed, pulling her deeper in the murky depths, far deeper than before. The tenacious current continued to tug her down, forcing her beneath the surface. Her board flopped against the jetty, and she reached for the strap around her ankle but couldn't grip it. She pushed her feet against the rocks, craning her neck upward, trying to break the water to catch a breath, but failing. Panic set in, and she kept kicking her legs, reaching her arms out for anything to grasp. Her chest burned as she breathed in water.

She panicked, arms thrashing, legs kicking as water poured into her lungs as if she were breathing in liquid fire. Her vision grew dark as her fingers fumbled the strap around her ankle loose, the Velcro giving way as she tugged. The last thought crossing her mind before everything went black was why the hell the Velcro hadn't come loose during her initial struggles.

THE FIRST THING Sam noticed was the calm, a dense quiet surrounding her, pressing against her ears, muffling her senses. She was shrouded in darkness, and then came a light, blinding in its intensity. Sam squinted as she sat up, the pain in her chest and limbs gone. Soft, sun-kissed grass tickled her bare hands, and she peered up to see the piercing light was emanating from the sun. She remembered a sharp pain clouding her thoughts, robbing her of any conscious movement. And now, she took in a meadow stretching out, rolling hills dotted with lavender blossoms and orange poppies. Sam rubbed her head, her hearing finally coming back after a long respite. The first sound she became aware of was a soft bubbling to her right, and she turned her head, noticing a shallow brook flowing through the tall grass, lapping at the riverbed.

"Welcome, kid," a gruff voice chimed from above her. Perched upon a large boulder covered in moss sat a woman. Nothing was outwardly peculiar; her denim jacket hanging open to display a band tee, blue jeans ripped in the knees, and Converse sneakers, which had seen better days, all appeared ordinary. But the fine hairs on the back of Sam's neck lifted when she met her piercing blue gaze. The woman was attractive and couldn't have been much older than Sam's twenty-six, her jaw chiseled, a metal hoop dangling from her nose, lips pursed, and blonde hair pushed back, a swoop of the ash locks hanging over her forehead.

"Where am I?" Sam stood, wiping the grass and dirt from her wetsuit. What was she doing wearing her wetsuit in the middle of a meadow?

"Okay, here's the deal," the woman said as she hopped down from the boulder. Her feet thumped heavily on the ground as she landed. She pulled a soft pack of cigarettes from a pocket on the denim jacket with long fingers before bringing one to her lips and lighting it. Her next words came out on a stream of smoke. "You're dead. I'm the Grim Reaper, Angel of Death, whatever the fuck you want to call me, preferably my name, Margo. This"—she gestured to the peaceful scenery—"is your in-between."

Sam's brows scrunched as the woman took another drag from her cigarette. "In between what?"

A long tuft of white smoke came out of her mouth as she cackled. "In between life and death. You decided to go play in the water, drowned, and got yourself as dead as a doornail."

"You're the Grim Reaper?" Sam asked. When Margo nodded, Sam burst into laughter as this couldn't be real.

Margo glowered, her expression unamused as she brought the cigarette to her lips again. Sam sobered. "Oh my god, you're serious?"

"As serious as the plague," she said. "You could say I'm *dead* serious." Margo laughed raucously. Sam stared at her. "Okay, enough puns for now. I've got an offer for you." Before Margo could speak further, Sam cut her off.

"Wait, if you're the Grim Reaper, what's up with the frolicking ponyville?" Sam surveyed the beautiful meadow again. "I'm sorry, but I would've expected something a little, well, darker I guess."

Margo quirked an eyebrow, a dimple creasing at the corner of her mouth. "This is your mentally concocted illusion; it can be whatever you want it to be. Let me fix that." She snapped her fingers, and the scenery transformed into a starkly different atmosphere. Black trees sprouted from the ground, their bare, burned branches raking an opaque sky. Knee-high fog wove between their legs, the smell of soot, ash and damp decay filling the air. Sam took in the acres of burned woods around them, a small murder of crows fluttering above their heads, cawing to one another. "Better?" Margo inquired.

Sam knew her mouth hung ajar, but she couldn't help it. The woman before her wasn't a normal person. Or, Sam was having an incredible hallucination. She hoped for the latter as she ran her fingers through her short hair and whispered, "Uh, yeah, I guess."

"Don't cut me off again. I don't do this often, and if it weren't for upper management being on my goddamn ass, I wouldn't even be considering this," Margo said, inhaling smoke from her cigarette. "But desperate times call for desperate measures. Like I said, you're dead. I'm going to offer you two choices."

Sam chewed her lip, confused about the entire situation. Was she dead or was this an elaborate dream her subconscious created? Oh, no. She remembered the storm coming out of nowhere, the riptide thrusting her into the jagged rocks of the black jetty, and her subsequent struggle to breathe. "This is a dream," she whispered, taking a tentative step away from Margo. What about Katie and Ben? How could she make sure Katie was okay if she was truly dead? How would Katie manage without her? Her pride would keep her from reaching out to anyone. Fear bubbled in Sam at the thought of what would become of her family. Not to mention Lauren. *Oh, Lauren.* Why hadn't she simply told Lauren about Bethany's little visitor?

Margo rolled her eyes as she snapped her fingers together. The dark setting around them vanished, instantly replaced by the very beach where Sam had been struggling to swim. A loud commotion behind her caused her to turn and she gasped. Numerous people crowded around a figure on the ground, one person performing CPR, another above her head positioning a mask over the face of the victim. Another individual struggled with a stretcher, its wheels caught in the sand. Josh stood by idly, his hands on his head, tears streaming down his face. "Oh, shit," Sam muttered. The prone figure was unmistakably her.

"Finally firing on all cylinders?" Margo's cynical response had Sam nodding her head, brown eyes wide as they met the Reaper's. "All right." She cleared her throat. "You're good and dead, bought the farm, etcetera. The thing is, I can bring you back."

"Really?" Elated, Sam smiled but Margo held up her hand.

"On one condition—I need your help."

"My help?" Her brows furrowed. What could she possibly offer the Grim Reaper? The whole notion of her standing in front of an imaginary person had Sam questioning her sanity. People talked about a white light when they had near-death experiences, not a cocky butch, who identified as the Grim Reaper, giving her cryptic nonsense about needing help. Margo stubbed the smoked cigarette out below their feet. Rain pelted the area, the drops leaving little divots in the sand. For the second time, Sam's skin broke out in goose bumps as Margo's cerulean stare met her own.

"Yeah. Upper management's been breathing down my neck because I've fallen behind on their quotas. One of those 'you do your job so well, you get to do someone else's too!' Let me explain the best way I can." She paused, scratching her head. The expression she gave Sam was condescending, one brow scrunched, the other lifting while she pursed her lips in contemplation. She sized Sam up, doing nothing to stifle her discomfort. "I guide souls to the afterlife. It's my life and I do a damn good job. But sometimes spirits aren't so willing to jump on the bandwagon and head on to the other side."

"Okay," Sam said.

"By this point, they're sick of seeing my mug, and I can't convince them that it's what they have to do. After a certain period of time, it's damn near impossible to get them to cross over. So, what I need from you is a little push."

"A push?"

Margo folded her arms over her chest. "Yeah. I need you to help me get these stubborn spirits to move on with their afterlife, so to speak, and go to the other side so I can go onto the next one."

"How do I convince them to move on? What's the catch?"

"Talk to them. Find out what they need to do to make them happy enough to get the hell out of here. No catch. After you help me for a few months, you're off the hook."

Sam considered this. The deal didn't sound terribly hard, but she was curious. "How am I supposed to do that when I can't see them?"

Margo chuckled. "So many questions. Don't worry your pretty little head; you'll see the spirits and only them."

Great, Sam thought. She wasn't sure how she felt about being able to see the dead, to have to help the Grim Reaper make souls move forward to...wherever. Margo was digging in her pocket, retrieving her pack of smokes again before bringing one to her lips. "Where do they go?" Sam asked.

"Wherever they're meant to go. It's not for me to know, nor do I give a shit." Smoke swirled around her face before she continued, "It depends on how they live their lives. It has to do with karma or something. Think of it as a temp job. I only need you for a couple months and then you can go back to your life, debt free."

Sam couldn't understand why Margo said all this with such nonchalance and cynicism. Again, her mind wandered to Katie. She was hardly getting through this divorce with Sam by her side; how would she survive without her sister? She would never ask for help from anyone. And poor Ben. The child had been through enough for his tender age of five, far more than he should have. Given the option, she couldn't willingly leave them, no matter how insane it seemed. Being the hand of the Grim Reaper sounded like hell, but what other choice did she have?

She stole another glance back at her lifeless body as the paramedics continued their efforts to revive her. They had cut off her wet suit and applied pads to her chest with wires leading to a small box beside her body that Sam recognized as an AED. The copious amount of blood pouring from her injuries obscured her view of her skin. Damn, the wet suit was expensive. Without thinking, Sam uttered, "Okay."

Margo's eyes widened. "Really?" Her lips curled, and she took a few steps, closing the distance between her and Sam.

"Well, yeah. I don't think I have much of a choice if I want to live."

Margo stuck her hand out. "Good. I thought I'd have to do a little coercion. Let's shake on it." Sam held her hand out, reluctant due to the fear it might hurt. It was the Grim Reaper, after all. To her surprise, Margo's hand was warm, albeit calloused and rough. When she let go, Margo rubbed her hands together and smiled wickedly. She pulled a small knife from her pocket. "Sweet. I'm going to give you some time to recover from your run-in with death. You've got two weeks."

"What are you doing with that?" Sam's eyes were on the dagger.

Margo ignored her and slid the knife over her palm. "Okay, now," she began, her hands out, palms facing Sam. The hand she cut was dripping with blood and Sam cringed at the sight. "Wake up." Margo's hands slammed against Sam's chest. The air left Sam's lungs, making her breathless as she fell backward, which was odd to her because she wondered how her "spirit," or whatever it was, could be physically pushed by Margo or how she could feel the air leaving her lungs.

Then, she was on the ground, her body frigid, damp sand beneath her, and people surrounded her from every angle. Sam tried to look around, but her movement was obstructed by a thick plastic brace around her neck. She was completely paralyzed, her body deaf to her mental commands to move. Margo's face came into view, blonde hair wavering into her eyes as she leaned in. "This is going to hurt a lot worse than anything you've ever felt before, okay?" Before Sam could respond, Margo pressed her cut hand over Sam's shoulder. Searing pain snaked through her body from Margo's hand. Sam tried to scream but her voice remained silent. A fire engulfed her, its origin where Margo's open palm sat, and it burned a trail through her veins. She thrashed her body, kicking her legs, arching her back. Gasping, Sam reached her arms up, finally free from her frozen state.

"We've got a pulse!" a voice boomed above her head. Plastic covered her mouth and she tried to yank her arms free from their restraints to remove the object over her mouth. Sand lay beneath her and she could see the face of her friend, Josh, standing over her as strangers crowded closer around her. Shooting pain filled her shoulder, the faint metallic scent of blood filling her senses. "Try to relax, okay? We're going to get you to the hospital. Don't move," the woman in uniform to her right commanded. Where did Margo go?

Sam blinked her eyes, chest heaving, the right side of her upper body throbbing with pain. The paramedics counted off and lifted Sam and the board where she lay onto a stretcher before wheeling her up the ramp from the beach, causing the pain to intensify. Josh was close behind, his face full of concern as he peered over at her. "Oh my God, Sam. If I hadn't been on the beach, you'd be dead." His voice wavered as he spoke. She tried to defend herself, but her lungs continued to feel as if she'd swallowed lava. Shit, she couldn't even shake her head at him.

The stretcher bumped over the boards of the boardwalk and she cried out each time the stretcher rattled. Pain radiated through her right shoulder and down her back, the leg that had gotten caught in the rocks shooting agony through her body. "Hold on, one more bump," said one of the paramedics as they pushed the stretcher up into the ambulance. The pain became unbearable and Sam screamed in near agony.

She closed her eyes, the face of Margo, the Grim Reaper, floating around in her head on a cloud of cigarette smoke before everything went black again.

Chapter Five

LAUREN WOKE TO the rambling of a crime show rerun on the television, the familiar voices hushed and eerie in the otherwise quiet living room. Lifting her head, Lauren noticed Jackie spread out on the love seat, bare feet kicked over the arm and a bowl of popcorn balancing on her chest as she slept. Midmorning sunshine streamed in through the large bay window in her living room, and a sliver of light threaded through the parted curtain. Lauren's phone rang for the fourth time, and she sat up, glancing at the table. The screen flashed, Bethany's name displayed on its surface. Memories of the previous day entered her thoughts and Lauren sighed heavily.

The evening had proved rougher than expected, Lauren running through their relationship mentally the entire time, desperate to cling to an answer for Bethany's behavior. She considered asking Bethany, but her anger prevented her. When Lauren thought she couldn't cry anymore, she curled up on the couch and hugged a pillow to her chest to ease the hurt. Jackie stayed, offering her the best wisdom she could: forget her. Lauren read over the text from Bethany.

Please call me.

Lauren didn't want to engage. The truth was too fresh, too painful for her. She knew eventually they would have to talk, though she was certain she was not going to allow Bethany back into her life after such an act of betrayal. "Hey, you okay?" Jackie asked.

Lauren looked up from her phone and feigned a smile. "Yeah. Bethany's trying to get me to call her."

Jackie snorted, stretching her long limbs to place the popcorn bowl on the coffee table. "Surprise, surprise. Don't let her weasel her way back in. You two discussed this at the start and she broke the trust. You told her about Maribel and your trust issues and yet she still did what she did. No amount of groveling can fix that."

"I know. I'd eventually like to know why she did it." Lauren worried her lower lip, wringing her hands in her lap. Jackie meandered over to the kitchen, helping herself to Lauren's pantry. The relationship between Lauren and Bethany undoubtedly became more complicated since their weekend in Cape May, Lauren struggling to keep their connection strong after the rejection. Their sex life was far from lacking, which kept Lauren from believing Bethany was sexually frustrated. Before the night in Cape May, they'd shared open dialogue with each other, especially after Bethany moved in. This added a magnitude of weight to the already distressing issues of her infidelity. Had Lauren inadvertently caused the infidelity by telling Bethany she loved her?

Jackie rounded the corner munching loudly on a piece of toast. "Does it matter? Don't think too hard about this, Lauren. She made the choice, and you don't need to go analyzing every minute of your relationship up until it happened to try to figure out what made her do it."

Lauren sighed again. "You're right. I did that with Maribel, and it got me nowhere."

Jackie clicked her tongue as she shook her head. "Don't you go blaming yourself, either." Lauren met Jackie's pointed stare. "I'm not an idiot—I know you. I bet you think it's your fault because you told her how you felt.

If that was the reason she cheated, you're better off without her." The truth in Jackie's words hardly eased the sting, but Lauren took comfort in the knowledge.

Jackie stayed most of the day, helping Lauren clean her house, ridding the residence of as many reminders of Bethany as possible. The pain was numbed by the action, and Lauren thanked Jackie countless times, prompting her friend to tell her to stop. There wasn't too much to remove from her house, with Bethany having recently moved in. When her lease ended, Bethany had decided to place her furniture in a storage unit rather than bring it to Lauren's house, hinting at them getting a place together to start fresh in the coming months. The move had brought on a level of commitment Lauren hadn't anticipated, but she went along, excited for their growth together. However, her excitement had vanished the night in Cape May. The remaining belongings were enough to remind Lauren of the ache of what could have been—what she thought could've been her happy ever after. Jackie stood in the doorway of the bathroom as Lauren tossed a few toiletries that belonged to Bethany into one of the boxes. "At some point, I'll have to let her come get her stuff."

"You tell me a time and I'll be here," Jackie said.

Lauren offered Jackie a sullen smile. "Thank you."

Jackie put a hand on her hip. "You need to stop thanking me. I'm your best friend and best friends are supposed to help scrub the essence of your ex out of your home when they cheat on you." When they both felt the house was free of any remnants of Bethany, the two friends ate dinner. Finally, Jackie bid Lauren goodbye, hugging her tightly and telling her to call if she needed anything.

After an hour of playing a video game, Lauren called it a night and headed to her bedroom. The last thing she wanted to do the night before was change the sheets on the bed, leaving the task to do before she went to sleep. Lauren yanked the sheets off the bed and when she did, something thudded to the floor. She ignored the item until the new sheet was tucked under the mattress. Then, she searched around to find the object. A sliver of green caught her attention and Lauren knelt, snatching the glittering piece of jewelry from the floor.

The necklace was as beautiful as the night Bethany purchased it, the same night Lauren professed her love. How could such a magical night turn into the beginning of the end for their relationship? Perhaps Bethany truly wasn't ready for commitment, Lauren's confession insinuating a fissure between them. Lauren ran her thumb over the sterling silver encased emerald, sighing with consternation. They came back to the city the following day, their weekend getaway shortened. Lauren had tucked the necklace between the mattress and box spring, refusing to be reminded of the painful night.

The epitome of romantic: a beautiful cottage away from everything, right on the water. Crashing waves, a sky full of stars, expensive wine, and warm company. Lauren naively thought Bethany was going to propose to her. Bethany holding her close, they watched the water lap at the shore, basking in the serenity of the tiny town. The words came tumbling from Lauren, and she pulled away from Bethany to study her face, to gauge her reaction. Instead of the beautiful smile she anticipated, Lauren received silence, Bethany's jaw slack, and her eyes blinking rapidly. No doubt she'd heard what Lauren said, however, she feigned ignorance, her gaze flickering from the necklace she purchased Lauren and then back to her face.

Tightening her fist around the necklace, Lauren shook the invasive memories away. After grabbing a small trash bag from her bathroom, Lauren tossed the necklace inside, tied the plastic, and flung the bag in the closet. She took a long shower before jumping into her bed, glad to have clean sheets without any remnant of Bethany's cologne. She rolled onto her back, staring at the ceiling. Her bedroom was darkened and the only sounds were the crickets outside her cracked bedroom window. Boo was cuddled by her side and a pang of loneliness washed over Lauren as she closed her eyes.

Maybe she should text Sam and ask for the book loan. All she needed was a good book to get her mind off the events of the last twenty-four hours. Lauren found her phone on her nightstand and sent Sam a quick text.

Hey, I'd love to borrow that book if you're still willing to lend it to me. I could use a high fantasy right about now.

She contemplated the thought of inviting Sam over but thought it would be weird. Her eyes widened. Sam was supposed to come over that evening, but Lauren had completely forgotten about it. Had Jackie canceled the planned game night? Lauren was supposed to have a few fellow teachers come over as well and nobody called her or had stopped by. Lauren immediately called Jackie.

"You okay?" her friend answered on the second ring.

"Yeah, I'm fine. Did you cancel game night with Liam and Bonny?"

"Of course, I did. I didn't want them showing up with junk food and good cheer while you're going through this shit show," Jackie claimed. Lauren smiled at the thoughtfulness of her friend.

"Thank you." But her answer still didn't solve how Sam knew. "Did you happen to mention it to anyone else? I invited Sam over too."

"Sam?"

Even though she sat alone in her darkened room, Lauren blushed. "She delivers my mail. She's really cool, and I figured maybe she'd have fun. I was just wondering because I didn't text her or anything and...I don't know," Lauren trailed off. Maybe Sam was a no-show. Bethany had acted strange when Lauren mentioned inviting her and she wondered if Sam held the same animosity toward her fresh ex-girlfriend.

"Are you sure you're okay, Lauren?" Jackie asked.

"Yes, I swear I'm fine. I think I need to sleep. Thanks again for being an awesome friend."

After they hung up, Lauren opened her social media app on her phone and scrolled until she found Sam's page. She smiled when her eyes ran over Sam's picture. She stood beside a woman slightly taller than her, but they were identical otherwise. Sam's short black hair was in a messy faux hawk, lips curled in a lazy smile. Lauren cleared her throat and closed out of the app. If Sam had decided not to come, she would've let Lauren know. *Maybe she forgot.* Lauren sighed as she placed her phone back on the bedside table and closed her eyes.

A SEARING PAIN shot through Sam's temples and shoulders as she tried to lift her head. "What the hell?" she said but her voice came out in a breath of a whisper, her throat parched and burning. Her eyes opened, and she squinted at the blinding lights coming from above her. The smell of rubbing alcohol and antiseptic filled her senses, a rhythmic chime sounding from beside her. "Hello?" She forced herself up and a shadow advanced toward her.

"Oh, Sam!" Katie's arms wrapped around Sam, provoking a cry of pain as she pressed on Sam's injuries. "Sorry." Katie pulled back and Sam's eyes finally focused enough to see her sister's mascara-streaked face.

"What happened?" Sam croaked.

Katie shook her head, her usually pristine ponytail disheveled, with black strands curling around her face. "You're an idiot. What kind of lifeguard goes surfing at dawn without someone there with you and no other lifeguard on duty? You could have died, Sam." Katie narrowed her eyes.

"I'm feeling the love, Sis. What happened? The last thing I remember was climbing on my board and trying to catch this sick wave."

"Josh got to the beach and saw you struggling in a riptide. You don't understand how close of a call it was. It scared me so bad, Sam." Fresh tears slid from Katie's eyes and Sam attempted to sit up enough to hug her but the sharp pain in her right shoulder stopped her. "You got a good fracture to your clavicle and the orthopedic surgeon already checked out the X-rays. They'll have to fix it surgically. As for your ribs, there isn't much they can do for them plus you have a significant pneumothorax."

"My ribs are broken too? And, you're going to have to break the last word down for me."

"A hole in your lung. What do you expect when you're thrown into the jetty a dozen times?" Katie gripped the railing of the hospital bed.

"I admit it was stupid," Sam lamented.

"You know better," Katie said as she pointed a finger at Sam.

She was right; Sam knew better. "Sorry."

Katie dropped her hand and gave Sam a weak smile. "I'm just glad you're okay. When Josh called me and said you weren't breathing, and the medics were trying to revive you, I..." Katie shook her head and cleared her throat. "Don't you ever do that to me again." Sam knew what Katie was referring to and the memory of their mother's death flashed into her mind.

In hindsight, she shouldn't have gone into the water. Guilt engulfed her as she realized how terrified her sister must have been. "I'm sorry, Katie."

"Don't do it again, okay?"

Sam nodded. She glanced at the damage and winced. There were countless tubes and wires trailing over the bedding. Sam couldn't distinguish which went where. Simply moving her head to investigate her right shoulder sent a sharp burst of fresh pain through her upper right side. A sling held her right arm limply against her chest and she could see faint bruising beneath the ugly blue gown she wore. Thick gauze pads covered the exposed skin and she remembered the blood pouring out of her arm when she looked at herself. Wait. That wasn't right. She had seen her body on the ground, watched them cut off her wet suit and try to revive her. Sam's eyes widened, and the beeping quickened on the monitor beside her. "Did they say anything about my head?"

"Your head?" Katie asked, one eyebrow quirked.

"Yeah. I had the weirdest dream...well, I guess maybe it was a hallucination." She blushed under her sister's scrutiny.

"The CT and MRI were all normal. It could've been a hallucination; you did almost die. I'm going to talk to your nurse to see what time they're taking you into surgery."

"Okay," Sam said and smiled at her sister. Katie squeezed her shoulder, the non-broken one before she left the room.

She banished the memory, taking a deep breath and closing her eyes. When she opened them, through the small gap in the curtain, Sam could see Katie leaning over the edge of the nurse's station chatting to one of the other staff members. God, Sam had scared the shit out of Katie. All she wanted to do was help Katie through her disastrous custody battle and here Sam was making her life more stressful. The scrub-clad woman on the other side of the counter came around and hugged Katie tightly. This was Katie's place of employment, and Sam knew her coworkers were like family to her sister.

The curtain in front of the glass-paneled doors shifted and an oddly familiar face peeked around the fabric. "Miss me?" Margo whispered.

Sam rubbed her eyes, sitting up. She recalled the deal she'd made with the blonde woman approaching her bed. She'd changed clothes, though, now sporting black scrubs. The Grim Reaper; Sam had to admit she kind of fit the part now. "You're real," she breathed.

Margo nodded. She placed a hand on the bedrail and fixed her gaze on Sam's shoulder. "Unfortunately."

"How is this possible?" Sam lifted her left arm and clasped the back of her neck in disbelief. There was no way she was having a conversation with the Grim Reaper. "This can't be real."

Margo took a cigarette from her pocket and put it between her lips. "It's real, buttercup. Get used to seeing my face more often. I was serious about giving you some time to heal, but after that, you'll be on my dime."

"You can't smoke in here; it's a hospital," Sam whispered. Who the hell had she made a deal with?

"Damn," Margo muttered, slipping the cigarette back in the pack. "Look, I'll give you a little break to recover from your dumbassery, but I'm giving you two weeks, got it?"

Sam blinked a few times to test whether or not Margo would disappear, but there she was, her blue eyes glaring at Sam. Maybe it's the pain medication. Assuming Margo was a figment of her imagination, Sam decided to play along. Maybe then she could go back to sleep and the pain in her arm would cease. She tried to take a deep breath but halted halfway through the inhale, the hole in her lung objecting. "Okay, two weeks," she whispered. Over Margo's shoulder, Sam could see Katie rounding the circular nurse's station as she headed back to Sam's room. "Here comes my sister."

"Got to go. I'll see you soon," Margo said with a wink before she slipped out the door to the trauma room.

Only moments later, Katie walked in. "Was that woman from X-ray?"

Sam shrugged. "What woman?" Did her sister see Margo? No, there was no way. Sam was losing it because Margo was a figment of her imagination, not a person.

Katie gave Sam a peculiar look before she shrugged. "Weird. I swear I saw someone leave your room and figured they were going to take you for some more imaging. Anyway, you've got about a half an hour before they'll be ready to take you over to surgery. You should relax while you wait."

Sam nodded and rested her head back, wondering if she was reading so much urban fantasy her brain was creating these bizarre hallucinations. She stared at the ceiling, counting the tiles to keep her mind off her delusion. Margo wasn't real. She wasn't the Grim Reaper, and although Sam had almost died, she was brought back by trained medical professionals, not a mythical creature. Pain medication. It dawned on Sam the pain wasn't as bad as one would expect with a broken collarbone. She peered over at Katie.

"Am I getting pain medication?" Sam inquired. Katie tilted her head and nodded.

"Is it not enough? I can grab the nurse and see if you—"

Sam held up her hand. "No, it's fine. I was only curious." Medication explained the dream. Margo appearing in the room had to have been a dream. It didn't explain how Katie had seen her, but it sufficed as an explanation for now. Sam figured once she researched near-death experiences, she'd probably discover it was a normal occurrence to have vivid dreams. Or, waking dreams. Sam sat, reaching for her phone.

"Where's Josh?" she asked, assuming her friend had it. Katie was sitting in a chair pushed to the wall with her head bent over her cell phone.

"He had to grab something to eat. He was here the whole time they were getting you stabilized."

"Oh crap," Sam muttered. Had she left her phone on the beach in her bag? She was itching to search her predicament on the internet, but she needed her phone to do so.

"What?"

"My phone. I had it on the beach with me. Did Josh find it?"

Katie shook her head and put her own phone on her lap. "I don't think you realize how bad off you were when they brought you in, Sam. I doubt Josh even thought to search for anything of yours on the beach because he was so scared you were going to die."

"I'm glad I'm here." Sam couldn't think of a better response to the seriousness in Katie's tone. The faint memory of slamming into the jagged rocks came to Sam's mind and she shivered.

"Me too."

LAUREN'S PHONE RANG, ripping her from her dreamless sleep. She squinted at the device. Bethany's name flashed on the screen and she sighed as it was almost time for her to get up for work anyway. At five thirty on a Monday morning, she was not going to engage in conversation with Bethany. She ignored the call and closed her eyes again, taking a deep breath. As she exhaled, her doorbell rang. "What the hell?" A hint of guilt jabbed Lauren, so she threw her blankets off and climbed out of bed. *Maybe she needs her clothes for work.* She wrapped a sweater around herself before heading to the front door. Five large boxes sat stacked beside the entryway, labeled for Bethany in Jackie's elegant cursive. Through the peephole, Lauren could see tufts of blonde hair pushed back, a pressed suit hanging on Bethany's lanky frame. She threw the door open with a scowl. The sky held a pink hue as dawn approached, the rosy tint a stark contrast to the dismal meeting.

"What do you want? I didn't throw your stuff away, if that's why you're here, even though I told you I'd let you know when I was ready for you to come get it," Lauren snapped. She took in the sight of Bethany, the white of her eyes now red-streaked, and the bags under her eyes were profound. Lauren had never seen her in such a disheveled state, although she had not a hair out of place. She shifted her weight on Lauren's doorstep, her face full of regret.

Despite Bethany's Armani suit giving her a pristine appearance along with her perfectly styled hair, she looked terrible.

"No, I came here to talk because you won't answer your phone. Lauren, please, just hear me out," Bethany pleaded.

"Why should I even give you the chance to explain yourself?" Lauren folded her arms over chest, more so to steady her breathing than to project her faux apathy. "How could you?"

"It was a moment of weakness."

"Oh, come on, Bethany! Are you kidding me?" The sadness and loss were immediately replaced with anger, Lauren's face contorting in rage. "'A moment of weakness?' You've barely been living with me for five months and you slept with someone in my house?"

Bethany's head dropped, her usual confident façade crumbling in front of Lauren. "You're right. Lauren, let me make it up to you. Please."

"There's no making up for what you did. I let my guard down." She waited until Bethany glanced at her, her cerulean gaze pained, but Lauren continued, "I trusted you and I shouldn't have made that mistake." Lauren's voice quivered, and she turned before the tears spilled from her eyes. "I told you I loved you, and now I know why you said nothing," Lauren added with her back turned. "I'll text you when you can come by for your stuff."

She closed the door, sliding down the solid surface to the floor as she began to cry, knowing she should've let Bethany take her things but unable to force herself to face her again. Damn, why did she have to hurt so badly? She figured she should be used to it by now, with her last relationship ending in a similar fashion. Covering her mouth to quiet the sob, Lauren hoped Bethany couldn't hear her cry. She didn't want to let herself become caught up in the promise of Bethany's artificial apology. Lauren recognized her own vulnerability, and she didn't want Bethany exploiting it. So, she sat there, silent tears falling as she waited for time to pass, unable to move or do anything other than just that. Only time would help her past the hurt.

The soft rumble of Bethany's car starting was muffled through the door. Lauren learned the hard way how time healed when she lost her first love, Maribel. Lauren and Maribel's relationship had started in college, shortly after she began the teaching program. Their love was swift and unyielding, Lauren quickly finding herself head over heels. Three years in, Lauren contemplated a proposal, as their blossoming romance had reached the level Lauren believed unbreakable. Until Maribel decided she wasn't as happy as Lauren and hadn't been for months, seeking companionship elsewhere behind Lauren's back. The aching memory, combined with her current state of events, elicited another sob from her.

Lauren let out a breath as Bethany's car retreated from her driveway. Twenty minutes passed before Lauren stood, wiping her face dry with the sleeve of her sweater. There wasn't an option to give Bethany another chance. Lauren had expressed her trust issues with Bethany when they became exclusive to each other. She knew what Lauren had been through, yet she still trampled over the sliver of trust Lauren had given her. Lauren took a shaky breath and got ready for work.

She wouldn't let her emotions cloud her mood or bleed into her day. Jackie had checked in with her numerous times on Sunday, Lauren persuading her to stay home and not fuss over her. She was determined to make it up to her friend at some point in the week, whether she bought her a gift or baked her something.

The first half of the day went by briskly. During her student's lunch, she headed to the teacher's lounge and found Jackie already sitting at the table beside the window overlooking the football field. Jackie's smile greeted Lauren. "Hey."

"Hi." Lauren took a cup from the cabinet, serving herself coffee from the carafe before adding two scoops of sugar. Although she usually took her coffee black, she needed the extra sweetness to get through the rest of her day.

"How are you?" Jackie's concern was sincere. Lauren stirred creamer into her coffee and sat across from her friend. Forgoing her usual eclectic attire for blue blouse and slacks, Jackie presented as the average teacher, save the clunky rock dangling from a chain around her neck.

"I'm okay. Bethany showed up this morning."

"She did what?" Jackie's mouth gaped.

Although the creamer was well mixed into her coffee, Lauren continued to stir the contents of her cup. The sound of the spoon scraping the ceramic surface was oddly soothing. "She apologized and wanted me to give her a chance to explain."

"And what did you do?" Jackie asked. Lauren met her eyes, fingers twirling the stone hanging from her necklace.

"I told her to leave."

Jackie exhaled through her nose, dropping the gem to pick up her own coffee mug. "Good."

Crossing the room, Lauren sat at the table with Jackie. "I can't say it was easy. She looked terrible."

"There's no excuse she could come up with to fix the trust she broke. She did it in your house, for Christ's sake, Lauren. Did she say where she's staying?"

"You're right and, no, I didn't bother to ask, either. I also didn't give her the boxes before she left, so we'll be seeing each other soon. I can't keep her stuff just because I don't want to see her again."

Jackie reached out and touched Lauren's arm. "You got this. You're strong and you need to remember that strength, no matter what she says. And don't worry about her crap—you tell me a time and day and I'll be there to hand over her stuff."

Lauren nodded, not trusting her voice to convey her thanks to Jackie.

Jackie slapped the table as she stood. "I've got to head back to the classroom to prep for the next project we're doing. You let me know if you need anything later, okay?"

"You rock, Jackie," Lauren said. Her friend grinned before she left the teacher's lounge.

Lauren took her phone out and checked her messages. No word from Sam. Maybe she'd forgotten. Sam wasn't one to ignore a text message and Lauren was getting concerned. She had to admit she wanted to talk to Sam more than to borrow a book. Their varied conversations and mellow banter were just what Lauren needed to get her out of her funk. Jackie was a wonderful friend, but she was too close to the situation with Bethany.

Finding Sam on her friend's list on Facebook, Lauren sent her a quick message.

Hey stranger. I'm sorry if I'm bugging you, but I missed you on game night. I tried to text you but hadn't heard back, so I figured a message would work. We still need to trade those books!

She hoped it wasn't too presumptuous, but she hastily banished the thought based off her and Sam's friendship. Sam was always polite, yet her humor shone at just the right time. Lauren smiled as she thought of Sam's quick-witted retorts and easygoing attitude toward most things. Her sweet smile, warm hazel eyes, lithe body. Lauren's eyes widened. She was attracted to her.

Chapter Six

SAM WALKED THROUGH the hallway, her arm searing with pain. Only five days had passed since her run-in with the rocks, and she was hating every minute of recovery. When she woke up after they'd taken her into surgery to fix her clavicle with a handful of pins, she felt a bit better, aside from the pain in her ribs. Unfortunately, there wasn't much they could do about her broken ribs other than to let them heal on their own. They'd kept her for three days as her right lung had been punctured from her rib fractures, but it seemingly healed itself within the first few hours after surgery, much to both of the doctors' astonishment.

Even with pain medication on board, Sam was hurting way more than she'd anticipated. She gripped the edge of the bathroom counter and tried to take a breath, a sharp burn spreading through her right side to her sternum. "Shit," she muttered, gritting her teeth. She glanced up in the mirror and scrutinized the marred skin of her shoulder, the sutured wound disappearing beneath her button-up. Unbuttoning the shirt, Sam revealed the wound. Though her skin was starting to heal where the surgeon had gone in and fixed her clavicle, the deep scarred groove between her breasts was a vivid purple and angry.

The surgeon told her she was lucky her sternum hadn't been fractured from the impact of the rocks. What the hell did Margo do to her? Sam hoped the whole thing had been an elaborate hallucination conjured up by her near-death experience. The lingering electrical waves still present in her brain when she had lost her pulse had concocted some fantastical illusion, right? That's all a near-death experience was, anyway, she figured from the research she did on Katie's laptop. There was no merit to the details of said hallucination, however, and if this were true, why did it feel so real?

"Sam are you okay?" Katie asked from behind her.

Sam managed a slight nod as she buttoned her shirt back up. "My arm feels like it's going to fall off, and I can't even take a breath without hurting." She turned, grimacing at her sister. Katie stood in the doorway of the bathroom with a worried frown.

"You look like crap but you're healing nicely already."

"I feel like crap," Sam chuckled.

Katie snorted and moved out of the way as Sam ambled out of the bathroom. "Well, seeing how much damage you did to the poor limb, you should be thankful it's still hanging around." They strolled to the kitchen, and Katie grabbed the can of coffee from the pantry. She filled the carafe and started a pot. Sam hissed through clenched teeth as any movement she made caused a fresh wave of pain to emanate from her ribs. She peered down at the counter, holding her breath.

"Sam," Katie said. Sam lifted her head and grimaced again as her sling dug into her neck. Sam was really beginning to loathe the thing, especially when it loosened on her arm. "I know it hurts but you have to keep taking deep breaths. The last thing you need is to develop pneumonia because you aren't breathing deeply enough."

Sam chuckled, the movement causing another wave of pain to burrow through her and she coughed. "Damn it, Katie," she grumbled but she was smiling. She knew Katie was only trying to help. As a respiratory therapist, it was literally her job to hassle people for not taking their lung health seriously. "I guess you're right."

"I know I am. You really have no idea how lucky you are. Dr. Kepler was about to put a second chest tube in you for the pneumo you had but it vanished," Katie said. Katie and the doctor were both taken aback by her recovery, but Sam didn't see what the big deal was.

Sam shrugged. "I wasn't lucky enough to avoid the damn jetty. And don't think my concussion made me magically forget about helping you with the attorney. I transferred the money last night when I used your laptop." Sam threw her a sideways glance. Katie bit her lower lip, her expression frustrated.

Brows furrowing, Katie put a hand on her hip. "I was wondering where that money came from. Sam, you—"

Shaking her head, Sam cut her off, "Nope. I told you I was going to help you, and you told me you'd take the money."

"Fine, as long as you let me return the favor eventually."

Sam smirked at her. "I'm sure you'll figure out how to do that." She took a deep breath and winced from the pain.

"How about I get you an ice pack and some pain meds?" Katie's smile was sympathetic, and Sam wondered if it was the smile she gave her patients when she was working.

"You don't have to wait on me hand and foot. I can get up to do it," Sam claimed, the sling tugging on her right arm and shoulder as she pushed away from the counter with her free hand. She grimaced as the pain thundered through her again.

"Quit or you're going to end up hurting your other arm. Go sit and I'll grab what you need. Take my help while you can because I'm going to run out of time off soon and you'll be on your own."

"All right, all right, I'll sit," she relented and walked over to the living room. Sam settled on the couch, her shoulder throbbing even worse as she reached for the remote with her uninjured arm and turned the television on.

A banana plopped in her lap. "Eat that before you take your pain med, or you'll be throwing it right back up." Sam nodded but rolled her eyes at her sister's motherly tone. Reluctantly, Sam ate the fruit and was thankful when Katie brought her medication to ease the pain. After gulping it down with a glass of orange juice, Sam rested her head back and closed her eyes.

What felt like only a few moments later, a gentle hand shook her uninjured shoulder. "Sam." Katie was standing in front of Sam when she opened her eyes. "Josh stopped by and dropped off your tablet."

How long had she been asleep? Sam took it from her sister. "Thanks. I don't know how I slept through his loud voice."

"He knows not to mess with me." Katie held up her fist in a pretend threat and Sam laughed.

With her phone gone, Sam hadn't been able to check her text messages and couldn't remember her password for Facebook to save her life. The first thing she did was open said app and scroll through numerous messages. The first one that caught her eye was from Lauren and her heartbeat quickened.

Hey stranger. I'm sorry if I'm bugging you but I missed you on game night. I tried to text you but hadn't heard back so I figured a message would work. We still need to trade those books!

Sam grinned. The message had been sent on Monday and it was already Friday. The game night hadn't crossed her mind since the accident and she felt like an ass for not reaching out to Lauren sooner. Not that Lauren would hold it against her. "What's got you grinning so wide?" Katie asked.

Sam shook her head and chuckled. "Just checking all my messages."

Before she could stop herself from potentially saying something embarrassing due to the medications hindering her good judgment, Sam typed her reply.

I had a bad run-in with some rocks out on the 11th Street beach and just got out of the hospital yesterday. I'll be out for a few weeks while I heal. I'm sorry I didn't text you; my phone is lost in the sandy abyss.

Her ears burned at the prompt reply from Lauren.

Oh my God, are you okay? Do you need anything?

Yeah, I'm okay. My sister is babying me back to health. You can come borrow that book if you're interested, though. I'm on Spruce, the third house from the corner with the yellow door. Don't ask. My sister likes yellow.

"Why don't you lie down? I'll keep Ben from bugging you if you want to chill here on the couch for a while," Katie said from behind Sam.

"That'd be awesome," Sam said, turning her head to smile at her sister. "I appreciate your help, Katie. You have no idea how much."

Katie laughed, shaking her head as she beamed at Sam. "Okay, you take a nap because I'm pretty sure those meds have gone to your head."

Sam obeyed, lying on the couch in a crooked, awkward position to keep her arm from hurting. The cushions offered her a lot more support than her bed and she swiftly relaxed. Closing her eyes, Sam let out a long breath, allowing the fatigue to wash over her. She hadn't been awake for very long, but the medication made her numb all over, including her thoughts. Sleep quickly grasped her.

LAUREN SMILED TO herself as she thought of Sam's message.

Yeah, I'm okay. My sister is babying me back to health. You can come borrow that book if you're interested, though. I'm on Spruce, the third house from the corner with the yellow door. Don't ask. My sister likes yellow.

She peered up at the condo in question. Lauren had contemplated whether or not to drop by but after school let out for the day, Lauren decided to go ahead. Although Sam invited her, Lauren didn't want to impose, given Sam was recovering from an injury. If anything, she'd drop off the cookies she'd bought on the way over, grab the book in question, and head out.

She hesitated before knocking on the canary-yellow door, holding the box of cookies in her hand. When the door opened, the woman standing there was not Sam. Her black hair hung loosely over her shoulders, and her eyes were the same beautiful shade of brown as Sam's. "Can I help you?" She eyed Lauren up and down.

"Oh, I'm sorry. I was looking for Sam. I heard she was recuperating from a run-in with some rocks?" Lauren was hoping Sam didn't send her to the wrong house, but the woman in front of her moved, a grin on her face.

"Sure, come on in. She didn't tell me she was expecting anyone."

Lauren stepped into the house, relishing in the instant air conditioning cooling her. "I'm Lauren."

"Katie, her sister. She's right in here," Katie said, showing Lauren into the cozy home.

There she was, on her back, sunk into the couch, eyes closed and breath even. Her dark lashes lay on her bronze cheeks, black hair disheveled from sleep, swooped over her forehead, lush lips parted. Lauren's cheeks burned with a blush as she realized how attracted she was to Sam. A white sling held her right arm up to her chest, a ragged incision peeking out from beneath her button-up shirt. "What happened to her?" she whispered to Sam's sister who ushered her over to the kitchen.

"She decided to go surfing during a storm she claims wasn't there when she got into the water, and she got thrown against the jetty a handful of times. Compound fracture to her clavicle, seven fractured ribs on the right side, punctured lung, and a gnarly concussion. She's on the mend now, though."

"That's awful."

"She's a brute. Do you want some coffee?" When Lauren nodded, Katie took a cup from the cabinet and filled it with the black liquid.

She took the offered cup. "Thank you. We had plans and I hadn't heard from her, so I got a little worried."

Katie smiled at her, taking a cookie from the box and nibbling on it. "Oh, she lost her phone on the beach during the accident. Thanks for the cookies."

Before Lauren could reply, a little voice echoed from the hallway. "Mama?"

Katie peeked around the corner. "Excuse me," she told Lauren and then disappeared. Lauren sipped the black coffee again before she set it on the counter. A shuffling from the living room caught her attention, and she stepped toward the couch.

Lauren smiled as Sam lifted her head, glancing around with confusion. Her eyes widened when they met Lauren's, and she grinned sheepishly. "Hey."

"Hey, you. How are you feeling?"

Sam ran her fingers through her hair and blew out a breath. "Better than I was this morning." She chuckled. "I'm a little embarrassed. I thought me texting you was a dream."

"Well, I'm glad it wasn't a dream. Free coffee is always awesome," Lauren grinned, lifting the cup in the air. Sam's tan cheeks held a pink tinge as she sat up on the couch, her hair adorably ruffled. "You really did a number on yourself, didn't you?" Lauren indicated to the jagged sutures visible under the collar of Sam's T-shirt.

"Yeah, I did. You won't be seeing me delivering the mail for a few weeks."

"I'm just glad you're okay," Lauren said, and she was surprised how much she meant it. "How battered are you?"

Sam scratched her head and shot Lauren a crooked smile. "I've got to keep this sling on for the next few weeks, but I can get around."

"How about we go see a movie? That new one you were talking about comes out this weekend." The movie in question was based loosely off one of the first books Sam recommended to Lauren and she couldn't think of seeing it with anyone but her.

Sam beamed at her. "I'd really like that. I promise to be a cool third wheel." Third wheel? Oh, duh, she didn't know about the abysmal end of her relationship. As Lauren opened her mouth to correct Sam, a small child came barreling through the living room, his little feet stomping on the old hardwood.

"Auntie Sammy, you're awake! Mama told me to leave you alone, but I had to show you my dinosaur drawing. Look, look!" the small child said, eagerly holding up a sheet of colorful paper.

Lauren giggled, and Sam winked at her, dropping her gaze to do as she was told. "Oh, my, this has to be the best dinosaur drawing I have ever seen." The child jumped up and down as Sam stood and headed to the kitchen. She located a magnet, securing the page to the refrigerator. Katie came into the kitchen, smiling at her sister and the child.

Lauren rose from the couch and offered a small wave. "I don't want to impose."

"Let me get the book I was talking about before I forget," Sam said. She led Lauren to the end of the hallway.

Sam's room was cozy, though bland and lacking any personal touches. Lauren was expecting much more than a bed and a small dresser with a handful of books adorning the top of it. "Wow, that's an impressive collection," Lauren said sarcastically.

Sam smiled with a nod, plucking the thickest book from the small stack. "You think this is a lot? You'd lose your mind if you saw the bookshelf at my place." Sam handed Lauren the book. "Katie begged me to stay with her for at least the first week of all this."

"I don't blame her. Your arm looks like it hurts," Lauren sympathized. Each time Lauren caught a glimpse of the injury, she internally grimaced. Sam was taking it as if her injuries were nothing, but from the visibly marred skin, Lauren knew she was playing tough.

"Yeah, but I could've gotten worse."

"I bet you're losing your mind not being able to go surfing," Lauren assumed. Sam's love of the ocean fascinated her, and as Sam scrunched her brows in a grimacing nod, Lauren figured her assumption was correct.

"Yeah, I've been itching to go to the beach, maybe simply sit on the sand and soak in the sounds but Katie would probably kill me," she chuckled with faux nonchalance. She tapped her finger on the book in Lauren's hand as she digressed. "I love this one because there's a great female lead, plus some phenomenal world building. Let me know what you think, and you can keep it as long as you want. Maybe Bethany would like it." Sam's smile was genuine as she handed Lauren the book.

Lauren took a deep breath. "Thanks, Sam. Bethany and I actually split up."

"Oh. Lauren, I'm sorry," Sam said, and she touched Lauren's shoulder, her eyes full of sympathy.

"It's okay." For the first time since her discovery of Bethany's infidelity, Lauren's answer was candid.

Sam's nephew bolted into the room and wrapped his arms around Sam's legs. "Auntie, come see what I made with noodles!" The little boy jumped up and down and Sam laughed at his antics.

"Thank you for the coffee. I better head out," Lauren said.

Sam's smile fell, and she walked toward Lauren. "Are you sure?"

"I've got some lesson plans I've got to go over before Monday, and I'd rather get it all done than wait until last minute. We'll have to get together to see a movie when you're feeling better."

"Absolutely," Sam said. The little boy tugged the hand of Sam's good arm and Lauren followed them out into the living room.

"Thanks again for the book. I'll see you later." Lauren reluctantly opened the door and stepped into the sunshine.

Chapter Seven

"SO, LAUREN?" SAM knew the inquisition was coming and although she found her sister's interest endearing, she was dreading the explanation she'd have to give.

Without lifting her head from the book she was reading, Sam said, "Yeah, she's a regular customer of mine, and we go out for coffee sometimes."

"Hm," Katie replied, clearly unsatisfied with the response she received. "You seem kind of off today. Are you sure you're okay?"

Sam lifted her head. "I'm fine."

Katie snorted at Sam's reply, pushing her hair over her shoulder and fixing her gaze on her sister. "Yeah, sure. Is your arm bothering you or, is this 'girl problems'?"

Sam dropped her eyes and closed the book in her lap. "Lauren and I are just friends." Sam mentally cursed her sister's intuition.

"She's super cute, Sam," Katie insinuated. Seeing Lauren had made Sam incredibly happy, yet the guilt of her aiding in Bethany's infidelity by omission was strong and couldn't be ignored. Sam wanted to tell Lauren about the woman in her house with Bethany but figuring they were no longer a couple, Sam didn't want to pour salt in the wound. Katie cleared her throat, throwing her arms over her chest. "Is she really just your friend?"

"She is."

"Whatever you say," she responded dubiously.

Sam decided she needed to get out of the house to clear her head. She placed her book on the coffee table and stood. "I'm going to take a little walk, maybe see if I can get some monkey bread on the boardwalk."

"As long as you don't go anywhere near the water," Katie remarked as she headed down the hallway to check on Ben, who was suspiciously quiet in his room.

"Yes, mother," Sam called back at her as she slipped on her flip-flops and grabbed a hoodie. She headed out the front door, feeling mildly naked without her cell phone. Maybe she'd walk over to the store and get a new one before she went crazy. The condo was located close to the beach and only a ten-minute walk to the boardwalk staircase. Her arm wasn't hurting at the moment, and Sam was happy for a hiatus. She was hoping she'd be able to return to work before the full six weeks were up. Thankfully, her short-term disability was covering things until then or she wasn't sure how she'd get by.

The echoes of laughter and whirling machinery from the amusement park filled the streets as she approached the tall steps. A steady wind blew from the ocean, and Sam closed her eyes at the top of the stairs, relishing in the feeling of the salty air caressing her. Nothing sounded better than a good run in the surf. Sam sighed with longing as she opened her eyes and stared out at the crashing waves. Of all the places she could have gotten injured, it had to be in her place of tranquility.

The boardwalk was crowded, and she scurried directly across the busy foot traffic, bounding down the stairs onto the beach. Kicking off her flip-flops, Sam scooped them up, the sand still warm from the sun's rays beneath her bare feet. She walked over the uneven terrain until she found the lifeguard stand. She'd spent many summers in this very spot as a lifeguard for extra money and the sense of nostalgia almost eased her mind.

The water lapped at the shore, spilling over and receding back into the ocean. Sam sank into the sand, her back leaning against an overturned lifeguard rowboat as a flock of seagulls dipped into the water. The sun was up, teasing the horizon as it lazily made its way below the water's edge. She should've been dead. She glanced at the injury, the sling far too heavy around her neck. How had she survived?

Sam took in a deep breath of the cool air, relishing in the serenity, closing her eyes again as a breeze tugged her hair. The vision she had was far too real to ignore the potential, and she wondered what to expect. Had she truly agreed to be the Grim Reaper's helper? When she opened her eyes again, the sky was becoming a deep purple, tingeing the scant clouds indigo. Waves crashed over the rock jetty shooting out of the water, a layer of white foam frothing around the black stone. The rock formation wasn't the same one responsible for almost killing her. Well, she was technically dead for five minutes. The sound of the ocean usually calmed Sam's mind but this night was different. A stray scream from the amusement park on the pier sent a shiver through her body, and she tried to shake the ominous foreboding.

Her bare toes curled in the cooling sand and she sighed. Another wave crashed over the jetty, sprinkling water over its surface. Maybe she imagined the whole scenario with Margo. Perhaps her subconscious didn't know how to process her injuries and conjured up the fallacy to cope. "Funny meeting you here," a familiar voice said from beside her. Or, maybe it really did happen.

Sam whipped her head around and met Margo's blue stare. "Holy shit, you scared me."

"Did you think I wouldn't be back?" Margo clasped Sam's back with a calloused hand and chuckled. The Grim Reaper wore a ratty hoodie over a gray button-up shirt, cargo shorts and black steel-toed boots in lieu of her sneakers, the ring in her nose glimmering in the low light. She sure had a strange sense of fashion.

Shaking her head, Sam took a deep, uneven breath. "No. I figured I had a nightmare after drowning. Now, I think I'm crazy."

"Come on, we've got places to be, people to see." Margo hooked her arm under Sam's, lifting her from her spot on the ground with surprising strength. *I'm going crazy*. She grabbed her flip-flops.

She had hit her head hard during the accident, and although the doctors reassured her that there was no damage, she was considering there was a possibility of it. "What happened to my two weeks?"

Sam let Margo yank her forward and they walked by the water's edge, the sun had set completely, shrouding the beach in darkness. "Shit happens; time restraints become a real thing."

"So, how does this all work again?" Sam tried to catch Margo's sight, but the other woman kept her head straight, vision poised ahead.

"I've got a problem child; you convince them to move on, and then we go about our lives until another one comes along."

"How many people am I going to have to do this for? I have a job and a life, you know."

Margo chortled. "You are not the only assistant. Okay, figure about one hundred and sixty thousand people die each day in this country alone. Narrow that down by state and population density, we're looking at about two thousand per state, give or take a few hundred. Do you really think I would be the only Reaper let alone you be my only helper?"

Sam chewed her lip. She hadn't given much thought to the logistics of being the Grim Reaper's assistant and the probability of helping a demon go around the world to get reluctant spirits to leave. Was Margo a demon, and if she wasn't, what was she? "I guess I didn't think about it." Their footfalls were muffled by the soft sand as they continued parallel with the water. "How many people do I have to help? And what do I help with?"

"It depends on the situation. Sometimes we get dry spells and other times, we can't keep up. You convince them they can cross, they've lived a great life, blah, blah, blah, and they go on to the other side." Margo's tone was becoming sharper.

"What's on the other side?"

"As I told you before, not for me to know. It's different for everyone."

The beach was silent for a few moments, the sound of a seagull's call wafting to Sam's ears and a siren somewhere close in the city. She didn't want to continue the barrage of questions but had to ask one more. "Why'd you pick me?"

Margo exhaled loudly. "I told you: upper management isn't happy with my monthly quotas, so I decided to find an apprentice. I could've let you die instead of offering you the job."

"But, why me?"

"Good God, do you ever stop with the fucking questions?" Margo stopped, searching Sam's face. Sam glanced at the sand, watching the sea water lap at their feet as the tide came in. Margo's gaze was far too intense to keep staring.

Margo sighed. "Because I decided you'd be perfect for this line of work." She took a few steps forward, throwing a glare back at Sam. "No more questions. We're starting out with an easy one tonight to get you into the swing of things."

"Okay," Sam stated.

Margo pushed through the boardwalk visitors, the amount having dwindled since the beginning of the school year. When they reached the opposite side, Margo hurried down the tall staircase, turning to gawk at Sam while she ambled after her, her legs still sore from her run-in with the rocks. When she made it to the sidewalk, Margo bumped her arm, making Sam curse as pain shot through her shoulder and ribs. "What the hell?"

"Where're you parked?" was Margo's curt reply.

Sam scoffed, rubbing her arm over the sling. "I can't drive for another six weeks."

"Well, shit. Guess we're taking my ride," Margo said, taking off toward an alleyway behind a busy restaurant. She dug out a key fob from the pocket of her white cargo shorts, the lights of a pale-blue MINI Cooper blinking. Sam tried to stifle her laughter and Margo glared at her as she opened the driver's door. "Get in."

The fifteen-minute drive was absent of conversation, as all Sam wanted to do was continue with her line of questioning, but she knew Margo wouldn't offer her the answers she needed. Why the hell was she alive and why did she choose Sam? Was Margo alive or was she a spirit? She wouldn't be able to drive a car if she were, right? What kind of spirits was Sam responsible for and how far did her area of responsibility fall? Margo drove through the affluent neighborhood in the northern tip of the island, the houses and lots much larger than the ones in town.

Margo stopped in front of a large Tudor-style home, the picket fence painted an off-white and the porch lights dimmed. She turned the car off and climbed out, Sam following her up the pathway. Wind chimes hung from the porch's awning and their delicate chime in the wind added to the ethereal feeling that was already overwhelming Sam as she let Margo led her to the back of the house.

She stopped abruptly, standing in front of a large bay window. "Take a peek," Margo whispered. Sam knelt in the flower bed below the window, the cool, damp earth beneath her knees spreading a chill through her body as well as the scene in front of her. To Sam, it appeared to be a plain bedroom. Floral prints hung on the pale-yellow walls, the lilies and tulips depicted matching the cream-colored carpet beneath an empty bed boxed in by bedside tables. She didn't see any ghostly forms hanging around, nor did she hear chains and moaning. What did a ghost look like, anyway? She wanted to ask Margo that very question but Margo's face held a stoic expression as she peered into the window.

Beside the bed in a tall wingback chair sat a distraught man crying, hands over his face. "Would you look at him?" a voice cracked from behind them. Startled, Sam fell back, landing on her butt in the damp soil of the flower bed. A woman glanced at her and Margo. The woman's back was significantly hunched, snowy white brows furrowed. Long, frayed white hair hung over her shoulder in a wispy braid, her knuckles bumpy as she pointed to the window.

"Ah, here's the stubborn old bat," muttered Margo.

The old woman shook her head, unaware of Margo's comment. "He's going to be lost without me. I don't know how he'll manage."

Sam turned to Margo, a brow quirked. "How am I supposed to get her to go with you?" she whispered.

Margo shrugged and lit a cigarette, her hand cupping around the flickering flame of her lighter to combat the slight breeze. "What would you want someone to say to you?"

This was a thought Sam had run through her head numerous times in the last few days when she humored the possibility that her 'hallucination' was real. If she hadn't taken Margo's deal, how would Margo have convinced her to go to the other side, especially when she hadn't a clue what this entailed? Sam cleared her throat and looked at the old woman. She seemed so real as if Sam could reach out and touch her gnarled, arthritic hand. "Who is he?"

The old woman sighed, the breath shuddering her body as it came out harshly. "My son. He's been caring for me the last year and a half after I fell ill, never leaving my side for more than a few hours. I can't leave him." It was strange, Sam standing beside the woman. She seemed so real, so physical. Sam reached out and touched the woman's back. A gasp left her mouth as she physically touched the woman, a tingle flowing up Sam's arm, lifting the hairs on her skin as it advanced to the rest of her body.

"He sounds like a wonderful son. You must've raised him well," Sam said despite the strange sensation. The old woman nodded at Sam's words, her face despondent, and her gaze fixed on her son. Sam turned her attention back through the window as the man stood, and another woman who appeared to be similar in age wrapped her arms around him.

"Who's the woman with him?"

"My son's wife. She's been wonderful through all of this and has been by Kevin's side since the start. I couldn't have asked for a better daughter-in-law."

An idea formed in Sam's mind and she threw a glance back at Margo who was staring at a cell phone, cigarette dangling from her lips as she moved her fingers over the glowing screen. What the hell—Grim Reapers had smartphones? Before she could lose her focus, Sam turned back to the troubled spirit. "So, she'll help him through your passing?" she ventured.

The old woman met Sam's gaze, tears sliding down her wrinkled face. "Yes, she will." She turned, took a deep breath, and set her shoulders. "All right. Where does your bossy friend want me to go?"

"Uh, Margo?" Sam was dumbfounded to find her scant persuasion had worked, and the woman was ready to go, just like that. The process seemed far too easy.

Margo grinned, slipping her phone into the pocket of her tattered hoodie and stubbing the cigarette out on the sole of her boot. With a cavalier flourish of her hand, Margo pointed to the road. "After you, my dear." Sam helped the old woman up the slight incline toward the street, and they walked down the quiet neighborhood road. "Now, you'll probably see a light or something soon. You'll want to follow it," Margo said. Her fingers curled, then spread, a flicker of glittery air coalescing around her hand. Sam moved closer, desperate to see more of the strange display, in awe at the sparkling air. When she stepped forward, she bumped into Margo's arm. A shock wave shuddered through Sam's body, causing her to draw a sharp breath. Power coursed through Sam, raw and biting, coiling in her chest underneath her breastbone, forcing its way through her body.

Enlightenment flashed across the old woman's face as she stared out at the empty street where Margo's glittering force was directed. The air wavered before Sam's eyes, the image distorting into an opaque surface. Dizziness washed over her, the sound of her heart thundering in her ears.

"Oh, my," the old woman muttered, moving forward with tentative steps. The atmosphere shifted, like curtains billowing in the wind, fluttering glimpses of another world, and she disappeared.

"Where'd she go?" Sam was frozen in place, baffled the old woman was no longer present, her skin tingling where she'd bumped Margo.

Margo dropped her hand, rubbing her palm over the spot Sam touched. Her gaze caught Sam's, her expression puzzled for a moment before she chuckled heartily, shaking her head. "To wherever it is she belongs," she said as she walked to her car.

Sam caught up to her, clutching the sling to lessen the impact of moving too fast. "How did you do that?"

"What, opening the door? It's the one bit of magic psychopomps have aside from basic illusion."

"That's what you're called? Not death or the Grim Reaper, crypt keeper?" Sam found herself intrigued. She'd never heard the term before. What little she knew of death was what she'd been taught at Sunday school when her mother forced her to go.

Margo folded her arms over her chest and leaned against her car. "No, smartass. We're called psychopomps or Grims. I'm done answering your questions for the day." She pushed off the car and yanked open the driver's door.

Sam barely made it to her seat before Margo was pulling away from the curb. "Wait, one more: what was that feeling?" She could taste the lingering electricity of it on her tongue, feel her arms vibrating and pressure in her chest.

"Just a taste of what it's like to open a portal," Margo said dubiously.

"A portal?"

"No more questions," Margo grunted, shifting the car into drive and speeding down the road.

The energy pulsed within her, a lingering flutter of power thudding through her veins, tensing her muscles. She was galvanized, bouncing her feet off the floor of the car, a pent-up sensation flowing through her. "Where are we going now?"

"I'm taking you home. Where do you live?" Margo asked without glancing at Sam.

After rattling off her sister's address, Sam asked, "Will I feel the same sensation every time you open a portal?" Margo turned the music up in lieu of an answer.

When they reached the curb in front of Katie's condo, Margo twisted herself toward Sam. "You weren't supposed to feel the energy, to begin with, and I'm still trying to figure out why the hell you did," Margo said curtly. "Now, get out."

Sam hesitantly left Margo. She climbed up the stairs and into the condo. The living room was dark, Katie and Ben having already gone to bed. A light above the kitchen sink lit her path as she snuck back to her sister's spare bedroom. She flopped on the bed without changing, throwing a pillow over her head before she allowed herself to fall into a heavy sleep.

A shrill scream echoed into the night, jagged and ceaseless, shrouded in anguish, strangled by water. Sam woke, her heart pounding in her chest, perspiration sticking to every inch of her body. Deep, heaving breaths did nothing to stifle the fear present in the room. The hazy images of the nightmare were staggered in the periphery of her mind, crashing waves, sharp rocks, any solidity in their context unreachable. Her breathing slowed, as did her heart, and Sam swiped her hands over her face.

She threw her feet over the edge of the bed and tried to recall the sequence of the nightmare. An untimely death. Was *any* death timely? Sam shook her head as she stood and padded across the plush carpet of her sister's condo. Margo had held true to her word, refusing to answer the questions Sam threw at her. The woman's confidence faltered upon Sam feeling the energy of her opening a portal. How had she brought Sam back anyway? Margo was infuriating, but Sam couldn't get her to budge. She did save Sam's life, and Sam owed her the terms of their agreement for her act. The glint of the dagger in Margo's hand came to her mind, the Reaper pressing her bleeding hand to Sam's wound. What the hell had she done to her? What did this make her, and did Margo even know?

Sam quietly grabbed a glass from the cabinet, turning the faucet. Her hand hovered under the stream of water as she filled the glass and it dawned on her: her shoulder wasn't screaming in agony anymore. She hadn't put the sling on before she left the bedroom and she lifted her arm, the action not eliciting the searing pain it had just hours prior. The glass under the faucet spilled over, causing Sam to hastily switch the water off before she placed the cup on the counter. She headed back to her room, confounded.

With the door closed, Sam flipped on the light. She carefully unbuttoned her shirt, let it slip from her shoulders, and stared at herself in the mirror hanging on the back of the bedroom door. The injury on her collarbone appeared substantially different than it had the day before as if another week or two of healing had passed. The redness was gone, replaced by pink blotches, the six-inch marred skin tucked and fused. A handful of the sutures had fallen out. She moved her limb up and down, side to side. Ran her fingers over the raised skin. A scant hint of pain. It didn't make sense. The day before, she'd been in agony.

Sam shook her head in disbelief. What the hell was going on? She clenched her fists and settled at the end of her bed, staring at her reflection. So many questions, the most pressing matter being when she would see the psychopomp, or Grim, again. With no way to contact her, Sam was left wondering when and where Margo would call upon her again, vainly hoping there wouldn't be a next time at all.

Chapter Eight

"OKAY, GUYS, WE'LL be going over the homework for tonight first thing in class Monday, so I expect everyone to be well versed in the topic. Have a good weekend," Lauren said as her students filed out of her classroom on Friday afternoon.

She sighed, gathering her belongings before wiping the board clear. Her phone buzzed in her pocket and she smiled when she read the text from a strange number.

I got a new phone! Yay! It's Sam, if you haven't figured that out. Are you free this weekend? I'm still debilitated but we could catch a movie.

Lauren grinned as she turned, tossing her grade book into her bag with her free hand.

A movie sounds great. How about tonight, the Boardwalk Theater around 8? We can figure out what to see when we get there.

A harmless date was exactly what she needed.

"Hey, what are you doing tonight?" Jackie poked her head through the threshold of the open door.

Lauren glanced up, grinning at her friend. "I have a date."

"You and Bethany have only been broken up for two weeks and you're already on the prowl?" Jackie chuckled. Lauren was sure her friend hadn't meant the comment in a demeaning way.

Lauren sighed, "It's not like that, though. We're only going to the movies."

"Enjoy yourself. Nothing *has* to happen. And if something happens, it doesn't have to go further than you want it to." Jackie crossed the classroom and put a comforting hand on Lauren's shoulder. "Don't let Bethany's shitty decision ruin romance for you, Lauren."

Her phone vibrated again, and Lauren took the diversion.

Did you finish the book?

"Is this date with Sam, your mail carrier?" Jackie asked. Lauren typed her reply with a grin on her face.

I consumed it. I was hoping I could keep myself from finishing it so fast because of the length, but I couldn't help myself! Want me to pick you up at 6:45 or have you been released to drive yet?

"Are you listening to me?" Jackie cut in. Lauren glanced up and blushed at her friend's gleeful expression. "Seems like I don't need to lecture you on having a good time. Any girl that makes you smile like that is okay in my book—as long as it isn't Bethany."

"It's just a movie, and yes, it's Sam. I don't know if she's interested in anything more than our friendship, and that's all I'm interested in right now," Lauren said. Honestly, she was hoping Sam wanted more, but wasn't sure if getting into a relationship was a good idea.

Jackie pulled her dreads back with a hair tie, smiling. "I want you to be happy and if this happens by hanging out with another bookworm and geeking on weird movies, then go for it."

"We'll see where the night takes me."

"Don't do anything I wouldn't do," Jackie said with a wink.

Lauren grabbed her bag and headed home, excitement coursing through her at the prospect of her date.

A FEW HOURS later, Lauren pulled up beside the curb and got out of the car. Sam bounded down the staircase of her sister's condo, head bent and dark hair slightly obscuring her face. The white sling she'd had on the last time Lauren saw her was gone, her arms both at her sides as she looked up, beaming when she noticed Lauren. "The movie we wanted to see isn't in our tiny, little theater. They've got a few others playing at eight, so I'm sure once we get there we can agree on one."

"How about the first one to the car gets to pick?" Sam said before darting to the passenger door. Lauren chased after her, giggling at the sudden childish behavior. When they both climbed in at the same time, Lauren grinned at Sam.

"I guess we'll have to toss a coin," Lauren laughed as she started the car. "The book was fantastic, by the way." Lauren glanced over at Sam as she drove, and Sam's face lit up.

"You liked?" Sam asked, and Lauren nodded. "Sweet. I've got the rest in the series if you're interested." Books were what sparked their friendship. Lauren remembered the day Sam asked her what she ordered from a large online bookstore when she'd delivered what was probably the fifteenth book in two months. Lauren had blushed and told Sam the author's name, thus beginning their book sharing and eventual friendship.

"What happened to your sling?" Lauren asked.

"My collarbone is healing already, so I don't need it anymore," Sam explained, glancing out the window to her right."

They spent over ten minutes trying to decide on a film, opting to see the latest horror movie offered. Finding a spot in the back, the two sat, chuckling over the previews preceding the film. As the movie started, Lauren put her hand on the armrest, her fingers brushing Sam's knuckles. "Oh, sorry," she apologized. Sam only smiled. Truth be told, Lauren wanted to hold her hand. No, now was not the time for her to start a relationship with anyone, especially not her friend.

She stole a glance at Sam, the profile of her face stunning in the flashes of light flickering from the screen. Jawline defined, long lashes touched her cheek as she blinked. Sam caught Lauren's stare and shot her a smirk before turning her attention back to the screen. Even in the darkness of the theater, Lauren worried Sam would see the blush creeping over her face.

They both laughed after the movie ended when they admitted to each other they hated it. "I'm not sure what was worse—the movie or the couple making out the entire time behind us," Sam said, shaking her head as she walked out onto the boardwalk. Night had fallen during the film, and the thick clouds above were illuminated by the various lamps adorning the edges of the long boardwalk. Lauren gazed out at the nearly barren boardwalk, a scant handful of people walking down the planks. The area always gave her such a strange, isolated feeling during the off-season when it lacked the normal flow of tourists.

"It was a pretty terrible movie but at least it made us laugh."

Sam nodded, a huge grin on her face. "Yeah, and that alone made the make-out session stop for all of five minutes."

They stood staring at each other for a moment, and Lauren didn't want the night to end just yet. "Do you want to walk a bit, or are you ready to head to my car?" Lauren ventured.

"A walk sounds really nice." Sam's smile caused Lauren's heart to quicken and her own lips curled into a crooked grin as they set off toward nowhere in particular. They were quiet for a few minutes, the sounds of waves crashing onto the shore coalescing with the distant sound of traffic. The two amusement parks were both closed for the night as it was nearing 11:00 p.m. They were alone in their easy pace, except for the occasional late-night walker. "I love when it's like this," Sam said. "I used to come here as a teen and sit at the arcade until they closed, watching people play. Then, I'd wander down the boardwalk, soaking up the quiet."

Without conscious thought, Lauren asked, "Wasn't the boardwalk lonely?"

"The quiet was better than being surrounded by all my little cousins. My aunt's house was what I like to refer to as controlled chaos without the control." Sam glanced over at Lauren, the eye contact stirring something within Lauren. Before she could figure out what it was, Sam turned her gaze forward, Lauren following suit. The long, winding boardwalk lay stretched out for miles in front of them. She wanted to know more about Sam's upbringing, actually, everything about Sam, but she tried to squash the feeling. Lauren had no business getting involved with anyone at the moment, certainly not someone as sweet as Sam.

"After my mom died, Katie and I stayed with our step-aunt. Considering we didn't have another place to go, it wasn't terrible," Sam said neutrally. Their conversations in the past were varied, but rarely did they talk about their childhoods. Her eyes were focused ahead, and Lauren stayed quiet while she waited for her to continue. "I used to hang out at the arcade on the end of the boardwalk. Even when I ran out of quarters to play, the owner never bugged me."

They continued walking, the faint creak of the wooden planks beneath their feet echoing in the silence. Lauren shifted closer to Sam and let her fingers graze over Sam's hand. Sam met her eyes and smiled as she intertwined their fingers.

A light wind swelled around them, causing Lauren's hair to sweep across her face and she stopped, struggling to tame her locks. Sam was laughing when Lauren tugged her hair back and forced it in a bun with the spare hair tie in her pocket. "That came out of nowhere," Lauren said, staring out at the beach, the surf white as it crashed upon the shoreline

"I think we're in for a windstorm," Sam said, her head tilted toward the sky. She was right; the sky was laden with nimbostratus clouds, and the wind whipped the loose awnings above the establishment to their right. Loose cattail tufts from the dunes blew past, caught on the strong gust tearing through the beach below where they stood. "Ah, we're being attacked!" Sam chuckled, flailing her arms around to displace the little cottony wisps.

Lauren laughed, enthralled by the cute behavior and wanting nothing more than to kiss her. Sam stopped, dropping her arms when she caught Lauren's gaze with her own. Lauren's giggles halted when she noted the staunch desire in Sam's brown eyes. "Lauren," she began, her voice raspy as she licked her lips.

Lauren tipped her head to the side, bringing her hands up to Sam's face, cupping her cheeks. Any rational or otherwise logical thought vanished at that moment, as she was taken over by need. "Kiss me," Lauren whispered. Sam pressed her lips to Lauren's, hands touching her sides gingerly. It was chaste, her lips brushing Lauren's, but Lauren lost herself in the contact, closing her eyes, and snaking her arms around Sam's neck. The heat of Sam's body radiated against Lauren, and she sighed, parting her lips as Sam did the same. Sam's tongue grazed Lauren's mouth and she cooed. Sam's arm grasped Lauren's back, drawing her closer as the wind threatened to break up their kiss.

Sam pulled back, breathless as she met Lauren's eyes. "Is this okay?" she asked, her hand brushing back the hair from Lauren's face.

"More than okay," Lauren murmured as she brought her fingers to Sam's short hair, grasping the strands and pulling Sam's face to hers. Sam's lips were pliable, delicate and warm on her own. Lauren sighed, opening herself to the kiss. Sam spread her fingers over the nape of Lauren's neck, sending a shiver through her body. Grasping fistfuls of Sam's jacket, Lauren tugged her closer, her own back hitting the wall of the closest closed storefront. Sam's body pressed against her own, teeth capturing Lauren's lower lip, gripping her hip with her hands.

A chilled gust whipped around them, stirring the errant leaves scattered on the ground. Lauren shouldn't have kissed her, but she couldn't stop. It was far too soon for her to delve into anything, but this didn't stop her from letting out a throaty moan as Sam's tongue grazed the roof of her mouth, the sensation provoking a fervor she hadn't expected. The kiss didn't have to *be* anything more than a kiss. She slipped her hands beneath Sam's hoodie and shirt, her skin hot under Lauren's caress. Sam arched as Lauren's fingernails grazed her ribs, edging closer to her bra.

Lauren would be lying to herself if she said she didn't want this to be more than just a kiss.

"Excuse me," a voice cut into their private moment. A uniformed police officer rode over on a bicycle. Lauren dropped her hands. "The boardwalk is technically closed."

Sam pulled back from Lauren, her face flushed, eyes heavy-lidded. "Sorry, officer," she mumbled.

"It's all right. Have a good night." The officer bid them goodbye as Lauren threaded her fingers in Sam's and headed toward the staircase closest to the parking lot. Sam was silent, her thumb running over the back of Lauren's hand as they walked down the stairs and onto the sidewalk. The massive structure of the boardwalk sheltered them from the wind pressing off the ocean and Lauren stopped to stare at Sam.

Sam was watching Lauren, eyes narrowed and still tinged with lust. The expression caused Lauren's heart to race anew. "I haven't got caught making out on the boardwalk since I was a teenager," Sam quipped, her smile rueful and adorable.

"Oh, did you make a habit out of that?" Lauren's eyebrow lifted, and she smirked. Sam pushed back an errant strand behind Lauren's ear, her hand lingering at the base of her neck. The gleam in Sam's hazel eyes was different, and it ignited a stirring within Lauren, a dangerous attraction she wasn't ready for. She couldn't start this, despite wanting it so badly.

"No, only once in a blue moon."

When they reached Sam's sister's condo, Lauren parked in front and turned to her. Sam brushed her fingers through Lauren's hair, and Lauren closed her eyes, relishing the sensation. Lips brushed Lauren's cheek and she smiled. As much as she wanted to hold onto the hope Sam wasn't like Bethany, Lauren had to be true to herself and not let her guard down. She was in no shape to step into a relationship, and she knew it wouldn't be fair to put herself at risk of heartbreak so soon. "Sam?" Lauren whispered. Saddling Sam with such baggage wouldn't be fair, either, and she had to ensure their encounter was casual, lest she ruin their friendship.

Sam drew back and smiled. Lauren steadied herself. "I find you extremely attractive, and you're an amazing person," Lauren began, and she hated what she was doing as Sam's smile faltered. "But I'm not looking for more than casual dating. Bethany and I just broke up two weeks ago, and I'm healing from it. I don't want to get into anything and not be there completely. It wouldn't be fair to either of us. Am I making sense?" Lauren noticed Sam's shoulders visibly slump and her brows furrow.

"Yes, it makes sense and I completely understand," Sam said hastily. "I had a great time, and I'd love to hang out again." Her words seemed genuine but Lauren could see a pained expression behind her bluff.

"We should. I'll let you know when I'm free again."

"Okay. Thanks for the ride," Sam said before slipping out of the car. She paused, her gaze cautious. "Lauren, I don't want you to feel pressured into anything. I'm okay with being friends."

"Thanks," Lauren murmured. Sam closed the passenger door with a short wave as she turned and walked up the sidewalk. As Sam's form climbed the stairs to her sister's condo, Lauren wondered if she ruined their friendship with her impulsive behavior.

Chapter Nine

SAM STRETCHED HER arm, testing the limits. The scent of antiseptic and the associated memories threatened to bring her breakfast back up. She knew her arm was healed but had to attend the doctor appointment regardless.

"It's remarkable, really," Dr. Kepler said as she examined the X-rays. The surgeon's face scrunched as she sighed. At her three-week follow-up, Sam's pain was nonexistent. Katie had been livid when she realized Sam wasn't wearing the sling anymore, her disbelief at her swift healing just as strong as Sam's own. "Your rib fractures are healed as well as your clavicle. The large pneumothorax you had prior to surgery surprised me with how quickly it closed on its own, but this is incredible. No signs of pneumonia, no lasting damage I can see."

Sam chewed her lip, unsure what to make of it. "Apparently you work miracles," she said. Margo had yet to reach out to her again and nearly a week had passed.

"And you're sure there's no damage to my head?" She considered confiding in the doctor about Margo and the weird events since her near-death experience, but she didn't want Dr. Kepler sending her to a shrink.

The doctor fixed her gaze on Sam. "No, your MRI showed all is normal. Is there a reason you're concerned?"

Sam's throat became dry and she shook her head. "No, I was just curious because of the random headaches and weird dreams, but if it's okay, then it's okay. As I said, you work miracles."

Dr. Kepler seemed unconvinced. "Okay. If these headaches get worse, please contact our office. In the meantime, I'll set you up with a referral to the neurologist and perhaps a psychologist to delve deeper. It could be a lingering effect from the accident." She glanced at the computer as she was typing her notes. "Well, at any rate, you can drive, but I still want you to take the full course of six weeks from work. And no swimming until your next follow-up."

"Okay."

When the appointment concluded, Sam went outside, taking deep breaths of the fresh air. Josh was waiting in his little Toyota, his lips moving and head bouncing behind the windshield. Sam could hear music blaring from the speakers even on the outside of the car, and the noise engulfed her when she opened the passenger door. "You're done already?" Josh yelled over the music before he turned it down.

"Yeah, thankfully. I'm all healed, and I get to drive myself around now. No more praying you get me from point A to point B without killing us both."

Josh stuck his tongue out at her as he started the car. "Next time I won't take the day off to drive you to your appointment, then."

"You're self-employed, so I don't feel bad." Sam fastened her seat belt and held onto the handle of the door as Josh pulled out of the medical center's parking lot and flew down the road. His driving was worse than Margo's.

"So, when can you surf again?" Josh asked.

The last thing on her mind was surfing. Sam loved the thrill of it, of course, but the whole situation was wearing on her. Her brain appeared normal so why was she hallucinating? She knew Margo wasn't a hallucination, however, she held onto the possibility as the Grim Reaper hadn't shown her face since the first soul Sam watched move on. Margo was real, flesh-and-blood real. Sam remembered the surge of energy when the portal opened, craved it like a drug. She cleared her throat to dispel the longing. "I'm not supposed to swim until I go back for my next appointment."

"Lame. Where am I dropping you off, your place or Katie's?"

"Mine so I can get my car. I was serious about not wanting to die."

The car was quiet save the faint music still playing through the stereo. "So," Josh began after the short verbal hiatus. Sam glanced over at him to find him grinning. "How'd the date go last Friday?"

Sam picked a piece of lint off the seam of her shirt. "It wasn't really a date, more like a platonic movie outing."

Josh snorted, shaking his head at her. "I'm sure."

"Okay, we kissed but—"

"Platonic my ass," Josh snickered.

"But, she doesn't want a relationship right now. They broke up a few weeks ago, and I can't blame her for not wanting to jump into anything right off the bat, can you?"

"No, but don't get hurt, Sam," Josh pleaded as they turned onto Sam's road. "I can tell you've got it bad for that girl." She lacked the strength to deny his words and she sighed. The date hadn't been what she expected by a long shot. Their kiss had been unexpected, and Sam wasn't surprised how much she wanted more. The delicate situation left her troubled, respecting Lauren's wishes but also longing for more. Sam hadn't been surprised by Lauren's response when she dropped her off—Lauren *had* just gotten out of her relationship with Bethany.

Her life was complicated enough without throwing in the added deal she'd made with Margo. A deal she begrudgingly could tell no one about unless she wanted to be committed.

She climbed out of Josh's car, bidding him goodbye. Without stepping foot in her own apartment, Sam got into her car and headed to her sister's condo.

She puttered around Katie's apartment without much purpose. There wasn't much to do, save some dishes, since Ben was back in school, and she wanted to let Katie know how her appointment went before she headed to her own apartment. Sam was drying the last of the clean dishes as Katie walked into the kitchen, pajamas wrinkled from a restless sleep, assuming she'd gone back to bed after getting her son on the bus. She rubbed her eyes, pouring herself a cup of coffee. "Sleep well?" Sam asked idly. Her sister shrugged and took a sip of the black liquid, grimacing. "Any news on your next hearing?"

Katie grinned. "Actually, yes. My lawyer seems fairly optimistic after the last meeting with John's attorney and our next hearing is planned for early next week."

"Sounds promising. What do you think will happen?"

Her sister shrugged. "All I want is for John to stop being so immature about this whole ordeal and realize what's best for our son. Taking him around the world while he works is not going to be good for him."

Sam nodded.

"How'd your appointment go?" Katie digressed.

Sam grasped the back of her neck. "Good. Dr. Kepler was surprised I'm healed up. I'm not allowed to go back to work, but I can drive now."

Katie gave her a skeptical grin. "Wow, that was quick, Sam. I expected her to give you a load of crap for not wearing your sling. I guess I must be jaded because I'm used to caring for an older generation, and they heal a lot slower than you would."

Katie settled onto the couch and sipped her coffee, obviously enjoying the respite of her son being at school while she woke up and began her day. Her sister and the doctor weren't the only ones astonished by her recovery; Sam had trouble believing her quick healing had to do much with her age but rather something more. Something like being resurrected by a demon.

"NO THANKS, BETHANY," Lauren murmured after she read the message. The text was much like the rest Bethany had sent her way:

I was an idiot. Please let me make it up to you.

Lauren was through and, although she wanted to have a mature, adult conversation with Bethany, she knew it would be unlikely when she continued to tell Lauren she could make it up to her. Nothing would redeem Bethany in Lauren's eyes, so she continued to avoid her. When Bethany came to Lauren's house to pick up her belongings, Lauren hid in her room as Jackie—true to her word—acted as a buffer for Lauren while Bethany packed her boxes into a borrowed truck. Even when she begged Jackie to talk to Lauren, Jackie refused and sternly told Bethany to leave.

Lauren hurried up the worn path to Jackie's loft. Peeling white panels revealed a gray undertone to the weather-beaten exterior of the two-story beach house, the rickety staircase unnerving as Lauren climbed up to the porch. The home could've been made for Jackie, the spacious second level perfect for her work space. She'd helped Jackie move her stuff from the dorms to the location after graduation. The absence of any family around Jackie always left Lauren curious, but she'd never ask outright. Though she'd disclosed her entire family history and upbringing to Jackie, Lauren couldn't say the same for her friend. Her knowledge of Jackie's pre-college life amounted to her having received a full-ride scholarship for her art and leaving her hometown behind. Jackie's tight-lipped approach regarding family matters perplexed Lauren, but she wasn't one to pry.

Lauren let herself in, the metal-framed screen door squeaking in protest. The front door opened to the crowded living room, where random pieces of furniture were strewn about, all in varying stages of age. An antique lamp stood beside a Walmart bookshelf placed in the far-left corner. Three couches were scattered around the living room, one a newer futon, another a torn mess, which could've been taken right from the early '80s, and the final covered with a sheet. To the right lay a large kitchen with no defining shift from the living room. A deep farm-kitchen sink sat beneath a window, and tall candles flickered on the sill. Beside the counter where a refrigerator might've sat, had this been a normal kitchen, stood a tall rack, shelves covered with painted canvases and sleeves of warped papyrus.

Lauren always wondered how Jackie afforded the home, as the property was set right beside the waterfront. The awkward split-level seemed to be to Jackie's liking, the top half of the building reserved for her art while the bottom floor contained her laundry room, bedroom, and full bath.

Jackie hunched over the massive oak table placed directly in the middle of the room, her denim overalls splattered with various shades of paint, the colors spread over her arms and hands. "What's up?" she shouted without lifting her head, moving the brush in her hand over the taut fabric. The amethyst hung from its chain around her neck, swaying as she stretched to the farthest corner of the canvas with the paintbrush. Music blared from a portable speaker on the end of the table, and Jackie reached over to turn it down. A black cat padded across the rough dining room table, pressing his face to Jackie's arm with affection. Another cat meowed at Lauren as he did circles around her ankles.

"Not much," Lauren said, stepping over the cat as she headed to the table. The canvas her friend was leaning over appeared to be almost the same size as the table it sat atop, the illustration a detailed landscape of the windswept beach. Lauren was struck by the brushstrokes twirling over the fabric, the grainy sand realistic and the billowing sail of the boat floating in the water uncanny in detail. "Wow."

Placing the paintbrush behind her ear, Jackie scoffed, "Yeah. I think the painting would've turned out better if Gollum hadn't trotted across it with his little feet." Jackie scratched the head of the cat in question, who in turn meowed loudly. The white, puffy clouds above the waterscape were marred, Lauren faintly noticing the tiny blue paw prints.

"I think they add character. Maybe you should lock them downstairs more often," Lauren suggested. *Jackie, always the perfectionist.* However, her perfectionistic attitude didn't bleed over into the rest of her life—she reserved this mindset for her art and only her art. "Is this one for a contest, a gallery, or for fun?"

Jackie shrugged, brushing her hands off on the front of her overalls before lifting the canvas and laying it against the leg of the table. "For fun. I got the idea when I was walking on the beach this morning." Her artistic ability had strengthened since the two friends took up jobs at the local high school, prompting their move to the island. Jackie seemed to thrive by the water, finding solace as well as inspiration from the ever-moving current.

Like Sam. Hm. She noticed her thoughts wandering to Sam quite often in the last few weeks. Since their date to the movies, Lauren hadn't texted Sam nor had she seen her, due to Sam's injuries keeping her from work. Her embarrassment and shame for rejecting Sam in such a way hindered any confidence she had to spark a conversation with her. "So," Jackie began. "You never told me about your little movie excursion. How'd your night go, and who did you go with?"

Lauren tucked a strand of her hair behind her ear as heat rose to her cheeks, the question coinciding with her internal dialogue. "There's not much to tell. I went with Sam."

"Which you have yet to fill me in with details on who this Sam is, other than she delivers your mail and she was supposed to do game night with us." Jackie pointed a finger in accusation.

"Yes, conveniently the game night when Bethany and I broke up. She delivers my mail and we've been swapping books almost since I moved here."

"What's cooler than a mail carrier who swaps books with you?" Jackie asked, leaning her elbows on the table. She batted her black lashes, smirking. "Let's hear more."

Lauren picked at a spot on the oak table between them, avoiding Jackie's direct stare. Sam wasn't her girlfriend; she'd made the point to tell Sam she wasn't ready to begin a new relationship so soon. To make matters worse, Lauren succeeded in admitting to herself that she'd developed a crush on Sam long before she and Bethany got together. Now she was given the opportunity, and Lauren was too fearful of ruining their friendship to act on her feelings.

"Lauren, are you okay?" Jackie's gaze was focused on her, and Lauren blushed deeper when she lifted her head.

"I'm fine. We've known each other for a little while now, and, like I said, we trade books, and we've gone out for coffee a few times."

"Sure. Is that what they're calling it these days—trading books?" Jackie folded her hands on the table and straightened. "I'm only teasing you. I hope you at least had a good time because you deserve it."

Lauren smiled. "We had a wonderful time. I kissed her and then I told her I didn't want to get into a relationship right now."

"Lauren!"

"What? Only a few weeks had gone by since Bethany and I broke up. I didn't want Sam to think I was getting involved with her because I was lonely after a crappy breakup," Lauren said. As much as she wanted to be with Sam, she couldn't imagine her thinking Lauren was using her as a rebound. "You're the one who told me the night didn't have to turn into anything more."

"How'd she react?"

Lauren chewed her lip. Butters hopped onto the table, rubbing his head on Lauren's hands. She opened her palm, allowing the purring creature to headbutt her hand. "She told me she understood and didn't want me to feel pressured into anything, but I could clearly see she was disappointed." Lauren had been upset by her own words. "We have a lot in common, and I just don't want to screw up a great friendship because of my newfound inability to trust people, thanks to Bethany."

"And Maribel," Jackie added. "You're my best friend and I want you to be happy. Don't screw up something potentially good because of fear," Jackie said with conviction.

"This is true…" Lauren trailed off. "I guess I feel bad because I realized on our date I've had a crush on her for a while, even while Bethany and I were together."

"Why do you feel bad? You never acted on it, and shit, you didn't notice until well after you two broke up," Jackie reassured. Lauren distracted herself with Butters, scratching him under his chin and avoiding Jackie's pointed stare. "Lauren."

She lifted her head. "I feel bad because I like her, Jackie. I like her a lot."

"What do you want?" Jackie grabbed the corners of the table as she awaited Lauren's answer.

What *did* she want? Lauren sighed with discomfort. Sam took an interest in her—why was she denying herself the possibility of a future with her because of poor timing? "I don't know."

"Have you two talked since your date?"

Lauren shook her head. "I don't know what to say after I all but rejected her."

"Send her a text. Ask her to coffee. Talk about those books you guys are trading," Jackie sneered. Lauren pulled her phone from her purse and flickered her eyes to Jackie. "Go on. Do it."

Taking a deep breath in, Lauren started her text to Sam.

Hey, you. Do you have any plans on Saturday? I was thinking maybe we could grab a cup of coffee. I'm dying to read the next book and would love to see you again.

Just as she hovered her finger over the send button, her phone came to life with a phone call. "Hello?"

"Lauren! How are you?" her brother, Aaron, asked with his usual enthusiasm.

Jackie threw up her hands, face scrunched. "Did you send it?" she whispered.

"I'm well," Lauren said to her brother as she shook her head at Jackie. Jackie rolled her eyes, moving away from the table toward the deep sink, her hands full of dirty paintbrushes.

"Gram told me about your breakup. I'm sorry," Aaron said with sympathy. "How are you doing?" Her brother was kind, a little too much at times, but Lauren appreciated his concern.

"I'm okay. Thanks for checking on me." She went on to listen to her brother chat her ear off about his youngest daughter. All the while, Jackie tinkered with her painting supplies, shooting Lauren amused glares. Eventually, Jackie moved across the living room, flopping onto one of the couches with a loud grunt. After agreeing to take her niece on an outing the following weekend, Lauren was able to end the call.

"Your brother is a talker," Jackie called from the couch. The piece of furniture she sprawled out on stood by the bay window and Jackie peered through the glass. Whipping around, Jackie clapped her hands together, offering Lauren a wicked grin. "You should totally let me consult the cards to see where this little romance with your mail carrier is going."

Lauren threw her head back, laughing at Jackie's joke. The cards she referred to consisted of a deck of tarot, their edges frayed and crumbling, the hand-drawn depictions haunting. Jackie believed in their wisdom, whereas Lauren held a strong skepticism toward the occult. She respected her best friend's beliefs, although Jackie was well aware of her dubiety. "Very funny," she chuckled. "I know you trust your almighty cards of creepy, but I'd rather see how things pan out. I'll send her a text later."

"You're a fun killer. Let's order some pizza and binge-watch a mindless show on Netflix."

DARKNESS CLUNG TO the room as Sam sat up in bed, disoriented and sweating. Her heart was racing, the faint swooshing of water in her ears resonating. The nightmare was gone from her consciousness, her thoughts jumbled and unable to grasp any contents of the dream. Not that she needed to remember. The fragments she held on to were clearly from her own death. She realized she was in her own apartment, the faint whirring of the oscillating fan by her bed familiar and comforting, rather than caught in the rushing undertow, and relief washed over her. The soft neon glow of a neighboring convenience store illuminated the windowsill. Darkness shifted by the window. She held her breath as she surveyed the room, the vibrant red tip of a cigarette suspended in air beside her window. She gasped. How the hell had someone gotten into her apartment? She ripped her blankets off, reaching behind her bedside table for her softball bat.

"Don't you hit me with that fucking bat, kid," Margo's distinct voice rasped in the dark. Sam blinked a few times, allowing herself to take the moment to make out the silhouette of Margo standing next to her window, arm dangling out the opening, the cigarette secured between two fingers.

"What the hell?" Sam snapped, noting the time on the digital clock on the bedside table. "You go MIA for two weeks and then show up in my bedroom at four o'clock in the morning?"

"Oh, did I wake poor sleeping beauty? Come on, we've got shit to do." Margo took one last puff of her cigarette before stumping it out on the sill and tossing the butt out the window. Sam rolled her eyes as she threw her legs over the bed. Margo flipped on the light switch, causing Sam to shield her eyes. Dressed in a crisp suit and hair slicked back, Margo looked like a totally different person as she folded her arms over her chest, staring at Sam impatiently.

"What kind of shit?" Sam asked as she rose from the bed.

"Business as usual. I'll explain on the way."

Sam yanked on a pair of sweatpants over her boxers and pulled a hoodie over her T-shirt as Margo left her bedroom without waiting for her to finish dressing. Sam barely made it out the front door before Margo was already in her MINI Cooper with the engine running. Locking the door, Sam hurried down the porch, jumping into the passenger seat with haste. "What're we doing at this hour and how the hell did you find my apartment?" The last interaction they shared Sam was still staying with Katie.

Margo's hands gripped the steering wheel and her brows were drawn. "I'm not sugarcoating this—the soul we're in charge of today isn't going to be as easy as the first. And finding your place wasn't very difficult. Maybe you shouldn't post so much shit on social media."

Great, Sam thought. The cryptic warning was not what Sam was hoping for in answer. "Can we at least stop at Wawa for some coffee?" Sam asked. Margo snorted but obliged.

They pulled into the parking lot of the convenience store and Sam climbed out, Margo right behind her as she entered the automatic doors. The aroma of freshly brewed coffee and doughnuts wafted over her and Sam breathed deeply. Copious amounts of caffeine were in order if she wanted to deal with Margo's antics so early in the morning.

Sam rubbed her eyes to stifle the obnoxious radiance of the overhead fluorescent lights as she walked over to the self-serve coffee carafes. A young man was pacing in front of the coffee, and Sam waited patiently, hoping he would move so she wouldn't have to ask him to get out of the way.

She wondered if he was homeless, the state of his rumpled clothing, the corduroy pants stained with dark substances and sweatshirt torn in various places leading her to this assumption. He was muttering something under his breath, hands moving animatedly. She chewed her lip, contemplating whether to go for a refrigerated caffeine substitute rather than bug him to get to the coffee.

"Excuse me," Sam said, but the man continued to pace. "Excuse me, sir." She tried to project her voice a little higher and the man finally stopped, turning to glare at her. His beard was scraggly, and he widened his eyes when she spoke again, "I'm sorry, I just need to get some coffee."

He moved out of the way, staring at Sam with bewilderment. "You can see me?" he whispered when Sam's back was turned.

Pouring her coffee into the red paper cup, Sam turned around, confused. "Yes, and I'm all done. Sorry." She briskly moved out of his way, his gaze on her the entire time while she grabbed a premade bagel and headed to the cashier. Margo was nowhere to be seen, and Sam was fine without her presence. The Grim Reaper was really beginning to get on her nerves and Sam was ready to rally for answers to her countless questions when they got in the car, heading wherever they were going. She paid for her coffee and walked outside, the man from the store standing under the awning.

Sam tried not to make eye contact, worried her interruption of his pacing could've irritated the stranger. "Hey, boy," the man called out. Sam ignored him, not just because of the mistaken gendering but because she was really starting to worry about his intentions.

Margo leaned against the hood of her tiny MINI Cooper, the posture along with her attire making Sam chuckle under her breath despite her concern for the man calling out to her. A cigarette dangled from Margo's pursed lips as she thrust her hands into the pockets of her suit jacket. "He's talking to you, kid," she said around the cigarette.

"We can go now," Sam muttered, reaching for the passenger door handle.

Margo shook her head, blowing smoke out as she lowered the cigarette. "No, he's a convenient add-on to our to-do list."

Sam stopped, glaring at Margo in confusion. "Huh?"

"Hey, you, hold on." The man was standing on the curb, waving his arms around, his tone loud in the sleepy city. Sam's cheeks flushed, and she looked around, hoping no one else was watching the bizarre interaction. At 4:15 a.m., the eerie desolate silence clung to the streets, their voices echoing against adjacent buildings.

"What?" she snapped, placing her cup of coffee on top of the MINI Cooper.

The man widened his eyes again, and when Sam stared directly at him, he touched his chest as he spoke. "You can see me?"

"Yeah. What do you want from me?"

Margo cleared her throat as she moved closer to Sam, bumping her arm. "He needs your help."

Then, the truth finally clicked in Sam's sleep-muddled mind. "Oh, shit," she mumbled. He was fully visible like the old woman had been, not mist shaped or blurry like in the movies. Prior to her own death, when Sam thought of a ghost, she envisioned the perception perpetuated by Hollywood films and television, not the flesh and blood form before her. "Hi, I'm sorry."

The guy clapped his hands together, gazing up at the sky before glancing at Sam. "So, you *can* see me."

"Yeah, I'm here to help you move along to, you know, the other side." Sam still wasn't sure how the process worked, embarrassed as she moved a few feet closer to the man. He didn't appear to be harmed in any way, and she wondered why the two ghosts she'd seen hadn't had any physical deformities from their cause of death. "Do you know you're dead?"

"I do. That lady over there won't leave me alone about going with her, but I haven't said thank you yet."

"Thank you to who?"

"The one who used to help me get by," he said as if this conveyed meaning to Sam.

She blinked, shooting a frown back at Margo, who in turn leered at her. God, she was fucking incorrigible. "Who is the one who helped you?"

"This kid who works in the deli here. She used to give me all the leftover food until I got hit. She even cried when she found out I died."

"Oh." Sam didn't know what to say. So, she was right in believing he was homeless, well, rather, used to be homeless. "Where is she?"

The ghost sniffled. "She comes in at four thirty, and she can't see me. I've tried to say thank you, but it's no use."

"Do you want me to say thank you for you?"

His brows rose, mouth ajar. "You'd do that?"

"I can. What's your name?"

He lowered himself onto the curb and kicked out his feet, the soles of his worn shoes scraping the asphalt. "Billy. She knew me as Billy. Please tell her Billy says thank you."

Sam checked the time on her phone. The worker in question would supposedly be at the store in less than ten minutes. "Well, we've only got a few minutes to wait."

Billy nodded, dropping his gaze to the ground. Sam let out a long breath. Now that she was closer, Sam noticed Billy couldn't have been much older than her when he died. The light stubble on his chin was a dark brown, his cheeks not yet marred with wrinkles. The revelation made Sam sullen. The first encounter she had with her new line of work had been with the older woman. She had lived a long, fulfilling life from the looks of her home, and Sam didn't feel guilty pushing her to move on.

But as she sat in wait for Billy's unfinished business to be completed, a sense of despondency fell over her. He was young and had his whole life ahead of him. But he didn't. He was dead.

Margo lit another cigarette, hopping onto the hood of her car as she met Sam's gaze. "Can other people see you?" Sam asked.

White smoke swirled around Margo's face, and she rolled her eyes. "You don't give up with the questions, do you?" She tapped her finger, a mound of ashes fluttering to the asphalt ground. "Yeah, people can, unless I put up a deception, kind of like an illusion around my body. I'm there but can't be seen, which is what I did the day we met. Right now, anyone looking can see me. But," she paused, taking a drag. "Generally, I choose whether or not humans see me."

Now it made sense that no one else could see her when she brought Sam back on the beach, however, it didn't shed light on how Katie saw her the day Sam was still in the hospital the day of her accident. "Wait, my sister saw you when I was at the hospital. Why didn't you use your...whatever it is, to hide yourself?"

"Bringing someone back from the dead isn't an easy task, Sam. Kind of made me run out of energy to conceal myself," Margo scoffed in a whisper.

"Would I be able to see you if you did the thing?"

"Deception," Margo corrected. "And yeah, you'd see me, but I appear a little different. The concealment sort of shields me in the shadows of this world, making me look extra creepy."

Before Sam could pry more, a car pulled into the parking lot. A short woman in her early twenties hurried out of the driver's door and dashed up to the store. "Is that her, Billy?"

"Yeah," he said as he stood from the curb. Sam followed him into the store. The woman came out of the back, slipping behind the deli counter.

Hastily gathering items around the counter, the worker met Sam's gaze. "Can I help you?" she asked.

Sam cleared her throat, unsure how to move forward. "Uh, do you happen to remember a man who used to come in around here by the name of Billy?"

The girl's jaw tightened as she nodded. "Yes, I do. What's this about?"

Sam cleared her throat, glancing over at Billy. "Just...just tell her thank you. I would've starved to death if it hadn't been for her."

She glanced back to the girl behind the counter. "Thank you," Sam said. She lowered her voice, taking a step closer to the counter, placing a hand on the glass case as she made eye contact with the woman. "He would've starved if you hadn't helped him like you did, so thank you."

The girl blinked about five times, her eyes watery when she looked up at Sam again. "Are you his sister or something?" the woman asked. Sam shook her head. "How did you know I was the one who helped him?"

Shifting her feet, Sam turned away briefly. "He told me about you a few weeks before he died." The lie wasn't as hard to tell as Sam expected.

"Oh." Sam turned back to the woman as she continued, "I watched him the night he died. He was only crossing the street. The car came out of nowhere, and then hit him and ran right into a streetlight." The woman sniffled, wiping away the tear with the back of her hand.

"I'm sorry." Sam wasn't sure what to do. She turned to Billy who appeared to be crying as well, and Margo was still outside sitting on the hood of her car.

"I hope he didn't suffer too much. He suffered enough." With that, the girl turned and began prepping the deli, cutting vegetables and effectively ignoring Sam. Billy walked out the sliding doors of the convenience store. Sam was frozen as the worker tried to conceal her sadness, and she bit her lip to withhold her own tears. Would her job be this hard every time? She ripped herself from her melancholy and went outside. Margo was perched on the curb instead of her car, neck bent over her cell phone.

Sam made her way over to Billy and put a hand on his shoulder, holding in the gasp at the solidity of his body. "Are you ready to go?"

He nodded, smiling at her as he headed down the street. Sam looked to Margo, hoping for her to beckon her forward. She wanted to feel the energy again, craved the ripple of electricity, but Margo flicked her wrist and the air fluttered and fluctuated. Sam held her breath, the energy barely grazing her face in shuddering waves, emanating from Margo's control.

Billy's face was in awe as he took a step, the iridescent light piercing the dark street, glowing brighter with each stride. He offered the women a small wave before he disappeared in a flash of light.

"Don't ask where he went because I don't know," Margo said. Sam scoffed as they both climbed into the car.

"That wasn't so hard." Sam was expecting a challenge with Margo's warning, but Billy seemed like an easy soul, even with the sadness both he and his unfinished business exuded. She wasn't an expert on the matter; however, it wasn't difficult to help him with his final thank-you. They stopped at a red light, the intersection completely deserted, except for them. When Margo went straight, instead of turning left to take Sam back to her apartment, she said, "You went the wrong way."

"No, I didn't. We aren't done yet."

Sam whipped her head around. "What do you mean?" The sun was beginning to lighten the sky, tingeing the clouds pink.

"There's the original wayward soul we're responsible for this morning."

"What?"

Margo rolled her eyes. "Billy there was a convenient coincidence. We were in the right place at the right time, which seems to be happening to me a lot lately."

The Ocean Drive bridge on the north end of the island was deserted as Margo drove across, save a handful of people fishing on the long dock at the opposite side of the structure.

"This isn't going to be fun, kid."

"Would you stop calling me kid? You're like, what, twenty-eight, twenty-nine? You can't have more than two years on me, so stop calling me kid." The sky was relatively dark despite the sun cresting the horizon. The ocean churned like black oil, the peaks of waves bubbling in the current. Maybe the ominous feeling in the car caused Sam to feel this way as she peered through the window at the rough sea, but her skin broke out in goose bumps.

Margo snagged Sam's wrist gently. "Okay, listen to me for a minute. This isn't like little old Beatrice not wanting to leave because her son is going to miss her or Billy wanting to thank a friend. This is going to make your stomach turn, and he doesn't believe I can help with his unfinished business." She let go of Sam's arm and turned back to the road.

"Does this always revolve around unfinished business?"

"Yeah, but it's different for everyone. No two spirits have the same exact unfinished shit, and his is messy," Margo said.

"How do you know where to find the spirits?"

"I've already tried my best to get this guy to move on, but I get a list once a week of the spirits from corporate with general vicinities. I don't know where they receive the information and I don't care."

Sam wondered why she was disclosing so much information, and she wanted to know more. "Corporate? You have bosses?"

Margo nodded. "Let's go." Well, her sharing was short-lived.

The lone man stood near the end of the bridge of the opposite side of Ocean City, his hands in the pockets of his khakis. To Sam, he appeared average, with his plain black polo shirt, salt-and-pepper hair sticking out from beneath his ball cap. What could be so difficult about the spirit to spur such a weird warning from Margo? "Hi, there," Sam said as she sidled up beside the man. He turned, tilting his head in acknowledgment of her presence before looking back out over the water lapping at the beach.

Sam wasn't the most social person. She made conversation with her customers but didn't actively converse with strangers. Standing at the edge of the bridge with the silent man was different, not only due to his ghostly state but the deep foreboding permeating from his stature. She cleared her throat. "I'm here to help you with, uh, your unfinished business."

"Is that so?" the man asked, his voice rougher than Sam anticipated. He was tall and burly, his large hands emerging from his pockets to grip the railing as he turned to glare at her. "What leads you to believe you could assist me?"

Sam glanced behind him in time to see Margo give her a shrug. "I'm going to do the best I can. What do you need help with?"

He relaxed his shoulders, shifting his feet. "Have you ever done something so terrible you never told a soul?"

Sam was thrown off by the question. "I can't say that I have."

The man snorted. "About a year ago, I caught my wife cheating on me with an executive chef for a restaurant in Atlantic City. I was furious, and I let rage consume me. The dirtbag didn't see me coming."

Sam took an instinctive step back. Was he talking assault or worse? "What happened?"

He shoved his hands in his pockets again and continued. "I snuck up on him one night in the parking lot of the casino he worked at. Told him I wanted to chat with him." He met Sam's gaze. The eye contact caused Sam to shiver, and she tightened her hoodie around herself. The sun breached the horizon, the clouds taking on a purple and indigo shade, but its warmth neglected to thaw the chill around her.

"Did you guys fight?"

"I killed him. Karen never found out about it. We reconciled, moved on and had a wonderful two months until I was diagnosed with metastatic colon cancer. They never found his body." The man moved his line of sight over to a copse of bushes and scant trees by the parking lot, and Sam's stomach twisted. His unfinished business was the body. Shit. "I don't feel remorse for the people I've killed, but his body is the only one that wasn't found."

"Okay," Sam said gently. Her jaw tightened, and her heart raced. A dead body. There had been numerous. She fought the urge to take another step back because she knew he had to pass on. The quicker she helped him, the quicker she'd get away from him. How the hell was she going to do this? "Do you know exactly where it is?"

He nodded and went off toward the parking lot. Reluctantly, Sam followed. He crossed the empty road and bounded through the thick brush. The area was dense with marshland and Sam's sneakers made an unpleasant squishing sound with each step she took. Colorful advertisements for the neighboring casinos in Atlantic City were plastered on the sixteen-foot billboards, and Sam shivered as a strong gust of wind blew off the wetlands to the left. "He's back here," the man said, pointing to a small muddy clearing behind the billboards.

Though the question was far too morbid for normal conversation, Sam asked, "How come they never found his body when they changed the advertisements out?"

The man chuckled as he scratched the stubble on his chin. "They only change them out every few months but this particular one has a twelve-month lease. It won't be changed out for another nine months." His smile was wicked, and another shiver ran through her body that had nothing to do with the chill in the air. She swallowed and took a step back as the spirit knelt among the brush and mud. "Yep, it's still here."

Sam was terrified. Why didn't Margo warn her? She took a tentative step forward and stopped when the heel of a dirt-covered tennis shoe came into view. "What do you want me to do?"

He shrugged and stuck his hands in his pockets again. "Aren't you the one who's helping me? Call the cops."

Sam breathed through her mouth, closing her eyes. "I *could* call the police." Opening them again, Sam walked away from the spirit, heading back up the bushy reed-covered hill to the road. Her legs were drenched in mud and her sneakers squelched as she made her way toward the Reaper. Margo was standing on the sidewalk, gazing out over the water. Sam was surprised to see she wasn't smoking a cigarette.

"What the fuck?" Sam furrowed her eyebrows and shot Margo a glare.

Margo looked at her incredulously. "What?"

"Why didn't you tell me I'd be helping a murderer?" Sam whispered, her eyes sneaking a glance back to the billboards where, thankfully, the spirit stood. Could a spirit hurt her? She thought about asking Margo but dismissed the notion.

Margo shook her head, clearly unperturbed by the spirit's deed. "So? He still needs to move on like any other spirit."

"Why couldn't you have done it? You didn't have to drag me into this mess. What if they suspect me of the murder because I 'found' the body?"

"He didn't think telling me was good enough." Margo scrunched her nose in disgust before she continued. "Telling a demon his sins wasn't what he had in mind."

Sam shifted uncomfortably.

"As for the body, be careful what you say." Her eyes gave Sam a once-over. "You look like you've been running. Maybe you slipped and fell into the marsh and found it. I don't care what you say, but don't get yourself in trouble."

Sam stared at her in disbelief and cursed. What the hell had she gotten herself into? She pulled her phone out and dialed 911.

A half hour later, Sam stood with her hands in the pockets of her hoodie as the police scoured the area. "So, you were going for a jog and you slid down the embankment?" The officer, Detective O'Sullivan as she announced upon her arrival, gave Sam a scrutinizing once-over, lips pursed as she raised her brows. Sam worried she didn't believe her.

"Yeah. I usually don't go for a run on this side of the bridge, but I needed a change of scenery, so I decided to come over to this side," Sam lied. Detective O'Sullivan scribbled in a leather-bound notebook she held in her hands.

There was something off about the detective, and Sam couldn't put her finger on it. Her blue eyes were a shade too blue and her facial features sharply edged. It wasn't only the sense of authority exuding off her, there was a predatory and ethereal feeling that caused Sam's skin to breakout in goose bumps when the woman glanced at her. She asked Sam a slew of questions, and Sam mentally cursed Margo with each feigned answer.

"I didn't think exercise would land me finding a dead body," Sam said, trying to insert some humor into the bizarre turn of events. A flash of jagged teeth when the woman smiled gave Sam pause and her eyes widened. Did she really just see shark-like teeth on the detective?

Sam shook her head, and the detective squinted at her. "Are you all right?" the detective asked.

"Yeah. This is crazy." Sam grimaced and glanced over to where a team of people were closing off the road, placing tape around the vicinity of the body. The yellow wrapped around the massive billboards, a tangle of vibrant webs. There were several dogs leading their respective officers around the area and Sam assumed they were searching for more bodies. Another rush of bile threatened to rise, and she pushed the heel of her hand into her forehead. She turned back at the officer whose lips were a tight line. She couldn't have seen the teeth. Sam brushed off her odd hallucination, attributing the sight to her sleep deprivation.

Realistically, Sam had only gotten about two hours of sleep the night before. It *had* to be fatigue because people didn't have shark teeth. "Okay. We've got your information. If we need more, we'll be in touch, but for now, I'm sure you want to get home and wash up," Detective O'Sullivan said as she snapped the notebook shut. Sam peered down at herself and nodded. Thick splotches of mud and grass covered her sweatpants and her hands were covered in dirt.

"Thanks."

Margo was sitting in the driver's seat when Sam climbed into the car. The heat was blaring, and Sam was thankful for Margo's silent conscientious gesture. "Why'd you disappear on me? You could've done the illusion shit and stayed close to me. This spirit gives me the creeps." Margo wasn't paying attention to Sam. Her gaze was fixed on Detective O'Sullivan who was directing another officer over to the taped-off area. "Do you know her?" Sam inquired. Margo nodded hesitantly and turned back to Sam. Sam thought about the teeth and she understood. "Is she like you?"

"She's not Grim—she's something else—but you shouldn't have noticed," Margo answered as she put the car in drive, her brows drawn and expression disconcerting. Sam wanted to ask more, especially given Margo's odd reaction, but she was too fatigued to do so. She yawned and stretched back in the passenger seat.

Although Margo wasn't sunshine and rainbows, Sam felt safe with her. Just as she was set to close her eyes for the drive home, she noticed they weren't going the correct way back to the island.

"Please tell me we're done for the day," Sam muttered. Margo steered the car past the investigation and drove to the scenic road toward Margate, opposite of Ocean City.

"We've got Chuck over there to deal with."

Instead of continuing toward the neighboring seaside town, Margo turned toward the long fishing pier that was deserted except for the spirit in question. The hair on the back of Sam's neck rose as she climbed out of the car and he looked over at them. A gentle breeze pushed off the bay and Sam tucked her hands beneath her arms. "Everything's all taken care of," Sam stated as she walked toward the spirit. Margo was so close to her, her shoulder bumped into Sam's and Sam was oddly comforted by their proximity. She took a mental note to ask Margo if spirits could cause her harm as she awaited the man's response.

The man nodded, his hands in the pockets of his jacket. It was eerie how normal he appeared even though Sam knew the truth about his past. The profound distress she experienced when he smiled at her was terrifying. "I saw. Thank you. I think I'm ready to go," he said.

Margo shoved Sam back a few feet as she advanced toward the man, her hands outstretched, the air around her fingers shimmering. The iridescent doorway materialized, blotchy and jagged. Sam resisted the urge to reach out, to touch the shifting energy, to allow the power to caress her skin. The light was tinged a muddy hue as the man stepped through, and Sam swore a shriek emanated from the portal before he vanished. Margo dusted off her hands and looped her arm around Sam's. "Let's get the hell out of here."

"Where do you think he went?" Sam asked. Her mind buzzed with questions again as they both got into the car. Margo blatantly ignored her.

Sam rubbed her hands together in front of the heat pouring from the vents as Margo started the car. Her clothes were damp from her excursion down into the brush and her tumble into the dirt to make her lie believable.

"We're done," Margo said. She drove the narrow route back toward the bridge where investigators continued to canvass the area around the body.

"Is there a heaven or a hell?" Margo's eye twitched at the question.

After they crossed the bridge and entered Ocean City, Margo sighed obnoxiously. "No, not in the sense you were probably taught in church. It's different. One doesn't stay in a particular spot for eternity." Margo turned to her as they stopped at a red light. "Ever hear of reincarnation?" When Sam nodded, Margo continued, "I told you before, their fate has to do with karma. Chuck did a lot of evil things in his life and he won't go unpunished. This isn't what you'd think, and that's all I'm saying because I'm tapped out for the day."

"Fine," Sam quipped, regretting her offer to Katie to babysit that morning because Ben's preschool was closed for the day. Her only solace was she had a change of clothes at her sister's house, and she prayed Katie wouldn't badger her for answers. "Take me to my sister's condo."

The remainder of the drive was silent. Sam sat with numerous questions assaulting her consciousness, questions she knew Margo had no intention of answering at the moment. When they arrived in front of Katie's condo, Sam scowled at Margo. "I don't want to do this anymore if it's going to involve murderers."

Margo broke eye contact and stared out the windshield, her face contorted in annoyance. "I'll see you later," she said, revving the car as Sam hopped out. She slammed the passenger door, turning sharply as she headed toward the stairs.

The condo was quiet as she stepped into the living room and headed for the kitchen. Margo's car sped away loudly out front.

Letting out a loud sigh, Sam walked to the kitchen. "You look like shit, Sam," Katie said as Sam washed her hands in the sink. She wanted to simply head straight for the bathroom upon her arrival, but she hadn't gotten very far when her sister advanced on her. Katie took in her appearance and scoffed. "What were you doing, clamming?"

Sam turned the faucet off and dried her hands. "No, I was going for a walk and I fell down this embankment." Sam perpetuated the lie she'd thought up for the police officers because she figured it was as good as any. *Oh, I was helping a spirit move on to the other side, and I had to find a dead body in order to help him.* This didn't seem like a suitable explanation her sister would take lightly or understand. In fact, Katie would tell her she needed a psych consult. "I'm going to take a shower." Sam stalked off to the bathroom before her sister could reply.

Things were getting weirder and weirder. She couldn't deny the reality of her plight. Truly, she had made a deal with some ethereal creature and now she was bound by the terms of their agreement. She switched on the shower, turning it to the hottest temperature as possible before she shed her clothing and hopped in. Margo refused to answer most of the relevant questions Sam asked her. Scalding water rushed over her back and Sam winced. She couldn't get the sight of those razor-sharp teeth out of her head the entire shower.

As she toweled herself off, Sam's phone chimed on the bathroom counter. The text message was from a number she didn't recognize.

Don't drop out of the deal just yet, kid. It isn't always this bad, I swear.

Sam rolled her eyes, putting her phone down to get dressed. She opened the door to allow the steam to billow out of the small room as she reread the message. The text couldn't be from anyone except Margo. The cocky, arrogant woman was starting to irritate Sam. Okay, it was more than irritation. It was verging on outright distaste. She put her phone on the counter, grumbling under her breath to herself. How would she even drop out of a deal anyway? Would her refusal result in her death? Of course, if she asked Margo, the Grim Reaper wasn't inclined to answer these questions.

Sam picked the phone back up, starting a new message.

Like I have a choice? This isn't what I agreed to.

But what *had* she agreed to? Helping Margo. Hadn't Katie's well-being been the sole reason Sam had made the deal with Margo? In hindsight, Sam understood her reasoning, but she admitted she'd made a hasty decision. Either take the deal or die. She toweled her hair off, shaking her head.

"You're awfully thoughtful in there." Sam bristled at the sudden voice, calming when she caught sight of Katie's reflection in the mirror. Her sister stood with her arm against the threshold of the bathroom door as she watched Sam dry her hair. "Is your shoulder hurting?" Katie asked.

Sam shook her head, turning to face her sister. "No, my shoulder's fine. I had a really weird morning, I guess." Sam caught Katie's gaze and for a fleeting moment, she considered telling her what really happened.

"Are you okay, Sam?" Katie furrowed her brows, laying her hand on Sam's shoulder.

"I'm fine. How'd your hearing go?" Sam maneuvered from under Katie's scrutiny and headed to the kitchen.

"The hearing went way better than any of us expected," Katie said as she followed Sam. "I was granted full custody."

Sam dropped the towel into the laundry hamper at the end of the hall and whirled around to stare at her sister. "Wow, that's...wow, Katie. How did you manage this?"

Her sister gulped down more coffee before she spoke again. "Well, apparently John realized he wouldn't be able to keep up with his end of the fifty-fifty custody with his travel requirements for work. So, we agreed he could have Ben when he was here for two days at a time under my discretion. I can't believe it's over," Katie chuckled as she placed her cup on the counter. Sam hugged her sister tightly, and Katie started to cry. "I can't thank you enough for always being there for me, sis. I don't think I would've kept strong and stayed stubborn if you hadn't helped me stand my ground."

"You don't have to thank me. I'm glad you took my help."

Katie held Sam's shoulders and pushed her back. "I do have to thank you. Ever since mom passed, I've worried about you, but you've matured so much and I'm proud of you."

"Thanks," Sam said bashfully. Katie couldn't know how important it was for Sam to hear those words, especially how her life was secretly panning out.

"Where's that little nephew of mine?" Sam digressed, eager to distract herself from the madness of the morning.

Chapter Ten

THE IDYLLIC THEME park on the mainland was cute, giving Sam an almost uncomfortable sense of nostalgia with its tiny lopsided cottages and tunnels toward nowhere. Their mother had taken Katie and Sam to the very same storybook-themed park numerous times as children, and she remembered holding a love/hate relationship for it. Although fun with its merry-go-round, yummy treats, and bumper cars, the park also had creepy depictions of storybook characters, like the evil witch from Hansel and Gretel and then Humpty Dumpty cracking on the cement. The demented images haunted her dreams after their visits, but they kept coming back to the park.

Sam hadn't seen Margo in close to a week. She prayed Margo would simply disappear from her life as if she were some strange illusion her brain configured post-concussion. Unfortunately, Sam knew deep down this wasn't the case, and part of her hoped she'd see the brassy woman again. She wanted to feel the electricity ripen in the air. Even recalling the sensation conjured a soreness in the middle of her chest where the energy had swirled.

"Auntie! It's a slide," Ben exclaimed, pointing to a narrow tunnel near the tall slide in the distance. Sam grinned at him.

The biting scent of cigarette smoke pierced her senses and as Sam turned, a Margo-shaped shadow spilled over the sidewalk in front of them. Speak of the devil. Clenching her jaw, Sam rolled her eyes, turning to Katie. "I'm going to run to the bathroom, but I'll catch up, okay?"

"Sure," Katie said before running after her tot.

Peering to her right, she found Margo sitting on the edge of a brick wall, right beside a cement Humpty Dumpty, pre-fall. Sam let out an exasperated sigh, which sounded more like a growl, as she brought her hands to her hips. "I thought I filled my quota for the month," she snapped, looking around to ensure no one assumed she was talking to herself. Surely Margo wouldn't be seen smoking a cigarette around children, right? Another glance at the Grim Reaper made Sam step closer. The blue of Margo's eyes wasn't nearly as vibrant as before, and a general dullness surrounded her features. As if Margo were slipped under muddled light, her body was invisible to the rest of the world. Sam recalled what Margo had told her their last time together: *I choose whether or not humans see me.*

Margo chuckled crudely. "There's no quota to fill for you, yet. Look, kid, the dead don't give a shit that you're having a nice little outing with your family and neither does upper management. I've got a job to do and I'm pretty sure we have a deal. You're here, the problem child is here; let's get it over with."

Sam shook her head slowly as she chewed her lip in disbelief. "If you had told me, before all of this, what kind of people I'd be dealing with..." She didn't finish her statement, but her unspoken words hung in the air between them. Agreeing to be Margo's temporary assistant seemed to be a moot point with Katie's issues becoming all but resolved. Despite her elation at Katie's settled court proceedings with her ex-husband, Sam wondered if her decision to help Margo had been a mistake.

Margo's face softened, and she turned her head, blowing smoke through pursed lips. "I've got an easy one for you today, so don't run away." She jumped down from the wall. Leading Sam through a thickly wooded area of the park, Margo directed her up a slight hill and over a patch of dead grass. Fallen leaves crunched under her feet as Sam stepped over a snaking root erupting from the damp earth.

"Why the hell are you smoking around these kids?"

Without a word, Margo stubbed the cigarette out and threw the butt in a trashcan.

The outline of a chain link became visible in the heavy brush and a small child huddled beside the fence—knees pulled to his chest, small brown hands wrapped around his legs, little PAW Patrol shoes on his feet, and scuffed knees peeking out from under shorts. Sam gasped at the similarities between the spirit and her own nephew as she approached him. "Hey, buddy. Are you lost?"

Margo put her hand on Sam's shoulder. "He's our target today," she whispered as if Sam thought the spirit child was alive. Sam ignored her, and Margo eventually moved away to give her and the child a wide berth.

"I can't find my puppy," he whimpered. Sam knelt, getting level with the little boy, and placing her hand on the child's arm. As unnerving as Sam found her ability to touch the spirits, she pushed her unease aside to comfort him. The poor child was frightened enough—dead or alive. He raised his head, his chocolate-brown eyes wide. "Make the scary lady go away. Please." Sam shot a scowl at Margo, so the Reaper took a step back and out of the child's line of sight.

"Where did you last see your puppy?"

The boy sighed and his whole body shuddered as he let it out and began to talk. "I was walking with my mommy, and I saw this pretty little bee and the bee got scared and the bee stung me, and it hurt really bad." The string of his run-on statement had Sam's chest tightening, and she turned to Margo again. Margo nodded, the swoop of blonde bangs dangling in front of her piercing gaze. "It's black and white with a red hat, and so fluffy, and I love my puppy. I can't go somewhere without my puppy."

Sam swallowed back her tears and met the child's gaze. "Let's find your puppy. Can you show me where you got stung by the bee?" The little boy bobbed his head enthusiastically, standing from his squatting position. Bounding through the dead grass toward the amusement park, the little boy squealed delightedly. Sam followed the child, Margo close behind them. He led Sam to a small alcove beside a ceramic white bunny with a waistcoat and a familiar pocket watch.

"Right here," the boy said, pointing to a copse of plastic daffodils and faux tulips. "Where is he?" the little boy whimpered, his lower lip trembling and his hands in tight little fists. Could the living hear ghosts sob? Sam didn't want to find out and she supposed if she didn't locate the puppy soon enough, she'd find out. Dropping to the ground, Sam combed the area for the toy, the soil dampening her knees.

A large group of children passed by with chattering voices, laughter, and a sporadic glow of flashing sneakers. "Sam, what are you doing?" a familiar feminine voice had Sam lifting her head and finding none other than Lauren staring at her.

Her chestnut hair was pulled back in a loose bun, errant strands framing her heart-shaped face. Sam's cheeks burned as she stood and smiled at Lauren. "I, uh, was looking for my nephew's stuffed animal. He dropped the thing down here somewhere." Lauren was smiling at her, emerald eyes glowing in the sunlight filtering through the trees around them. Sam's breath hitched as she was reminded of how beautiful Lauren was. The fabric of her red blouse appeared soft. Sam wanted to touch her to assure herself that Lauren was real and not some ghostly apparition as the child had been.

A little girl tugged at Lauren's hand, trying to urge her forward. "Aunt Laurie, come on. We're going to miss the next train ride." Her brown hair was identical to Lauren's, but it was pulled up in a little ponytail at the top of her head. She let go of Lauren's hand and darted under the bushes.

"You're going to get all muddy," Lauren said to the child before meeting Sam's gaze. "I didn't know you'd be here."

Sam swallowed her desire and nodded, Margo's sharp grunt reminding her of the task at hand. She ignored Margo's impatience, thankful Lauren presumably couldn't see her. "Yeah, I decided to tag along with my sister and my nephew. How are you?"

"It's been a busy start to the school year, but I want to read the next book if you'll lend it to me. We should get together." Lauren grinned, her smile reaching her eyes.

"I found it!" Sam glanced over to see the little girl beside Lauren, holding a soggy little stuffed animal triumphantly in her hands. "It's all gross and wet but I found it. How did it get all wet? Did it get lost just today?"

As Sam took the offered stuffed animal, the boy behind her exclaimed, "That's my puppy!" It was, in fact, damp and covered in dirt, causing Sam to wonder how long it'd been sitting beneath the bushes.

"Thanks," Sam said, choosing not to respond to how long the toy had been lost.

"Now can we go to the line for the train?" the little girl said to Lauren.

"Sure." Lauren met Sam's eyes, her freckled cheeks flushed. "Do you want to grab some lunch tomorrow?"

"I'd love that." Sam nodded.

"All right, lover boi, let's go. You've got shit to do, remember? You can flirt with the cute girl later." Margo's tone was sharp. Sam's smile faltered, and she hoped Lauren hadn't noticed the shift in her mood.

"I better get this back to Ben. Text me when you have a place in mind," Sam offered. Lauren chuckled as her niece yanked her forward, giving a short wave to Sam as she disappeared down the path.

Margo whistled and clasped her hand on Sam's back, a little too close to her healed collarbone. "Do you have to cause me pain every time you visit me?"

"She's a cutie, Sam. And, knock it off, you big baby. I know you're healed. Now, come on." Margo linked her arm with Sam's and dragged her along, the little boy bouncing beside them.

"Can I have it, can I have it?" he shouted. Margo led them back off into the wooded area, snatching the toy from Sam, handing it to the boy. He grabbed it eagerly, smiling as he hugged the toy to his chest. Sam thought to ask how he was able to hold the physical toy but didn't want Margo yelling at her for asking too many questions. Instead, she turned her attention to the child as he gazed up, a bright light shimmering midair. Margo lifted her hands, creating the familiar shimmering across the trees. Sam wanted to feel the sensation, to allow the energy to coil in her chest, hot and fierce, but she kept herself back.

"Wow," the child whispered. His sneakers crunched on the leafy ground as he moved toward the glimmering spot between two evergreen trees. He turned, apprehension clear on his chubby face. "Do I really have to go?"

Sam nodded. Smiling as genuinely as possible, Sam knelt to his level. "Yeah, you do, bud. You've got your puppy, so it's time to go."

He lowered his vision to the ground and kicked a stray leaf before he sighed, "Okay." He whipped around with his gaze on the radiance in the trees, the door to wherever. With careful steps, he walked to the entrance as the brightness grew. His body diminished into nothingness the closer he got. With a soft plop on the forest floor, the puppy hit the ground, and the child vanished. Sam's lip trembled slightly, and a tear trickled down her cheek, causing her to swipe at it with impatience.

"You did good, even though you had help this time." Margo gripped her shoulder, more gently than before. Sam stepped forward, plucked the plush toy from the ground, and shoved it in the pocket of her hoodie.

She brushed the tears from her face, cleared her throat, and glanced at Margo. "Am I done?" Margo nodded sullenly.

Sam turned away from Margo.

"Sam, wait," Margo called. The expression on Margo's face was apprehensive, her eyes narrowed and pained. "There's something we've got to talk about, but it can wait until later."

"Whatever." Sam left Margo standing in the trees as she hurried down the slight hill toward the cobbled path. She meandered around, taking in the familiar sights of the park as she searched for Katie. A gentle stream of water gushed off a tiny windmill to her left and Sam stopped to soak up the soothing sound. What could Margo want to discuss with her? All of the cryptic talk she gave Sam was becoming increasingly infuriating and she didn't know how much more she could handle. She hoped the talk would shed some light on what was happening to her or she feared she would sincerely go crazy.

Katie stood beside the haunted house, her head moving from side to side as she peered around the park. Little Ben was by her side, kicking a small pile of leaves with his untied shoes, stirring an uncomfortable resemblance to the spirit of the child she just helped cross over. "Hey, there you are. Where'd you run off to?"

Sam ambled up to her, shooting her sister a rueful smile. "I thought I saw a cat in the woods."

"Leave it to you to go tromping into the woods to find yourself a stray cat. We're going to head out and grab something to eat."

SAM PACED AROUND the small space of her living room, bare feet thudding against the hardwood floor with each step. When the outing with her sister and nephew was over, Sam went back to her place and tried to unwind, but she couldn't keep her mind off the talk Margo spoke of. The subtle tick of her wall clock beside her bookshelf was louder in the void and she fixed on the sound. Just after eight in the evening. Margo would be there any moment per her text message earlier. Sam tried to pull more information from the Grim Reaper on what they were talking about, but Margo refused to elaborate.

Her phone buzzed in the pocket of her jeans and she yanked it out, surprised to see a text from Lauren.

How about lunch on the boardwalk? We could do pizza around noon on 14th Street.

She'd forgotten about seeing Lauren earlier in the day and her gut fluttered to life as she reread the words. Why did everything have to happen at once? Nothing sounded better than having lunch with Lauren and forgetting all about the bizarre world she'd been thrown into.

Heck yes. She replied.

Slipping her phone back into her pocket, Sam continued to pace her living room. Her unease had grown from a gentle annoyance to a gnawing anxiety in the pit of her stomach as the day grew into night. Something was bothering Margo. Since the moment Sam met the woman, nothing seemed to phase her up until this point.

A sharp knock on the door cut into the silence of her living room and Sam froze. "Sam, it's me," Margo's voice called.

Sam drew a deep breath through her nose and let it out gradually before she crossed the room, ushering Margo in. Margo glanced around the space with appraising eyes. "Nice bookshelf," she said, nodding to Sam's expansive collection of fantasy novels.

"Thanks. Uh." Sam swallowed back her apprehension. "What are we talking about?"

Margo jingled her keys. "We're going to see a friend of mine." She led the way outside and Sam followed her to the MINI Cooper.

When they were heading toward the bridge, Sam turned in her seat to face Margo. "You're not going to tell me where we're going, are you?"

A smile teased the corner of Margo's mouth. "Nope." She kept to her word and the twenty-five-minute trip was quiet.

The driveway led deep into the woods, and Sam's trepidation continued to climb. Night had fallen hours ago but the darkness seemed heavier the deeper they drove down the sloped gravel path. Gnarled branches raked the side of the car as the trees became denser. The vehicle dipped to the side, a wheel catching a pothole in the rough rocks so hard Sam had to save herself from hitting her head on the window. "Who is this person?"

"I told you, a friend," Margo said. Although the response was curt, Sam could tell there was something on Margo's mind. She was less talkative, her crass attitude diminished, her face thoughtful.

Then, the house came into view. The brick-built home wasn't exactly what caught her eye; it was the lofty glass-encased greenhouse to the left of the structure, the moon hauntingly reflecting off its surface. "Holy shit," Sam mumbled as Margo parked the car.

Margo chuckled as they both exited the vehicle. Grass spilled over the pathway leading to the house, blades pushing up between the cracks and reaching across the concrete. English ivy coiled around the pillars holding the archway of the porch, wisps poised toward the sky. The red brick of the building around the doorframe was splintered and worn. Margo knocked twice on the emerald door and shoved her hands in the pocket of her fraying hoodie. Sam's gaze was downcast. Margo's behavior had her on edge. More ivy threaded over the porch, the leaves upturned. A chill ran over Sam's shoulders as a breeze pushed through, causing the vines to ruffle in an eerie dance at their feet.

The door opened abruptly, and Sam looked up. The man who answered scowled at them. His dark-russet skin was illuminated in the low lighting coming from the small entryway of the home, and he swiped impatiently as his shoulder-length black hair fell into his face. An obsidian gaze glared at Margo with menace. "You're late."

"Yeah, well..." Margo trailed off as the man turned and headed inside the home, leaving the door ajar. Margo stepped inside, and Sam followed, closing the heavy oak door behind them.

"I'm in the middle of something, so make it quick," the man said as he continued through the cozy living room. Sam's damp sneakers squeaked against the dark-finished hardwood beneath her feet. They walked past inviting beige couches and a massive wall bookshelf Sam eyed jealously.

"Oh, please don't tell me I interrupted again," Margo blurted, a faint hint of red creeping up her pale neck. Sam smirked at the reaction. She'd never seen Margo blush before.

The man snickered in front of them. "No, not that, but we *are* working in the greenhouse."

"Great," Margo growled.

He pulled open a pair of French doors and the humidity hit Sam instantly. She was right to be impressed by the size on the outside, but nothing could've prepared her as they walked inside the greenhouse. There were plants everywhere. Exotic flowers spilling from baskets hung on long poles stretching the perimeter of the circular building. Reds, blues, and oranges filled the space. The aroma of earth washed over Sam, thick and heady. A handful of flowers she recognized—bird of paradise, sage, hibiscus, orchids—but the majority she'd never seen in her life. Tall, spindly plants curling around extravagant trellises, vivid green vines wrapping around the wooden posts, leaves upturned like the ivy outside the home. A narrow walkway looped the interior of the building, the rest of the space obscured by the exorbitant foliage.

"So, is this the one?" He finally turned around to face them again, jerking his thumb in Sam's direction.

Margo nodded. "Yeah, this is Sam. Sam, Brent."

"Nice to meet you," Sam said, holding her hand out. Brent hesitated before he returned the gesture, his grip firm and chilled. The hair on her arm lifted, brushing the sleeve of her thermal.

He strolled around the circular path, disappearing behind a fern bush, so they followed the winding curve. Five minutes passed, and Sam was wondering how the hell they'd been walking for so long. Granted, the building was large from the outside but not as large as it seemed to be as they continued on their path, passing stranger and stranger plants. A bird swooped over her head and Sam ducked. When she recovered, Sam could hear the faint lift of bird chatter a few yards in front of them.

They encountered a small clearing, an empty splay of patio chairs situated around a glass table. A solid wooden workbench was positioned a few feet from the patio furniture, a black cast-iron pot sitting atop what appeared to Sam as a camping stove. Mist rose from the pot, the thin tendrils dissipating instantly in the hot environment.

A white mortar and pestle gleamed in the light beside the stove. When she was a small child, her mother kept a set in the kitchen to crush peppers she grew in their garden along with different herbs and Sam remembered the cold weight of the ceramic bowl in her hand with nostalgia. Dried leaves were scattered over the table's surface, and Sam couldn't name a single one on display.

Brent gestured to the chairs. "Please, sit." Sam found a chair, the wicker back creaking in protest as she sat. Margo perched on the edge of another across from Sam, pulling a cigarette from her pack. "Don't you dare," Brent grumbled as he took a chair one over from Sam.

Margo tucked it back in her pack with an exaggerated roll of her cerulean eyes.

"So," Brent said, folding his leg over the other and leaning forward. He reached over to the decanter of dark liquid sitting in the middle of the table and poured himself a glass. "What the hell did you do, Margo?"

Margo mirrored his action, filling two tumblers to the top. "It was a simple blood bond," she said with nonchalance as she brought the glass to her lips. With her free hand, she offered Sam the glass and reluctantly she took it. The scent of rosemary mixed with something foreign filled Sam's senses, the aroma spicy and dizzying.

"God, you can be such an idiot," Brent chuckled.

"What do you mean a blood bond?" Sam interjected, placing the glass on the table.

Brent opened his mouth but before he could speak, Margo cut him off.

"How am I an idiot? You helped Mark do the same the thing!" she protested.

"No, I didn't. Yes, I helped Mark with the proper elixir to create an assistant, but I ensured it would be a temporary situation. He only needed the help while his throat healed from his interesting run-in with his Empusa friend."

"What the fuck are you talking about?" Margo snapped.

Sam sat back as the argument unfolded, unable to comment. Her foot bounced nervously on the ground, and she chewed her lip as she tried to dissect the conversation.

Twirling the liquor in the glass, Brent smiled. "Let me guess: you initiated a full blood bond at the cusp of death?"

Margo folded her arms over her chest and snorted through her nose. "Yeah, that's what the book says..." Sudden realization flashed across Margo's face, and her shoulders slumped.

"What?" Sam breathed.

Margo clutched her pack of cigarettes, bringing one to her lips as Brent scoffed. She lit the tip and inhaled deeply. Standing from the table, Brent left his beverage, crossed the few feet to the long wooden bench, and picked up the mortar.

"Who translated the literature for you?" Brent asked after a long pause.

Margo blew the smoke in front of her, the acrid scent wafting in Sam's face. "A friend."

"If you'd gone to an actual ethnobotanist, you know, like me for instance, you could've saved yourself the mistake. You don't need a blood bond for an assistant, all you need is a simple elixir, with the effects lasting no more than forty days." Brent shook his head with a smug grin as he crushed leaves into the bowl. "What do you need an assistant for, anyway? Mark only needed one because he decided to get kinky and had his throat nearly ripped out, leaving him voiceless and in dire need of a translator. You can't undo what you've done."

"What does this mean for me?" Sam asked desperately.

"You're an idiot," Brent muttered, gaze on Margo.

"It means this isn't a temporary gig," Margo said after flipping off Brent.

"Excuse me?" Fear bubbled within Sam and she gripped the ledge of the table, her knuckles whitening.

"Margo unintentionally altered you into one of us." Brent cupped the white mortar in his hand as his dark gaze met Sam's. "It's not the end of the world, but it isn't going to be an easy transition for you."

Sam blinked. "How does that even happen?"

Brent turned to Margo. "Have you told her nothing?"

"She knows what we do, and she's seen me open a portal."

Brent sighed through his nose as he brought the pestle to the bowl. "I'm sorry you have such an incompetent mentor, Sam, and I swear we're not all like this." He tipped his head in Margo's direction. The pestle scraped against the marble bowl as he crushed a dry substance into a powder. "As you already know what we do, I'll give you a quick breakdown. Unlike you, we're born into this and haven't much choice when it comes to reaping souls. We're technically demonic descendants but not in the traditional sense as our bloodlines mesh with a few different races. Other demonic creatures can't create a metaphysical door on their own just as we can't do many of the things they're capable of. It's our unique attribute to the paranormal community and it's crucial. If it wasn't for the Grim, human spirits would not pass on." He crumbled another leaf over the mortar.

Margo scoffed. "You make it sound like such an austere occupation."

"Some of us consider it as much," Brent countered. "You're going to piss a lot of people off with what you did, Margo."

"Fuck you." Margo threw him a venomous glare, fists clenched at her sides, stance threatening.

The leaves around them shifted and fluttered as if a gust of wind rattled through the room. "I'm going to have to ask you to refrain from doing that," a deep voice echoed.

"I meant no offense, Collin," Margo sputtered. Sam followed Margo's line of sight until she took in the owner of the voice. Shaggy crimson hair framed his angular face, his piercing green eyes on Margo.

Margo's apathetic façade faltered, and she sank back into her seat. He was menacing, Sam had to admit. His broad shoulders tensed as he and Margo continued their stare-down, the muscles in his arms rippling from simply placing his hand on the table. It was terrifyingly quiet, and Sam shifted with discomfort.

Finally, he turned to Brent, his rigid expression softening instantly. The leaves around them stirred again, a collective sigh carrying throughout the space.

"Is this almost done?" Collin inquired, his previously sharp tone honeyed, and he touched his hand to the small of Brent's back.

Brent nodded, pouring the contents from the bowl into the simmering pot. "Yes. A few minutes in here and it'll be finished."

"Good. She'll be here soon." Collin glanced at Margo. "Brent's right; you're going to upset quite a few people, specifically the corporation when they discover what you've done."

"*If* they find out what I did," Margo corrected. "They never found out about Mark's."

Brent shrugged. "It flew under the radar because I didn't turn the guy into a full-fledged Grim. Plus, he wasn't dead when I did it. Why didn't you come to me?"

Sam glanced at Margo, curious as well. The new knowledge was disturbing, and her irritation flared. Margo offered no response, stubbing the cigarette out on the bottom of her boot.

"What does this mean for my life?" Sam voiced after the question became too unbearable. Margo obviously wasn't going to give her the answers she needed, and Brent had already given her more information than Margo had in the few weeks since they'd met.

Scratching the scruff lining his chin, Brent leaned back against the table, sighing. "It's hard to say for certain. When corporate finds out—"

"*If,*" Margo interrupted but Brent ignored her.

"They may simply add you to the roster and line you up with your own charges once a week, like the rest of us."

"And if they don't, then what happens?"

"They'll kill you," Margo added casually.

Sam whipped her head around. "Kill me?"

"She isn't lying," Brent said, pushing off the table. "Saying they disapprove of blood bonds is a huge understatement. Their belief is any psychopomp created under such circumstances isn't neutral enough to follow protocol. They aren't considered part of the Grim."

"They consider any Cur unreliable to complete their tasks," Collin added.

"I know that's the term given to halflings and blood-bond psychopomps by the Grim but, yuck, don't use that word," Brent scoffed.

"What was I supposed to do when I was sacked with twice the work when Roz disappeared?"

"She's still missing, by the way. You should've come to me. I would've provided the elixir, you could've found a live, willing participant, and we could've avoided this problem," Brent emphasized with a jerk to his head in Sam's direction. Normally Sam's interest would've been piqued with the mention of someone's disappearance, but due to her predicament, she didn't want to halt the conversation simply to satisfy her curiosity. She knew by "problem" Brent meant her.

"The Grim?" Sam inquired.

"The name we're given as a whole. Individually, we're Grim, psychopomps, death, helping souls pass on but our race is *the* Grim. I know, sounds pretty pretentious, doesn't it?" Brent chuckled.

Margo grumbled something inaudible, standing again. "How do we fix this?"

"Keep a low profile, get your assignments done in a timely fashion and maybe this will all blow over."

"There's no way to undo it?" Sam inquired.

Brent shook his head sullenly. "I said that already. In all the literature I've read, there's no way to reverse the blood bond, barring death."

Sam flickered her gaze to Collin as the strange man scraped the pestle in the mortar, adding bits of a cherry-colored substance. He stared at her, the eye contact provoking a shiver. Sam concluded he was definitely not human.

"I'm sure Sam over here would rather not die to fix your mistake. Not to mention it isn't going to be an easy feat to kill her anyway," Brent noted.

Snatching her coat from the table, Margo tugged Sam up by the arm. "Cool. We'll be heading out now."

Their footsteps were muted by the strange sounds of the greenhouse, and Sam struggled to keep pace with Margo as she sped through the winding pathway. They went through the French doors back into the main house, the cool air washing over Sam's face, the space devoid of the humidity in the previous room. She paused to take in the climate change, her mind whirling with the new revelations revolving her life. After she'd made the deal with Margo, Sam had been correct in assuming her life would never be the same. Margo was already halfway to the front door, Sam hurrying after her.

As Margo reached for the knob, the door opened, revealing a woman with her head down, dark tendrils of dreadlocks obscuring her face until she looked up. Her gray rumpled T-shirt was covered in splotches of colorful paint, the words *For Fox Sakes* written over her breasts with a depiction of a small fox prancing over a log beneath the inscription. Her lithe body froze when she noticed them, and she snarled. Sam gasped at the flash of vicious incisors gleaming in the low light.

"Jacqueline, nice to see you," Margo sneered as she moved out of the way.

The woman's glare was intense, and Sam stepped back, her dark gaze moving from Margo to Sam and back. Placing a hand on her hip, her steely focus narrowed. "I wish I could say the same thing," she admonished before she pushed forcefully past Margo.

Though Margo wasn't the most social person or the kindest, Sam was startled to realize just how many people disliked her company.

"THAT WAS...INTERESTING," Sam mumbled as the car careened out of the driveway.

"Yeah, real enlightening." Margo's brows were knitted together, her lips a thin line.

"What's a Cur?"

Margo cleared her throat, scowling before she answered, "It's a nasty term given to Grims who aren't pureblood or who were created from a blood bond."

"How'd you know something was wrong with me?"

"Well, for starters, you healed way too fast from your accident. The energy emitted during a portal opening can't be felt by humans. You shouldn't have been able to see the selkie working for the police," Margo stated flatly. "And before you ask, because I know you will, Collin is a little overprotective of Brent, and frankly, he scares the shit out of me. The whole plant thing weirds me out, too, but he's Fae and it's his way of being close to his heritage when he can't go home."

"Why can't he?" Sam inquired, wondering where home for him would be.

Margo sighed, gaze on the road. "He's a halfling, half human, half Fae, so he's not welcome."

"Oh. That's sad." She paused. "Fae as in like a fairy?" she finally asked with a hint of skepticism.

"Yeah. Our world is as diverse as any. Shapeshifters, faeries, selkies, kelpies, witches, vampires, Empusa, which are like vampires but don't call them vampires unless you want your throat ripped out. Or, in my case, my shin kicked so hard, I bled."

"Oh, so that's why we had the weird interaction by the front door?"

Margo nodded, blowing smoke from her nose. "Yep, Jacqueline hates my guts. They prefer Empusa, but at the time I met her, I didn't know the term or the fact they're different."

"I'll keep this bit of information in the back of my mind." Sam laughed even as she pictured the unnaturally sharp teeth the woman possessed. Margo chuckled and shook her head, a lightness softening the edges of her gruff attitude.

They remained quiet until they were cruising over the bridge onto the island, the only sounds coming from the stereo. The information revolving around Sam's new existence was disconcerting. She didn't know where to begin or how to accept the fact her life would never be the same. Her mother had taken Sam and Katie to church as children and she had trouble believing the things they were taught. At first, she'd tried to convince herself Margo was a hallucination, but she kept coming back. Now, seeing was believing. How could Sam deny the incredible sensation of energy coursing through her body when she opened a portal with her?

The short answer was she couldn't, nor could she deny the power, raw and biting, emanating off the three other individuals she'd met during their visit. Sam checked her phone for the first time since she'd left her apartment with Margo. One message from Lauren.

I hope it's okay if another friend joins us. She wants to meet you anyway.

She grinned as she typed her reply.

That's perfectly fine. Should I plan to make a good impression?

"Lover boi, one more thing," Margo said. Sam lifted her head before she continued. "Don't tell your little girlfriend about any of this."

"How'd you know I was texting her? And she's not my girlfriend." Sam grimaced. Margo smirked. "It doesn't take a psychic to know you're talking to a girl. With that shit-eating grin, who else would it be? I don't care whether or not she's your girlfriend; don't tell her or anyone else about this, okay?"

"Sure." Lauren believing her was unlikely, to begin with, so Sam wasn't in a hurry to tell her anyway.

"God, I'm starving," Margo said as they entered the city. "You want something?"

Sam laughed, the thought of a Grim Reaper eating seemed ridiculous and she blurted, "You eat?"

Margo gave her a peculiar stare before her lips contorted in a smirk. "Sometimes the souls of small children don't cut it and I need a goddamn cheeseburger."

Sam's eyes widened, although Margo's face held mischief.

Margo chortled and slapped the dashboard. "Yes, I eat, don't you? I told you we're like humans with added obligations. Even Empusa and Fae have to eat and sleep. You get the point." She pulled up behind a small line of cars in the drive-thru of a fast food restaurant.

"You're telling me a lot, all of a sudden," Sam remarked.

Margo's smile vanished, and she stared pointedly at the car in front of them. "Well, seeing as you're stuck with this lot in life because of my fuckup, it's the least I can do." The red brake lights shined eerily in Margo's eyes, causing them to take on an odd lilac hue.

Sam realized the longevity behind her new occupation was an accident, and Margo's intent hadn't been malicious. The guilt was visible in her avoidance and her swift change in demeanor.

"Margo..." Sam began sympathetically. While she wasn't excited about her new life as a Grim, she was happy to be alive and given another chance.

The car moved up, Margo opening the window as she tilted her head to Sam. "What do you want to eat?"

Chapter Eleven

THE CROWDED PIZZERIA was a stark contrast to the calm boardwalk at midday in September. The influx of tourists visiting for the summer was dwindling as fall took over the seaside town, and Lauren was amazed at the number of people who were crammed into the establishment, despite this. The scent of tangy sauce and garlic hit her senses as she waded through the patrons to find Jackie. Her friend was tucked behind a dozen raucous family members celebrating a birthday, foil balloons glimmering in the fluorescents recessed into the ceiling. Jackie faced the wall, twirling a straw in a glass of water.

The table she sat at was situated by the back door of the eatery, and Lauren squeezed around the family's boisterous activity to find a seat across from Jackie. "I thought about finding us a spot outside, but the clouds look a little too unpredictable for that," Jackie explained, throwing her hair over her shoulder.

"It's okay," Lauren shouted over the noise from the table nearest to them that jumped an octave.

Jackie grinned impishly, rubbing her palms together, her various rings clinking together. "You have no idea how excited I am to meet this *friend* of yours."

"I'm sure you are. Please don't embarrass me," Lauren pleaded.

"*Me*, embarrass you? No way!" Jackie smiled broadly as the waiter arrived.

The waiter offered to give them a few more minutes while they waited for Sam. The waiter left their table and Sam appeared through the horde of people, and Lauren was stunned by the beauty of her androgyny anew. Sam pushed her unruly hair to the side, the length grown out from her usual pixie cut, and she peered around the venue before meeting Lauren's gaze. "Here she comes," Lauren whispered without taking her sight from the woman who had her so transfixed. Jackie turned around to check her out and her body stiffened as Sam approached.

Sam skidded around the crowded table beside them and stood still when she reached them. "Hey," she said breathlessly. Her eyes were wide as she took in Jackie, but she smiled.

"You can sit wherever," Lauren said, indicating to the two empty chairs around the square table. "We aren't expecting anyone else. Sam, this is Jackie."

"Hi," Jackie said as Sam sat beside Lauren. A strange expression flashed across Sam's face, leading Lauren to wonder if the two knew each other.

Her notion was dismissed when Sam reached over the table and shook Jackie's hand. "Nice to meet you," Sam said.

After their perfunctory introductions, they all fell into a comfortable conversation, Sam and Jackie clicking instantly. Lauren smiled as the two women engaged in an animated conversation picking apart the different pizza establishments in the surrounding cities. After their pizza was finished and the bill was presented, Jackie covered the cost against Lauren and Sam's protests.

"You've got dinner duty next weekend anyway. Oh, and by the way, Liam and Bonny can't make it," Jackie said, gathering their trash as they all rose from the table. The two she spoke of were fellow teachers at the school and were good company during their monthly game night.

"So, just you and Caleb, then?" Lauren asked. Jackie nodded. "You should come since you missed the last one I scheduled," Lauren said to Sam.

The trio of women exited the noisy pizzeria, stepping onto the boardwalk. "I'd love to," Sam said.

Lauren draped her sweater over her arm as they stepped outside. The dense humidity in the air left a fine mist clinging to everything, condensation lining the planks beneath their feet and the windows of storefronts.

Jackie turned to Sam. "Well, it was nice meeting you. I'm sure I'll see you at Lauren's next weekend for her game night."

"Yeah, that'll be awesome."

With a wave, Jackie walked down the boardwalk, slipping around a corner in the direction of the staircase.

"Want to go to the arcade?" Sam asked.

"Why, so I can beat you at Skee-Ball?" Lauren teased, relishing in the soft smile spreading on Sam's face.

Sam chuckled. "No, so I can beat *you* at Skee-Ball."

Puffy nimbus clouds drifted overhead, pushed by a cool breeze off the water. The heat was unseasonable, causing a sticky layer of perspiration to form on the nape of Lauren's neck.

"I have a random question for you," Sam said, tucking her hands into the large pocket of her hoodie, her gaze set ahead of them.

"Okay," Lauren said, curious what the question could entail. She half wondered if Sam was going to inquire about her and Bethany's demise. The possibility didn't frighten her, but she didn't want the atmosphere of their day to change.

"Do you believe in ghosts or spirits?"

At first, Lauren laughed, assuming it was a joke until she saw the sincerity as Sam turned her head. She'd never seen a ghost, nor did she believe in the stories people told. Any digital evidence brought about was disgustingly altered and easily disputed as forged. "Honestly, no. There isn't a lot of the occult or supernatural I believe in. Why do you ask?" Lauren couldn't think of one item in either category she believed in.

Sam shrugged and shot her a crooked smile. "No reason."

Perhaps she and Jackie knew each other from something revolving around the occult. Jackie may have considered herself Wiccan, but Lauren never knew her to partake in any group activities, however, the strange look the two women shared upon Sam's arrival had her questioning. Before Lauren could ask Sam if the two women had a link she was unaware of, they arrived at their destination.

The arcade was animated, and Sam bounded through the wide doorway with enthusiasm, clutching Lauren's hand as she towed her along. Lauren gazed up at the dome-shaped ceiling, the sounds of the arcade reverberating over them, clinking of air hockey pucks, the ringing of a won game and varying bits of music mixed with endless chatter. "How have I never been here?"

Sam smirked as she fed a couple dollars to the coin machine. "I'm wondering the same thing. I know you didn't grow up here, but didn't you and your parents come down during the summer?"

Lauren nodded. "My dad brought my brother and me here every single summer. It was our little tradition, and I loved it so much that when I graduated, I had to move here. Not to mention Jackie landed a job so quickly, and I was excited to know someone in the area."

"I'm glad you became a permanent tourist." Sam winked at her and Lauren sighed out loud. Sam threaded her fingers in Lauren's hair, Lauren's breath stalling in her throat. Kaleidoscopic lights flashed over Sam's face from a nearby game, her eyes shifting in an ethereal dance as her pupils dilated. "Lauren," Sam murmured. Lauren must've taken for granted how delicate her name sounded with the slight rasp of Sam's voice, and the single word caused her to sigh with longing. She wanted to hear Sam say her name again and again.

A group of children ran past, one of them bumping their shoulder into Lauren. Sam dropped her hand and cleared her throat. Damn, the moment was gone. They moved over to the pinball games after Sam suggested it and she started to play.

"So, what does a science teacher do on a lazy Sunday if they aren't doing teacherly things?" Sam inquired as she slapped her hand on the button. The pinball flew up the shaft and hit a target, causing a cacophony of music and a clattering as it was catapulted through a series of obstacles.

"If I'm done grading papers or trying to figure out how to tweak my lesson plans so I can pique my students wavering interests, maybe laundry or reading," Lauren began and leaned her hip against the game and titled her head as seductively as she could muster, which didn't feel like much.

WITHOUT TURNING AWAY from Lauren, Sam tapped the button on the game, her gaze causing an aching in Lauren to ravish Sam. Wow, where did such a thought come from? Lauren wondered. The pinball tumbled down the shoot and the game ended. "You lost your ball," Lauren nodded to the game. "Why don't we go for walk on the beach?" So much for Skee-Ball.

SAM ALMOST KISSED Lauren in the arcade full of people and she refrained from kicking herself in the ass for missing the opportunity. Despite Lauren voicing she didn't want a relationship, she wasn't going light on the flirtation. The way Lauren's gaze smoldered when Sam said her name, the slight curve of her crooked smile, her gentle touch—all had Sam wondering what Lauren's intentions were if she wasn't interested. A couple of joggers passed as they walked, Lauren grazing the back of Sam's hand with her fingertips.

"Have you been in the water since the accident?" Lauren asked as they headed down the staircase onto the sand.

"No, I haven't." Not that she hadn't wanted to. The near-death experience was still too fresh in her brain to consider stepping foot into the water. No, it wasn't near-death; Sam had died; she was sure of that after learning of how her life would change forever. What did this mean for her budding relationship with Lauren? Margo was adamant on her concealment of the circumstances, and Sam knew she had good reason. The corporation, whoever they were, looked down on individuals like Sam. Margo hadn't apologized outright, but the guilt was obvious and unwavering.

Speaking of Margo, Sam pulled her phone out with the intent of sending the woman a text, but she had one waiting for her.

We've got a job. Where are u?

Sam quickly typed her reply, feeling unbelievably rude to be texting while with Lauren.

I'm busy. Can't you do it yourself?

Margo's response was almost instant.

Ah, having fun with ur gf, lover boi?

She's not my girlfriend.

Was Lauren her girlfriend? The fine line between friends and friends with benefits seemed to have been crossed when they'd Frenched on the boardwalk after the movie a few weekends before, but Sam was sure they weren't officially a couple. Given the conversation when Lauren dropped Sam off, they were definitely not a couple. She wouldn't know until she asked Lauren where they stood. Plus, her life was far too complicated to drag Lauren into it. On this thought, Sam remembered the recognition on Jackie's face when she saw Sam, why she intended to text Margo, to begin with. Lauren's life was unwittingly complicated enough.

I think we need to talk about something later.

Too many secrets. Sam couldn't tell Lauren she'd been turned into a Grim Reaper, that her best friend, Jackie, was a vampire crossbreed, but she *could* disclose the awkward run-in she had with Bethany during her delivery to Lauren's house pre-accident.

Coolio. I'll see u later.

Fingers intertwined with her free hand, and Sam peered down to see Lauren's hand in hers. She looked up and smiled, a faint blush creeping into Lauren's cheeks. Shit, Sam wanted to bring it up but couldn't. She wanted to savor their moment together with the way it was, without worries. "Was it scary?"

"Was what scary?"

"Your accident," Lauren said.

Sam pursed her lips and they continued their pace before she spoke, the sound of water pouring over the shore filling the silence. "Yeah, I was pretty scared. The storm came out of nowhere, and the water just kept crashing over me." Sam swallowed the sudden lump in her throat as she recalled the salty water filling her lungs. "I didn't think I'd make it out alive." She chuckled dryly. Lauren's thumb rubbed the back of her hand, the gesture more soothing than Sam anticipated.

"I'm sorry if my question brought back bad memories."

"No, you're fine," Sam sighed, raking a hand through her hair. "I'd love to get back on a surfboard again, but I think my sister would kill me." Sam wasn't lying either; Katie would kick her ass, no doubt.

"I've got to tell you something," Sam said.

Lauren tilted her head. "Okay," she said gently.

She had to tell her. Despite the relationship ending in its own time, guilt stirred within Sam for witnessing Bethany's deception and withholding the incident from Lauren. "A week before my accident, I was working my normal route, and I had a few packages for you, but you weren't home. Instead, Bethany answered the door, and I saw another woman in your house, who called Bethany 'baby.' I'm so sorry I didn't tell you before. I was planning on telling you face-to-face when I came to your house for game night, but my lovely run-in with the rocks took away the opportunity."

Sam stopped talking, shifting her weight while she waited for Lauren to speak, her expression unreadable. Without warning, Lauren moved, pressing her lips firmly to Sam's. She threaded her wrists around Sam's neck, pulling their bodies flush together. Sam wrapped her arms around Lauren's waist, reveling in their closeness. She wanted Lauren, every single part of her. "You don't have to apologize, Sam. You weren't the one who cheated on me," Lauren whispered beside Sam's cheek. Sam let a long breath out. One secret down.

"I feel like such an ass for not telling you right away—"

"How are you this sweet?" Lauren asked, pulling back. "My track record with women hasn't been the best, but I hope my luck is about to change." She closed her eyes, bringing her lips to Sam's once again. Sam sighed into their kiss, parting her lips as Lauren's tongue probed. What did she mean? Sam had to reign in her elation at the prospects of Lauren's statement. Could she possibly mean what she and Sam shared or was Sam simply getting her hopes up?

Thick, fat raindrops fell upon them, one falling directly on Sam's forehead. "I swear the weather is out to get us," Lauren murmured against Sam's lips.

"Let's hide under the boardwalk until it stops," Sam offered.

Shards of light threaded through the planks of the boardwalk from the streetlamps above, casting eerie splashes of yellow on the dark sand. The waves at the shoreline were muffled as they stepped under the eight-foot clearance, and rain thudded lightly on the wood overhead, adding to the serenity of the darkened space.

Sam laughed at a memory of herself at seven years old, hauling a flailing orange tabby clutched to her chest from beneath the boardwalk, begging her mother to take him home. When Lauren shot her a perplexed expression, she elaborated. "I used to chase the cats down here, determined I'd catch one and take it home with me. One day, I caught one and begged my mom to let me keep him."

"Did she let you?" Lauren's smile caused a flurry of longing within Sam, nearly distracting her from the question.

"No, my mom was allergic, so I had to let him go. I came back and visited him all the time," Sam recalled with nostalgia.

"Well, if we find one, we should catch them. I bet Boo would love a friend," Lauren suggested. Sam shook her head with a grin, following Lauren deeper. Ten feet in front of them stood a freshly painted rowboat, announcing OCNJ, in crisp black lettering on its side.

The water vessel appeared recently refurbished, the inner workings stripped of benches, fresh wooden panels lining the base. Lauren clambered into the boat, giggling madly, and Sam chuckled herself, enamored by her. Locks of thick hair fell into Lauren's face as she bent to pull off her shoes. As she rose, she pushed the strands back and reached for Sam's hand.

"Oh, are we going for a row?" Sam asked, laughing.

Lauren flapped her hand at Sam, sticking her tongue out. "You never know if the rain out there will stop, and we'd better be safe than sorry if it decides to flood. Come on."

"I'm no expert, but I know there are supposed to be benches in these things," Sam said as Lauren grasped her hand, allowing her to help Sam climb into the oversized rowboat. The stern was reconstructed with various shades of wood spanning the siding.

"I was on the crew team in college, and not to toot my own horn, but I was pretty good." Lauren yanked Sam to her, their bodies colliding together, shaking the boat as Sam tried to steady herself.

"There aren't even any oars!" Sam retorted, reaching for the sides. The boat tipped in the loose sand beneath it causing them to fall to the bottom. Sam scooted herself to the stern, laughing as Lauren tried to regain her balance but ended up on her butt a foot from Sam.

She leaned back and crossed her arms, shooting Lauren a smirk. "Did you lie when you said you used to row because I wouldn't go anywhere near the water with you," Sam teased.

As if she hadn't heard Sam's retort, Lauren's face was still, her emerald gaze brimming with yearning. "Sam, I want you so bad," she whispered as she crawled toward her. The thudding of Sam's heart boomed in her ears, and when Lauren touched her cheek, she blew out a throaty sigh. She smelled amazing, like a steaming cup of chamomile and lavender tea during a spring shower. Lauren searched her face, her lips parting, breath hot over Sam's skin.

Sam ran her fingers through Lauren's hair and urged her closer, claiming her lips, her digits securing a handful of silken hair. Unlike their most recent kiss, this one was one of urgent exploration, ferocious and unyielding. Sam slid down the stern of the boat, easing them both to the floor, Lauren positioned over her body. Lauren canvassed her torso with her deft hands, Sam's excitement rushing through her, dampening her core, intensifying the desire that was already well stoked.

Lauren dug her fingers into Sam's hips, urging her against the wooden base of the rowboat, causing Sam to throw her head back and reach for Lauren. Sam pulled Lauren to her, kissing her lips fiercely as Lauren continued her crusade to feel her bare skin. She unzipped Sam's hoodie, roaming Sam's abdomen under her T-shirt, raking her nails over her ribs. Lashing her tongue against Lauren's, Sam brought her hands to Lauren's sides, scrunching her blouse up, needing to touch her silky skin. Lauren cooed as Sam dipped her fingers beneath her jeans, their kiss halting briefly.

This beautifully broken woman above her was swiftly engulfing Sam's heart, and she couldn't do anything to stop her ardor. Lauren's eyes closed as Sam skirted her hands under Lauren's shirt, unclasping her bra before bringing her hands over Lauren's breasts, teasing hardened nipples. Lauren moaned, laying her head on Sam's shoulder. Sam eased her shirt up, tugging it over Lauren's head. Lauren met her gaze, chest heaving. The splash of freckles over Lauren's face didn't stop at her neck but sprinkled her shoulders, her collarbones, spreading across her pale breasts.

Hunching forward, Sam took a nipple into her mouth, and she fluttered her tongue over the pebbled nub. Lauren took a sharp inhale, shifting herself over Sam, hips straddling Sam's waist. Fingers softly caressing her neglected breast, Sam nibbled the nipple in her mouth, earning herself another lovely sound from her lover. She grazed Lauren's exposed sides with her nails, easing Lauren's jeans down slightly. Evidently, Lauren had other ideas. She lifted herself away from Sam's mouth, shaking her head.

With renewed vigor, Lauren brought her mouth to Sam's neck, kissing a path up her jaw, her exhales deafening beside Sam's ear. Sam hadn't predicted this, too accustomed to taking the lead, but she didn't want Lauren to stop. The change, although unexpected, proved to be what she longed for. Need unfurled within her as she grasped Lauren's neck, pulling her face to hers, claiming her lips once more. Sam placed her hands back on Lauren's hips as Lauren pressed her knee against her core, eliciting a low moan from her.

When Lauren pulled back breathlessly, Sam murmured, "Are you sure this is okay?"

Nodding, Lauren kissed her again harder with a brutality that stole Sam's breath and had her grabbing desperately for Lauren. Lauren skimmed her stomach with her fingertips, ascending her bra, and grazing her palms over Sam's breasts. Sam groaned, and Lauren took the opportunity to capture her lower lip between her teeth. Footsteps thundered above their heads as Lauren moved her lips over Sam's collarbones, tongue swirling back up the slope of her neck. Her need throbbed as Lauren pushed her knee harder, a burst of pleasure coursing through Sam.

Lauren hovered over Sam, her hair tickling Sam's neck and face, cheeks reddened, chest heaving as she stared at her. Featherlight touches to Sam's waistline made her dizzy, Lauren dipping beneath her jeans, testing the elastic of her boxers. Sam held her breath at the sound of her zipper sliding open. Lauren quirked an eyebrow at her as she halted her progress, waiting for Sam's approval. "How bad do you want me to touch you?" Lauren breathed, her expression taunting.

"Fuck, Lauren," Sam replied, raising herself on her elbows, urging Lauren's mouth to her own. Sam lifted her hips as Lauren yanked both obstacles out of the way, raking her nails over her naked thighs, scorching a path back to the apex of Sam's legs. Breaking their lip lock, Lauren lowered herself down Sam's body, trailing her fingers across the peaks of Sam's breasts over her shirt, down the curve of her abdomen. She planted wet kisses on both of her thighs with soft lips, and taunted Sam's curls as she grazed her fingertips over Sam's core. Parting her legs, Sam welcomed the yearning Lauren's touch elicited, allowed her to be consumed by her need. Sam closed her eyes, resting back just as a hot swipe of a tongue dashed over her clit. Warm breath poured over her and Sam arched, wanting, no, *needing* more of Lauren as she took Sam's clit into her mouth, Sam's body tightening at the sensation.

Sam cupped the back of Lauren's head with her hand, gently encouraging her efforts, the pleasure washing over Sam in a torrent. She steadied herself with her other hand, grasping hold of the side of the boat as she neared her cusp, too soon, way too soon.

Her fingers laced through Lauren's glossy hair, rocking her pelvis to meet each stroke of her wet tongue. "Lauren," she hissed, tendrils of her climax filling her limbs, her muscles rigid and taut. Arching her back, Sam moaned, clamping her teeth down on her lower lip to stifle her cries as Lauren devoured her, the pleasure crashing over her as if the rowboat were in a turbulent sea rather than in the stillness under the boardwalk. The trickle of rainwater sounded around them, the storm picking back up where it'd left off, and Sam writhed, her body shaking, breath coming in short rasps. Lauren gripped her thighs, working her tongue harder, shoving Sam over another crest. Letting go of her lip, Sam groaned, awash in ecstasy, lifting her hips from the rough wood of the rowboat. She slowed her breathing, euphoria settling over her, resting back. Lauren crawled up Sam's body, straddling her belly, and Sam met her soft gaze.

Perspiration prickled the skin of her forehead, and Lauren pushed the errant hairs out of Sam's face, beaming down at her. She kissed her, Sam relishing in the taste of herself on her lover's lips. As Lauren deepened the kiss, Sam snuck her hands below, unbuttoning Lauren's jeans and sliding them over her thighs. Sam edged the waistline of Lauren's panties with her fingertips, provoking a jagged sigh from Lauren. "Now, how bad do you want *me* to touch *you*?" Sam mumbled as she toyed with the skin above Lauren's mound, barely brushing her soft curls before moving away. Lauren made an impatient sound in the back of her throat, causing Sam to chuckle.

"You have no idea how bad," Lauren whimpered. Lowering her hand farther, Sam met dampness and Lauren sighed, head lolling to the crook of Sam's neck as she ran her fingers over her lips. "Yes," Lauren exhaled. How did this woman seize Sam's heart so? Running her thumb over her clit, Sam pressed a finger into Lauren's warmth. Lauren moved her hips, relaying her need, kissing Sam's neck. "More, baby," Lauren breathed, the sound along with the words tantalizing. Obeying, Sam slipped a second digit into Lauren, earning herself a throaty moan, Lauren shifting her hips to meet her thrust. Her kisses turned to nibbles, nibbles turning to sharp bites against Sam's neck.

Lauren threw her head back, and Sam relished in the bliss on her face, her body writhing above Sam, nails digging into the skin on her shoulder from her strong grip. If she hadn't healed as promptly as she had due to Margo's altering of her physical makeup, Sam figured the pressure would've hurt like a bitch. However, Lauren's painful vicelike grip only added fuel to the fire, igniting her desire to please her to a boiling point. To bring Lauren a semblance of what she did to Sam. Sam rounded her thumb roughly over Lauren's clit, causing Lauren's brow to crinkle.

"Sam," Lauren moaned, her chestnut hair falling away from her face, her pale skin flushed crimson. She was stunningly beautiful, and Sam's chest tightened with affection. "Oh, Sam," Lauren cooed, rocking her body in motion with Sam's movements, tightening around Sam's fingers. Sam cupped the back of Lauren's neck, pulling her downward for a searing kiss to quiet the enticing noises coming from her as she reached her peak. Hips bucking, Lauren moaned loudly against Sam's open mouth as the climax tore through her, and Sam closed her eyes, reveling in the pleasure she brought her.

Lauren lay her head against Sam's shoulder, her breath settling, and her body spent. "I know autumn is here, tourist season is over and all, but there are still plenty of noisy bystanders traipsing the boardwalk at this hour," Sam muttered in Lauren's hair. Lauren giggled, the sound reverberating and beautiful. Sam breathed in Lauren's scent, cherishing the closeness of their bodies after their shared bliss. She combed her fingers through the length of Lauren's hair, mesmerized by the natural highlights illuminated by the faint lamplight peeking through the planks of the boardwalk overhead.

"We should probably get out of here before we get caught," Lauren mused, and Sam snorted, taking Lauren's face in her hands.

"Afraid we'll get booted out by a cop again?"

Lauren smirked, kissing Sam before whispering, "Something like that."

"SO, HOW'S IT going on the romance front with Lauren?" Josh asked as he lifted a box full of groceries from the warehouse store up onto the counter.

Sam lifted her shoulders nonchalantly. "It is what it is. Lauren isn't interested in anything more than what we're doing, and I guess I'm fine with what we have." It really wasn't fine with her. She wanted more with Lauren but didn't want to risk losing what they shared by expressing her desire. She came so close to sparking the conversation as they said goodbye to each other earlier in the afternoon. Lauren had kissed her before walking to her car, and Sam lost her nerve when those lips met hers again, even with their incredible experience. Her cheeks burned with the memory of Lauren's hands caressing her body, the rough wood on her bare skin, Lauren uttering her name in the darkness under the boardwalk.

"Are you sure about that? Because your face tells a whole different story."

Sam sighed and forced the image down. "No, of course, I want more but I'm not pushing it. We enjoy each other's company and beyond that, I don't know if she's ready. Plus, I'm too chicken shit to ask her if she's ready to be with me." Sam took a sip of water and Josh leered at her. She'd been so transfixed by her time with Lauren she almost forgot about her planned shopping trip to the grocery store with Josh who leeched off her membership card for cheap food.

"Speaking of strange things," Josh began, and Sam punched him in the arm. "Did you hear about the big car accident?"

Sam quirked an eyebrow at him. "What car accident?"

"There was a big pileup on the Black Horse Pike this morning and like five people died."

"Yikes." Sam didn't want to hear about death. If she could get through the rest of her life without talking about death, her world would be perfect. She knew better than anyone how imperfect the world truly was. Deaths close by meant her and Margo could possibly have a new spirit to help. Sam threw perishables into the fridge, hoping the conversation would die down and he'd go home. She needed time to think about, well, everything. Maybe read so she wouldn't have to think about it.

"Apparently, the accident was caused by some faulty truck from a big box store."

Sam nodded, taking another sip of water. "Lauren invited me over next weekend. She does this little get together with her coworkers and they play stupid board games and get tipsy; said I could bring you. Want to come?"

"For someone in a 'not relationship,' you sure do talk about her a lot," Josh joked, and Sam rolled her eyes. "I'm flattered she remembered me, but I'll pass. Brad and I are heading up to do some free-spirited gambling in Atlantic City. Don't have too much fun, though."

After more teasing on Josh's part, he left Sam. She wandered around her apartment for a while, debating whether she'd text Lauren or not, and then deciding to sit and read instead. By midnight, Sam deduced Margo was a no-show and went to bed.

Hours later, Sam woke to the soft rap on her bedroom door. She ignored the sound, turning over in bed and pressing the pillow over her head. Only moments later, she was woken again. "Sam, wake up," Margo's voice cut through the oscillating fan on Sam's bedroom floor. With an exaggerated groan, she rolled over. She considered tucking the pillow over her head again and ignoring the Grim, but she knew this would get her nowhere.

They had things to discuss anyway. "Do we have to keep doing this in the middle of the night?" Sam sat up and rubbed her eyes.

Margo stood in front of her with her arms crossed over her chest. "Technically, it's morning. Plus, the last one was smack dab in the afternoon, so quit moaning. Get up, get dressed, and let's go."

Sunlight crested overhead, and Sam recognized it was indeed morning. It was Monday and all she could think of was sleep as they walked over to Margo's car and got in. "What happened to seeing me later?" Sam grumbled.

"I was a little preoccupied." Margo offered her a sheepish grin. "My bad."

Sam pulled the hood of her jacket over her head and closed her eyes.

The Ocean City animal shelter lay on the outskirts of town with a huge soccer field down the long driveway to the facility. The early morning sun shone bright, far too bright for Sam's sleepiness. Tiny black birds peppered the blue sky, their flock shifting as a unit in the morning breeze as they fluttered over the field below. Margo parked at the end of the road and got out with a curt prompt for Sam to follow. "What're we doing here?"

"Work. What else?"

Sam rolled her eyes at Margo's half-ass response and followed her through the grassy field to the building. A handful of workers walked dogs a quarter of a mile away behind a large fenced area. Sam's breath left her mouth in a coil of mist, the air around them crisp. A lone figure leaned over the fence with their face turned toward the animals. "There's your target," Margo said quietly. "Today, it's all on you. I'll walk you through it, but I want you to try to open the door for this one by yourself."

The woman appeared to be in her late fifties, her blonde hair dappled with strands of gray and white. The blue scrubs she wore were frayed at the hem on the pants and a name was embroidered on the white coat tucked over her arm. Sam approached with caution as she felt the woman radiate authority. "Hi," Sam said. The woman either didn't hear her or was ignoring her. Sam shot a questionable glance back at Margo who gestured forward with her hands as if telling Sam to get closer. Sam took another step and placed her hands on the cold metal of the fence a couple feet from the woman.

In the fenced area, five dogs were off leash, trampling around the grass taking in the scents. Sam smiled to herself as a chocolate lab bounded over to where she stood and sniffed the woman next to her through the chain link. "Hi, buddy," Sam said, sticking her fingers through the holes to meet the dog's eager advance, but it ignored her for the ghost before it ran off again at the sound of a whistle.

"He's a cutie, huh?" the woman beside her asked.

"Yeah, he is."

The woman turned to Sam and jutted her hand out. "Meg Karo." Sam cautiously accepted the handshake, shocked she could grasp the spirit's hand.

"Sam."

When they let go, Meg stared ahead and sighed. "Life is funny sometimes. You dedicate your life to saving lives, and then one night you experience symptoms that you'd berate a patient for ignoring. Then, you end up dead."

Sam noticed the words on the embroidery. Dr. Meg Karo, Cardiothoracic Surgery.

"His name is Lance. Sweet boy. He's kept me company for the last five years, and I hate to leave him."

Ah, her unfinished business. "I don't blame you. Do you think he'll get adopted?"

Meg smiled at Sam and the gesture caused the wrinkles around her eyes to deepen. "He's got a home lined up and he's leaving today."

"That's fantastic." There went her assumption. "He looks like a good dog." Sam kicked a loose rock at the base of the fence as unsure as she ever was at what to do next. Distantly, Margo cleared her throat, and Sam turned to see Margo tapping her finger on her wrist. Damn, she was impatient. "So, the family—the ones who're taking him—do they seem nice?"

"They seem like a nice couple." Meg sighed and pushed off the fence to straighten her back. She fixed her gaze on Sam. "Take time to consider your life before you make a monumental decision."

"Okay," Sam said. "Do you want to talk about anything?"

Meg chuckled and wrung her hands together. "Are you a therapist or something?"

"No." Sam blushed, gazing out toward the animal shelter. What the hell was she supposed to say to get this woman to move on?

"Her name was Alice. We'd been dating for about four years, and I was madly in love with her. I was offered a fellowship at John Hopkins. We lived in Oregon at the time, and we argued about it for weeks." Meg paused and shook her head. "I was so stubborn and headstrong. It was Johns Hopkins—I couldn't refuse the opportunity because Alice didn't want to leave her nursery. See, she was a botanist and her plants were like her children. I just wish I could've seen past my pigheadedness. I lost her because of my conceit."

"I'm sorry." Sam rubbed her arm. Now she understood why she couldn't leave. The regret and loss were clear on Meg's face and Sam felt for her. "What happened?"

Meg let out a long exhale. "I left. I never saw her again. I was so frustrated with her for not going with me, I refused to even consider continuing our relationship. I immersed myself into my work, and when I finally reached out to her, she was happily married." She glanced down at her hands. "You know, when they say you see your life flash before your eyes when you die, they're lying. I didn't see anything but Alice's face. Don't make stupid mistakes because of pride," Meg pleaded.

Sam knew she was right. The only thing Sam saw when she died was a sassy Grim Reaper and her own dead body. No, that wasn't true. She'd seen Katie, little Ben, and, of course, Lauren, in her mind's eye.

"All right, you're up," Margo announced. Sam was hesitant, uncertain if she could do it although she was eager to feel the power again. "Close your eyes, let the feeling engulf you." Margo's voice was a whisper.

Sam closed her eyes, breathing in deeply. A spark lit within her, instantly spreading to her arms, goose bumps stirring her skin. Her exhale was ragged and forced, the scorching fire deep in her chest branching outward, tendrils of energy shocking her. Her eyes snapped open to see Margo staring at her, eyes wide and jaw slack. "Keep going," Margo mumbled.

A spot ahead of them in the field fluctuated such as heat radiating off hot asphalt in the summer, the telltale sign Sam had come to recognize as the precursor for the portal. She lifted her hand, spreading her fingers as the electricity wavered and bowed forward. Sam was drowned in power and she relished in the sensation, wanting more, longing to feel it swirl around her, encompassing her body.

Meg walked toward the fluttering space, and with a slight tilt of her head at them, she was gone. "Fuck," Sam hissed through clenched teeth. The swirling mass of electricity vanished as quickly as it came, leaving her nauseous and dizzy. She bent, gripping her knees as she heaved, dizziness shuddering her body.

A comforting hand touched her shoulder and Sam shook her head, trying to dispel another wave of nausea. "Is this going to happen every time?"

Margo patted her back and chuckled. "Nah, things will get better after a few. Pretty awesome though, right?"

Sam clambered into the car and rested back as fatigue hit her.

"That woman saved almost as many souls as I've helped cross over," Margo said as she shoved the key in the ignition. "Like a sick stroke of irony. The heart surgeon who ignores symptoms, something she'd rag on a patient for doing, goes home, and dies of a massive aneurysm tearing open her aorta."

"How do you know what killed her?" Sam asked.

"She told me. The info we get from corporate is usually bare minimum." Margo slipped on her seat belt and started the car before adding, "You really make a good psychopomp."

Rather than the words dripping with sarcasm, Sam noticed the candor in Margo's praise. "I feel like I'm a fucking ghost therapist or something," Sam muttered.

"What did you want to talk about last night?" Margo asked. With the early morning interruption and excitement from opening the portal, Sam completely forgot.

"The Empusa who hates you—Jacqueline, right? She's Lauren's friend."

"Ah, Lauren. Is this the *not* girlfriend?" Margo chuckled, tapping her fingers to the beat of the song pouring from the stereo as she pulled out of the gravel.

Sam threw her head back and scoffed. "Seriously?"

Margo put a hand up in faux surrender.

"Lauren has no idea. Shit, she doesn't even believe in ghosts let alone all the other crap out there. I just find the fact she's friends with Jackie weird."

"Weird because we try to live normal lives separate from the ones revolving around our preternatural traits?"

Sam considered this. Was it possible for her to live a normal life away from the reaping of souls she'd become responsible for? Did Lauren know her best friend wasn't human?

Would this even matter to Lauren?

"You mean there's a possibility I can live a normal life?"

Margo chuckled, slapping her hand on the dashboard. "I didn't say you'd live a normal life, but you can try to add some normalcy. Work your boring job, live your boring life, get yourself a boring girlfriend. I don't care as long as you keep quiet about what you can do. We don't need anyone finding out you can open portals. The wrong person finding out will open one hell of a can of worms."

Chapter Twelve

RAIN THUDDED AGAINST the windshield of her car as Sam pulled up to Lauren's little bungalow. Sam sighed, staring up at the home, the dainty rhododendron bushes trimmed neatly and the green lawn clean and void of weeds. Lauren's car wasn't in the driveway, but another was, so Sam got out and made her way up the walkway. Lauren's friend Jackie opened the door and grinned at Sam.

"Hey, come on in. Lauren just ran to the store. She should be back any minute," she said casually. She nonchalantly returned to the kitchen, as if she and Sam didn't know each other's monumental secrets.

Sam took in the home she'd only seen through the open door when delivering Lauren's mail. The living room to her right was pristinely clean, the cream-colored couch and love seat facing each other with a moderate-sized television in the far corner. To the left, a heavy oak desk was shoved against the wall, a tall bookshelf positioned beside it. Everything was neat and tidy, from the placement of the bindings on the shelves to the alignment of the charcoal rug atop the light gray carpet.

"You want a beer, Sam?"

"Yeah, I'd love one." Sam headed in the direction of the kitchen and took the offered bottle from Jackie. When her dark gaze met Sam's, Sam became frigid. She ran her free hand over her sleeve to smother the shiver that started at her neck and turned into a primal fear settling over her shoulders from Jackie's stare.

"Does Lauren know what you are?" Sam asked, instantly cursing her curiosity as the uncouth question came tumbling from her mouth.

Jackie didn't seem to take offense. She sighed, placing a hand on the edge of the island, her face unreadable. "No, she doesn't, and I'd like to keep it that way. I've considered telling her in the past, but she wouldn't believe me, even if I were in the act of biting someone in front of her."

Sam nodded, popping the cap off the bottle to take a swig.

"Brent told me what Margo did to you," Jackie stated. "I'm sorry."

"Beats being dead," Sam said, shrugging her shoulders. She hadn't realized how true the words were until she spoke them. If Margo hadn't royally fucked up by unwittingly turning Sam into a Grim, she would've stayed dead. Sam couldn't be angry with her, not when Margo was the sole reason she was standing in the kitchen of the woman she adored, sipping a beer, alive and breathing.

There was a long pause where neither spoke, Sam picking nervously at the paper wrapping around the beer bottle. "Lauren really seems to like you, but if I were you, I wouldn't tell her about the whole Grim Reaper thing. We've been friends for six years but there's no way she'd believe me if I told her the truth about myself," Jackie confessed.

"Thanks for the warning. I didn't know how I'd word something like that anyway. Don't think it would help in the wooing process." They both laughed at the prospect,

Sam thankful for their sudden amity. The distaste Jackie obviously had for Margo wasn't bleeding into her impression of Sam.

"No. You don't know her as well as I do, but I'll tell you, she holds strong to seeing is believing," Jackie explained. Although Jackie had known Lauren longer than Sam, Sam was also aware of Lauren's stance on the unexplainable. Sam studied Jackie, taking in the subtle details of her face, her long dreads yanked back with an oversized hair tie, glittering gemstone fixated to a long chain adorning her neck. Nothing about her screamed "vampire," nor did anything lead Sam to label Jackie anything other than a quirky art teacher, but weren't all art teachers a little eccentric?

Her preconceived notions of the occult held no truth regarding Margo either. Obviously, appearance had nothing to do with the inner workings of their preternatural traits. Every interaction Sam had with Margo showed her appearing as if she were ready to go to a punk rock concert rather than to reap a restless soul.

"You're curious, aren't you?"

Chuckling, Sam grimaced with a nod. "I'm sorry. I didn't mean to be rude. Margo doesn't tell me anything, and I just wondered how things worked with being an Empusa."

Jackie sighed, leaning against the refrigerator. After taking a sip of her beer, she stared at the bottle, and started peeling back the paper label. "You can think of my situation as being a vampire, but it's not really the same thing. I don't hate who I am, but I loathe the act of hurting people, and biting them and drinking their blood isn't painless. I don't have to drink blood all the time, maybe once, twice a month. Brent and Collin are great at concocting all kinds of shit for people like me—making elixirs, potions, tonics to keep weres from shifting—restricts my need to consume blood for a little while."

"Wow, so you don't have to, uh, drink blood to survive?" The picture her brain painted of a vampire was one constructed with the fictitious representation of Hollywood, same as her idea of a Grim Reaper, fairies, and ghosts.

"Right, not all the time. I'm not immortal. I live the same life span as the rest of society but heal pretty fast, like you guys. I don't burn up in the sun. I actually love being outside," Jackie chuckled, a piece of the label fluttering to the floor like an injured moth. "I don't kill people for their blood, nor am I a straight-up vampire. We're extremely different. Unlike them, I can hold in my need for a while, especially with help from Brent. Sometimes, the elixir isn't enough, but I can find plenty of willing volunteers if things come to that."

Sam stood staring at Jackie. Of course, she believed her after seeing her very real fangs at Brent's home. There was no reason to distrust her thoughtful explanation. Sam knew the woman didn't have to disclose so much information, her own experience with Margo proving their secrecy was of utmost importance. "Thank you for telling me so much."

"A secret can easily become someone's weakness, and I hope I can trust you not to say a goddamn word." Jackie met Sam's stare, her gaze penetrating.

"I won't," Sam reassured. "You have just as much dirt on me. Margo says if corporate finds out about me, I'm as good as dead."

"She's probably right. When Brent told me what she did, I was surprised you weren't already taken out. You've got to be careful."

Those words were being thrown around a lot lately, and Sam didn't know what they meant. How was she supposed to be careful? She figured after dying and being brought back, she'd be golden in her second chance at life. Now, she reconsidered her expectations of where she was headed. "I don't know how Margo made such a huge mistake, but I can't say I'm sorry she did. I wouldn't be standing here right now. I wouldn't have gotten the opportunity to tell Lauren how I feel about her," Sam said, cursing herself mentally for her verbal spillage.

Jackie chuckled, curling her lips in a crooked smirk. "She really likes you, Sam. Don't mess this up. Don't hurt her. Don't cheat on her. If you do, I'll kill you myself."

Before she could defend herself, the front door opened, admitting Lauren and another person into the living room. Jackie winked at Sam as she moved from the refrigerator, heading to help Lauren with the bags in her arms. Sam planned to heed Jackie's warning because she had a feeling Jackie was one to keep to her threats.

LAUREN SIPPED GINGERLY at the glass of wine cupped in her palm, a soft smile on her lips as Sam twirled the lingering contents of her beer. After two rounds of a card game, which left them laughing loudly, and a round of poker, the group of friends sat around Lauren's coffee table. Thankfully, Lauren's friends accepted Sam into their group, although it was only Jackie and Caleb, a history teacher, who showed up. At first, Lauren was disappointed in the small turnout but quickly had a change of heart as the night proved enjoyable even with just the four of them.

Jackie continued to ramble on her long tangent regarding a photography project she did in college, the piece consisting of numerous shots of flowers. "When the professor critiqued the work, he scoffed at me, literally scoffed at me because every flower looked like a vagina," Jackie said. "I told him that's the fucking point!"

Lauren glanced at Sam as they both laughed, the sound rich and decadent. The low lighting set an eerie glow over Sam's face, her gaze hauntingly beautiful as she met Lauren's stare.

The bass of a new song began, and Sam's body moved languidly to the rhythm. "I love this song." She grinned at Lauren. "We should dance."

Lauren put up her hands and shook her head, cheeks flaring from the wine and being put in the spotlight. "Oh, no. I don't dance."

"I'll dance with you!" Jackie put her beer on the coffee table and rose from the couch. Reaching for Sam's hand, she yanked her off the couch and they both began to dance. Lauren laughed as Jackie took both of Sam's hands and they shimmied around the room. Sam twirled Jackie in a circle and let go of her hands. Jackie tugged Caleb from the couch and directed him into an easy rhythm. Lauren absently wondered if the two shared something she was unaware of. For as long as she'd known Jackie, she'd never been in a steady relationship. Lauren inquired about this on a few occasions, but Jackie always deferred the answer, citing she was happier being single.

Sam wiggled her backside as her cavorting led her in front of Lauren. She reached her hands out, beckoning Lauren forward. "Come on. You know you want to," she sang. Lauren's cheeks heated further, resulting in a heavy blush, as she took Sam's hands and let herself be lifted from the couch.

"I'll make this easy; put your hand here," Sam placed Lauren's hand on her hip, "and this one here," she said, her other hand draped over Sam's shoulder. Lauren could feel the warmth of Sam's skin through her soft shirt, and she longed to be closer. As if Sam sensed the cue, she wiggled nearer, her body moving to the music and her lips in a wide grin. "Let the music flow through you."

Lauren let the beat engulf her. Sam's hands on her waist guided her along and she promptly moved with her, their bodies mere inches apart. Her forehead touched Sam's as Sam pressed her body to Lauren. Lauren's heartbeat quickened and she brazenly brushed her lips against Sam's. Sam brought her hand to Lauren's face and cupped her cheek, her fingers a tentative caress on her skin. Although Lauren could hear Jackie saying something about their dancing, all she could focus on were Sam's lips until they met her own in a delicate kiss. She wanted to feel her closer, to taste her again.

The warmth that began when Sam first touched Lauren raged into a fire, burning through her with desire as she surrendered to Sam's lips with a soft sigh of satisfaction. Their hips were moving, Sam pulling back, her mouth ajar. She searched Lauren's face with heavy-lidded eyes. Lauren presumed she was searching for a sign to stop and Lauren nodded slightly, drawing Sam to her for another kiss. Sam's palm flattened on her back, their bodies meshing together as they continued to follow the beat long after the song changed. Sam grazed her tongue over Lauren's lower lip, and Lauren held her breath, wrapping her wrists around Sam's neck.

Jackie cleared her throat obnoxiously, and Lauren halted their kiss. "I think I'm going to head out," Jackie said.

"Yeah, me too. Thanks for inviting me," Caleb added. Lauren disengaged herself from Sam, offering Jackie a hug.

"You're welcome. Do you need a ride?" Lauren asked Caleb.

He shook his head. "Nah, Jackie's going to drop me off. Thanks for the food, and nice meeting you, Sam."

The two slipped out the front door, leaving Sam and Lauren staring at each other. Sam chuckled, running her fingers through her hair. "How about that dessert?"

"Good idea." They both headed to the kitchen in silence.

"Are they together?" Sam asked.

Chuckling, Lauren shook her head. "No. Jackie doesn't really get into relationships. As long as I've known her, she sticks to a handful of one-night stands and enjoys her personal space."

Lauren opened the cabinet, her arms reaching high as she retrieved two plates from the top shelf, causing her blouse to rise and expose an inch of her abdomen. Warm hands touched her bare skin, and she shuddered as they met at her midsection. Lauren nearly dropped the plates and they clattered when she placed them in front of her. "Do you know how beautiful you are, Lauren?" Sam's voice was husky behind her and Lauren gripped the edge of the counter.

"Maybe," she whispered. Sam moved a hand to Lauren's neck, sweeping her hair aside before her lips met skin. She sighed, the brush of Sam's lips hot on her sensitive neck. Sam's hands were around her waist, urging Lauren to her. The swell of Sam's breasts pressed against her back, and Lauren surrendered to the onslaught of sensations coursing through her body as Sam's hands shimmied beneath her shirt, caressing her bare skin.

One by one, Sam unfastened each button of Lauren's blouse, her nails tantalizing her torso. When the blouse hung open, Sam slipped the material from Lauren's body and let it fall to the floor. Lauren moaned as Sam taunted the straps of her bra, easing them down her shoulders to trace the prominence of her collarbones. Impatiently, Lauren reached behind herself and unclasped her bra, needing to feel Sam's hands on her. Sam cupped her breasts and Lauren dropped her head back, Sam kissing her neck. Her nipples hardened under Sam's hands, as Sam pinched gently. She raked her teeth over Lauren's neck and she moaned, abruptly turning to face Sam.

"You okay?" Sam murmured.

"Yes, but I need to kiss you." Lauren pressed her mouth to Sam's, darting her tongue over her lips. Sam groaned, pressing her hips to Lauren's, caressing Lauren's breasts. Moving her hands, Sam unzipped Lauren's jeans before she slid them and her underwear over her thighs. Without thinking, Lauren hopped onto the counter and pulled Sam flush with her body. Sam needed no more instruction, kissing Lauren fiercely, guiding her hands over Lauren's freshly exposed thighs. She kissed a trail down Lauren's chest, briefly taking a nipple into her mouth, dancing her tongue back and forth. Head back, Lauren closed her eyes, pressing her breast deeper into Sam's mouth. Sam's thumbs circled her prominent hip bones, the movement eliciting a profound sensuality, making Lauren's head spin. She kissed downward, easing Lauren's legs apart as she met her mound. Lauren's breath caught in her chest as Sam's tongue flitted over her slit. A jagged sigh left Lauren's lips and her back hit the cabinets behind her.

Sam traced her dampened lips as her tongue focused on her clit, easing a finger into her. Bucking her hips, Lauren moaned unabashedly, greedily wanting more from Sam devouring her.

"You're going to fall off the counter," Sam murmured between her legs. Lauren peered down at her, the sight tantalizing as Sam's gaze met her own. Her cheeks pressed against her thighs, her lips parted, breath still pouring over Lauren's pussy.

"No, I'm fine...I'm fine," Lauren breathed. Sam continued, dipping her head back, lashing her tongue over Lauren's clit once again. Lauren lolled her head back, closing her eyes as her head hit the cabinet. Sam slipped a second finger inside and Lauren moaned, tightening her grip in Sam's hair. Pleasure swirled within her, branching out into her limbs. She bucked her hips, wanting more of Sam. "Oh, Sam," she moaned, threading her fingers in Sam's hair, her other hand clutching the counter's edge. The movement over her clit ceased, causing Lauren to open her eyes, meeting Sam's.

"I don't want you to fall," Sam stressed, a soft smile present on her face.

"Sam," Lauren whispered. "I mean this in the nicest...way possible," she moaned. Though she halted her tongue's work, Sam continued to pump into her, causing Lauren's climax to hang in her periphery, just out of grasp. "Stop...talking."

Sam chuckled, kissing Lauren's inner thigh, much too far away from where she needed her mouth. Sam rested her palm on Lauren's leg, thumb caressing her sensitive skin. "You're going to fall to the floor right on your ass." Her kisses moved upward, nearing Lauren's aching center, her nose grazing her need.

Twisting her fingers in Sam's short hair, Lauren whined, "Please, Sam, stop talking." Her words provoked more laughter from Sam as her kisses landed on Lauren's mound, the vibrations from Sam's mouth rumbling over Lauren's lower lips, causing a stirring against Lauren's clit, intensifying the delayed gratification. Sam gripped her thigh as she continued, her mouth resuming. Lauren gasped as Sam's tongue pressed hard to her clit, teeth catching the hard nub. She moaned her name again, breath hitching and body tensing as Sam's tongue thrashed. The orgasm throttled her, ripping the breath from her lungs and she pushed Sam's head harder to her core, feeling herself tighten around her lover's fingers. Ecstasy poured through her, limbs weakened by the swiftness of her climax, head leaning forward. Sam ceased her movements, wrapping her arms around Lauren as her breathing gradually normalized. Sure enough, Lauren's backside teetered off the counter, and Sam caught her before she fell.

"Told you," Sam whispered in Lauren's ear. Lauren never thought she'd be standing naked in her kitchen, a slight draft coming in from the window facing the alley. She absently hoped her neighbors hadn't heard her in the midst of pleasure. Pulling back, she caught Sam's lustful gaze—smirking and quirking an eyebrow.

Sam widened her eyes as Lauren fisted her shirt in both hands, yanking her into a bruising kiss, before leading her backward toward the living room. The lighting was dimmed, Lauren having turned the lamps off after Caleb and Jackie left, and Sam's hazel gaze glimmered in the soft light, lids heavy. "Lauren, I want you." Lauren pushed her gently onto the couch, lifting herself to straddle Sam's hips. Smiling down at her, Lauren worked the button loose on Sam's jeans before skirting her hands up Sam's T-shirt. Sam reached, grabbing the hem of her shirt and tugging it over her head.

Scanning Sam's torso, Lauren noted the white scar etched across her chest beneath her bra, extending over her right collarbone and disappearing over her shoulder. She traced a finger over the skin, shaking her head in disbelief.

"You healed so fast."

Nodding, Sam closed her eyes. "Yeah, I did."

Lauren continued to trace the lightened skin, fascinated she healed so rapidly. Hadn't only five weeks passed since her accident? Surely, more time was needed for her skin to be so intact, the scar faint and flat. She remembered the angry mark the first day she saw Sam after she'd gotten home from the hospital, the sutures present and her collarbone discolored. Although she had the chance to see the spot during their enthusiastic tousle under the boardwalk, she hadn't taken the time to look at the wound. "Lauren," Sam mumbled. Lauren met her eager gaze just in time to see Sam lick her lips. "I need you."

Taking the hint, Lauren chuckled and concluded her staring. She snuck her hand under Sam's bra, meeting hardened nipples and sighing as Sam groaned. Scooting down her body farther, Lauren kissed Sam, catching her lower lip with her teeth, pushing her bra up. Another heavy exhale came from her as Lauren dipped her other hand beneath her boxers, fingers grazing her curls. Staring down at Sam's breasts, Lauren kissed the peaks, circling a darkened nipple with her tongue before sucking it into her mouth.

What she'd planned as a slow night of exploration had shifted into this ravenous lovemaking. Lauren descended her hand lower, sliding against Sam's lips. Sam's hand was on her face, caressing her cheek tenderly as her chest heaved beneath Lauren's mouth. Lifting her head, Lauren kissed her, longing to hear Sam utter her name again. She was wet, so wet, because of Lauren, and this satisfied Lauren more than the earth-shattering orgasm Sam had given to her moments before.

Sam broke their kiss, her head pressed to Lauren's, her hips twitching as Lauren stroked her clit. Lauren stole a glance at Sam beneath her, Sam's teeth clamped tightly on her lower lip, eyelids fluttering, chest heaving.

She wanted Sam, every bit of her, the good and the bad. The feelings swelling within were far from just lustful; Lauren found herself enamored, frighteningly yearning to capture Sam's heart. Would the woman in her arms treasure Lauren's ardor, or would she turn away in silence? Banishing the thoughts, Lauren kissed Sam, upping the speed of her fingers, filling Sam with two digits. Rotating her thumb over Sam's clit, Lauren kissed her damp forehead. "Oh, fuck, Lauren," Sam groaned, writhing, gasping. Grasping Lauren's back, Sam arched, meeting Lauren's thrusts. Lauren continued her efforts, thriving on Sam's pleasure, quickening her pace over Sam's clit.

Body taut, Sam stretched her neck, breath halting, digging her fingernails into Lauren's back. Finally, she let out a breath, the euphoric sound cinching around Lauren's heart. Lauren was going to have a difficult time trying not to let herself fall in love with the woman beneath her if she wasn't already too late. Sam's body shook as she gasped for air, and she clutched Lauren's sides, riding the passion.

"You're incredible." Sam's voice was hardly above a whisper. Her head leaned on Lauren's chest as her breathing slowed and threw her arms around Lauren tightly.

"Let's go to bed," Lauren murmured, wanting nothing more than to lie beside Sam and bask in her affection.

A FURRY BODY heaved itself onto Lauren's chest and she opened her eyes, coming face-to-face with her cat, Boo. Light streamed in through her bedroom window, paneled beams trailing over the floor and foot of the bed. Sam lay beside her, cheek pressed to the pillow, arm tucked under her. She was even more striking while asleep. Lauren touched her face with elegance, tracing the lines of her jawbone. The featherlight caress caused Sam to stir. "Hi," she murmured, opening her eyes and smiling at Lauren.

"Hey," Lauren said before she kissed her. Sam stretched, pulling the covers from herself.

"I've got to go to the bathroom, and then I want to make you breakfast."

"Okay." Lauren beamed at her. Sam wrapped the sheet around herself before heading to the bathroom. Her bashfulness was adorable, and Lauren sighed, smiling broadly.

Taking her phone from the charger, she opened her news app and began her daily ritual while she waited for Sam. Their night together had been unbelievable, and Lauren wanted nothing more than to spend the day in a similar fashion. She scrolled through the news, absently reading over the headings. There was no doubt in her mind she was experiencing strong feelings for Sam, and

Lauren was scared. No indication was present to point to Sam being the same as the last two women she'd given her heart to, but her apprehension couldn't be ignored.

She opened an article on the recent car wreckage on the Black Horse Pike a few days prior and the list of victims caught her attention. She scrolled through the news article, heart racing, sweat tingling the back of her neck. No, there was no way. "Oh, my God," she whispered as her gaze went over the names of the deceased. Five people passed in the wreckage, but one name stood out, taking Lauren's breath away. She read the list again, and again, to be sure she read the names correctly.

"Are you okay?" Sam asked as she came out of the bathroom. No, this wasn't possible. Lauren reread the name a sixth time, swallowed, blinked, read it again before she tilted her head at Sam.

"Bethany's dead."

Chapter Thirteen

"HOW'D YOU FIND out?" Jackie questioned gently as she passed Lauren the bottle of ketchup, the glass skidding over the tabletop. A clattering echoed from the kitchen of the diner, causing Lauren to jump. Sleep had eluded her the night before, mostly due to her and Sam's unbelievable time together; her fatigue was only heightened by the emotional turmoil of Bethany's death.

"A Facebook news article," Lauren managed, shoving a French fry into her mouth. Lauren didn't believe it at first until she called Bethany's brother. He informed her it was fact, and they weren't holding a service for Bethany because she requested not to have one in her will. Lauren knew the yearly casualties from motor vehicle accidents totaled in the millions, most of them occurring in adults under fifty, but it still shook her to the core that Bethany was no longer alive. After the initial shock settled like dust around her mind, the guilt snuck in, dark and sickly.

Jackie frowned, touching Lauren's arm. "Are you doing okay?"

Feigning her calm, Lauren gave a soft smile and nodded before shoving more food in her mouth. If her mouth was full, she couldn't talk and if she couldn't talk, she was unlikely to cry. Jackie released her arm and turned her attention to her own plate.

It wasn't as if she and Bethany were a couple anymore. Hell, she refused to give Bethany the time of day to speak to her, and she finally gave up trying to apologize to Lauren a few weeks prior. Lauren's attempt to keep the guilt at arm's length was faltering. The emotional response Lauren experienced was normal at any capacity, and she tried to rationalize this, to allow herself to acknowledge the guilt and loss she felt without dwelling on it. However, as with most occurrences recently, she was having trouble removing herself long enough to analyze the situation. There was normalcy in the grieving process and, given the circumstances, wasn't uncommon for Lauren to feel the way she did. In hindsight, she could've been mature and talked with Bethany, even to simply let her apologize and the two women go their separate ways. She could've tried to be friends with her. Instead, Lauren ignored her in her anger and betrayal like a petulant child. Now she was dead.

"I'm here if you want to talk," Jackie said quietly, her offer almost lost in the noise of the restaurant. Lauren dipped her head at her friend as she took a gulp of her soda.

Sam had given her the same sympathetic look as Jackie when they both discovered the news of Bethany's untimely death. Her response had been gentle, taking Lauren into her arms as Lauren fought the tears and stayed stoic, her mind still numb and unable to process.

"I'm okay. I called her brother after Sam left, and he said there won't be a service."

"Sam stayed over?" Jackie's tone wasn't playful or teasing in any manner and held only sincerity in the question.

Lauren smiled. "Yes, she did. I kind of gave her the boot after we had coffee because I had to make the phone call and felt a little awkward."

"I can't say I blame you," Jackie remarked. She was unusually untalkative and Lauren knew it was due to Bethany's death. Her friend didn't know how to approach it nor did Lauren. "No service or funeral?"

She nodded at Jackie. "She didn't want one, apparently. God, Jackie...our relationship never reached the point of discussing things like this because she never let us progress. This is so sad," Lauren admitted. She couldn't continue because she'd cry. There was no fairness in her death or any death for that matter but, Bethany was young, barely having started her career.

Jackie held Lauren's hand, tears trailing down Lauren's cheek when their gazes met. "I shouldn't be this upset."

"Stop, Lauren. You're allowed to grieve. You loved her despite how things ended."

Lauren's phone buzzed in her purse and she dug around.

I hope you're okay, Lauren. I'm here if you need me.

Sam's text said. Lauren appreciated her kindness but didn't want Sam to see her this way. What she needed was time.

Thank you. I appreciate you offering. I think I just need a little time, a little space to get through this week. Maybe dinner Friday, if you're free?

I'm free and dinner sounds great. I'm here if you need anything before then.

In reality, all she wanted to do was snuggle up to Sam and cry, however, crying into her current girlfriend's arms over the death of her ex-girlfriend didn't seem appropriate in her grief-ridden mind.

SAM SHUT THE metal front of the locked mailbox server with a resounding slam, grateful for her last stop of the day to be completed. She'd been back to work for only four days, and she was already exhausted, ready for the day to come to an end and the weekend to start. Mostly because she wanted to see Lauren again. They'd chatted throughout the week, but she needed to see her, to hug her, to kiss her. After the devastating news, Sam knew Lauren needed space, and she didn't take the gesture personally. Although she and Bethany had a rocky breakup, she knew Lauren cared for the woman strongly, and her death was completely unexpected.

Though Sam was a couple weeks short of the entire time her doctor requested for her to take off from work, after some pestering on her part and a clean bill of health, her doctor allowed her to resume her full duties. A cold wind blew in off the shoreline, pushing the side of her little mail truck as she pulled into the parking lot of the post office. Sam also hadn't seen Margo since the week before. After starting back at work on Tuesday, she expected to have an impromptu visit from the Grim but had yet to receive even an uncouth text or foulmouthed phone call. With her questions mostly answered, Sam was sullen but accepted she was going to be aiding spirits for the rest of her life, so Margo was bound to be around shortly. Bethany's recent passing put things a little too clearly into perspective for Sam. To convince these people to move on when she, in the same predicament, hadn't. She'd been given the option to stay along to ensure that

Katie and her nephew were okay. To inadvertently be given a chance to be with a woman she had hidden feelings for. She felt like a hypocrite, telling the restless souls to move on to the other side, to give up their lives, to say goodbye to everything and everyone they loved.

Her phone rang in the cup holder, and she answered it reluctantly, shoving the headphones into her ears. "Hello?"

"Hey! How was your first few days back to work?" Katie asked joyously.

"Exhausting," Sam chuckled, taking a corner as she approached the post office. "How's everything with you?"

"Awesome," Katie said before going into full detail on the happenings in her life. Sam listened quietly, happy her sister was in such good spirits. "Oh, and Ben has been asking about you. I figured I'd beg you to come over for lunch, say tomorrow?"

"I'll be there," Sam said before they ended the call. Her own life seemed to be in a strange position, but Sam found solace in the fact Katie's was finally settling into something more stable. She couldn't be jealous of her sister's normalcy, but she did long for her life to be plain again.

When Sam reached her car, she immediately grabbed her jacket and tugged it over her shoulders to combat the chill in the air. Just as she made to enter the driver's seat, a whistle sounded over the parking lot, making Sam glance around.

"Sam, you done?" Margo called. She leaned against her MINI Cooper with her hands in the pockets of her jacket, lips pursed, brows knitted. Sam strolled up to her, searching the post office parking lot again, nervous a coworker would see her with the likes of Margo. Her attire was back to the way it had been their first visit; jeans ripped at the knees, denim jacket, and an additional hoop in her eyebrow that hadn't been there the last time Sam saw her.

"Yeah, what are you doing here? Couldn't this have waited until I got home?" All Sam wanted to do was go home, change, and watch television. Maybe figure out what Lauren wanted to do for dinner if their plans were still on. But, no.

"I figured we'd save some time because the spirit in question is up the road from here." Margo jutted her chin in the direction of the sidewalk and started walking without waiting for Sam to respond. Sam caught up to her and tucked her hands in her pockets such as Margo had her own. The streets were busy with rush hour traffic as they waited at a stoplight heading away from downtown. "Where are we going?" Sam asked.

She hadn't anticipated Margo would answer her, but she did. "We're heading to the high school."

Wonderful, Sam thought sarcastically. She could only imagine what the next spirit was and prayed their newest charge wasn't a depressed teen or equivalent. Her heart couldn't take something so painful.

Instead of explaining further, Margo continued to walk until she reached the stoplight. When the light changed, they crossed the street and stopped at the next red light just before the high school parking lot.

A familiar figure stood beside the tall fence enclosing the lot and Sam's stomach dropped. Ruffled blonde hair, fancy suit jacket, lanky posture poised with confidence. "Oh, no," Sam said out loud, halting her feet.

Margo chuckled and turned to her, cars zipping past them on the curb. "Yeah?" she asked dubiously.

"Can't I pass? Margo, please don't make me do this. I can help with anyone else, anywhere. I'll travel to another city if you need me to but don't make me do this," Sam pleaded in a whisper.

Margo rolled her eyes and as soon as traffic stopped, she made her way through the crosswalk. "What's the problem? You're being a drama queen, Sam."

Sam reluctantly followed, cursing under her breath as they crossed the street and stepped onto the curb. Bethany Walters turned, her icy blue gaze completely overlooking Sam to shoot a glare at Margo. Sam stayed back a few feet, avoiding the situation for as long as possible.

Even in death, Bethany oozed affluence. Her suit jacket appeared freshly pressed and the sun reflected off her polished Italian loafers. "I told you I'm not going anywhere," she said curtly.

Margo lit her routine cigarette and chuckled. "*I* didn't say anything about going anywhere, sweetheart."

"Yeah, but you're going to try to talk me into going to the light or something stupid like that. I told you I'm not going anywhere right now." Bethany waved her hand around the coil of smoke Margo blew at her. "And, could you not smoke around here? It's a school zone, and there are kids everywhere."

She finally noticed Sam, her finely trimmed eyebrow raising as she peered around Margo. "You've got a shadow." Her eyes widened when she met Sam's gaze, and she swiftly looked away. "Holy shit, it's Samantha Diaz. God, I used to tease the hell out of her in high school."

"Yeah, I'm pretty sure you called me a handful of racist choice words too," Sam snidely remarked, moving a few feet closer.

At Sam's words, Bethany's mouth hung gaping. "What the fuck? You can see me?"

Margo backed up, linked her arm with Sam's, and dragged Sam toward Bethany. "Glad you two know each other. Now, Sam here is going to help you with your 'unfinished business' so you can get the hell out of here," Margo said, air quoting the phrase with her fingers.

Bethany shook her head, taking a step backward. "Uh, no."

"Uh, yeah, she needs the practice. What's the problem?"

"I guess you could say there's a bit of a conflict of interest," Bethany stated, shoving her hands in the pockets of her pants.

Sam cleared her throat, hands balled in tight fists. "Yeah, that's for sure." What was she going to do—fight a ghost? Her reaction to Bethany was absurd so she relaxed, unclenching her hands.

Margo turned to Bethany and then back to Sam, her inquiring gaze noting Sam's annoyance. With a loud scoff, Margo shook her head. "Okay, I'll see you later then, I guess," she said with a bow of her head in Bethany's direction. She tugged Sam away from the spirit, heading back across the intersection.

When she'd learned of Bethany's death, her first selfish thought was Bethany would become her and Margo's charge and, since Margo was handing over the ropes, she'd be responsible to bring Bethany's unfinished business to a head. Although she expected the very circumstance she was in, nothing could've prepared her for this.

"Are we going to talk about this?" Margo jabbed her elbow into Sam's side as they neared the post office parking lot.

"I thought things were pretty self-explanatory. Bethany was a bitch to me during high school; she's also Lauren's cheating ex-girlfriend." Sam shot her a grimace. "Her *dead* cheating ex-girlfriend. Wouldn't you call that a conflict of interest? Do I *really* want to help her?"

Margo clasped her on the back and sighed. "Yeah, I hear you," she said, her hand falling.

Bethany hadn't simply been a bitch to Sam—she'd made her life a living hell during her entire junior year. The endless teasing over trivial matters such as her lack of designer clothing and sense of style wasn't what hurt her the most. Her outing Sam to the majority of their peers had been the precursor of Sam's grudge. For Katie to find out about Sam's sexuality from hearsay rather than Sam's own admission had been painful. Katie accepted her regardless of how she came to find out, but the hurt she expressed to Sam for finding out in such a way was disheartening. Not to mention, her destruction of Lauren's trust.

When Sam opened the driver's door, Margo gently grabbed her wrist. "Don't worry about this one," she said, her eyes soft. "I'll take care of Bethany, and you can get the next one."

"Cool. Thanks," Sam muttered, climbing into her car. If only things were so simple.

"I'M IGNORING YOU," Sam muttered, flipping a page in the book she held and lifting it to cover her face. Bethany snickered and moved around the living room to stand directly in front of her. Sam should've expected Bethany to grace her with her presence at some point during the evening. In a matter of two hours since she'd gotten home from work, the woman had startled Sam by appearing in front of the television. One moment, the living room was empty, the next, Bethany stood there, glaring at her. Even with the book obscuring her face, Sam could still feel the annoying presence. The hushed drone of her television wasn't loud enough to tune out the disturbance. Her phone buzzed, and she read the text from Margo.

Incoming. I think you might get a visitor soon.

Sam scoffed as she texted her back.

Too late. She's already here.

A steady blue gaze was on her when Sam lifted her head over the top of the book. At first, Sam hoped and prayed Bethany would simply leave like a speckle of dust in a breeze, but nope, she was there, standing as stoic as ever. Sam's eye twitched and she hopped off the couch.

Heading to the kitchen with faux purpose, she poured herself a glass of water and turned her back to Bethany, who quickly followed. The fact Bethany was in her home was odd enough for her, but the annoyance was exacerbated by Bethany trailing her. Their mutual distaste for each other was palpable, and Sam didn't know how the hell she was going to get Bethany to move on if Margo couldn't do it after two tries. She headed to her room, Bethany close behind. Sam plopped on her bed and reopened her book, determined to overlook Bethany's meaningful stare.

Eventually, the silence became too heavy. "So, why'd you do it?" Sam kept her gaze on the open book in front of her when she spoke.

Bethany glanced up and quirked an eyebrow. "Do what?"

"Why'd you cheat on Lauren?" She wanted to spark Bethany's irritation; perhaps Sam would be able to get her out of her apartment before Lauren showed up for dinner if she could piss her off enough.

Bethany scratched her head as she folded herself onto the floor of Sam's bedroom. Sam was still confounded by the solidity of spirits to not only be present and visible but how they could seemingly manipulate the world around them, walking through doors and walls but able to settle to the floor without slipping through. "She told me she loved me."

Sam snorted as she snapped the book shut with a resounding boom. "You've got to be kidding me right now. You cheated on a girl because she told you she loved you? What the hell is wrong with you, Bethany?"

Bethany combed her fingers through her hair and avoided Sam's glare as she mumbled, "She scared the shit out of me." The sincerity in Bethany's words softened Sam's attitude, and she swung her legs over the edge of the bed to give Bethany her full attention. Bethany's eyes were watery when she looked up at Sam. "Her admission scared me because of how much I love her and the vulnerability of admitting it. I couldn't admit to myself how much she means to me."

"Why not?"

"Because it meant that my own heart could be broken," she said and chuckled crudely. "I guess I figured if I broke her heart first then I wouldn't hurt as bad when the inevitable happened."

"Your excuse is incredibly childish. You say this like you assumed she was going to leave you."

"You're right, and she was going to leave me, eventually. I was too deeply involved in work, not ready to settle down or get married. She was bothered by my avoidance, and she voiced as much to me. I thought moving in together would kind of stall the rest of it, but then she told me she loved me."

"Doesn't mean she was going to leave you."

Bethany raised her eyebrow at Sam. "She wanted more than I was willing to give. Commitment wasn't my thing, as stupid and asinine as that sounds now. I tried to change for her, and I let myself fall for her." Bethany's gaze was downcast as she sniffled. "I wonder sometimes if I hadn't been an idiot if I'd still be alive. I wonder, what would I have been doing if things were different? Would I have gotten behind that truck? Would I have even been out so late at night when, normally, I would've been at Lauren's?"

A painful sympathy burrowed itself within Sam's chest, causing her to exhale. Bethany hadn't deserved to die because she was unfaithful. She was barely over thirty, and now her life was over, literally. "You didn't die because you cheated on her." A thought occurred to her. "Is she your unfinished business?"

"My what?" Bethany glanced up at Sam.

"What's keeping you here, Bethany?"

Shrugging, Bethany crossed her arms around herself, crinkling her suit. "I need Lauren to know I'm sorry for hurting her. I can't go anywhere until she knows how much regret I hold for breaking her trust, for hurting her so badly. She loved me, and I love her."

"What do you want me to do about it?" *...and I love her.* Sam hadn't missed those words.

"I know you shouldn't want to help me. I mean, damn, I was so horrible to you in high school you have every right to hate me. But..." Bethany trailed off, looking dejected.

Sam rose, shaking her head as she began to pace her bedroom. "She'd never believe me even if I could prove it to her somehow. I'm already on thin ice with this whole Grim Reaper thing, I don't want to blab about what I am, even to Lauren. Not the smartest thing to do when my second shot at life is already at risk of being shot down."

"What do you mean?"

For reasons she didn't care to delve into, Sam told Bethany everything. She detailed her death, meeting Margo, the unintentional transitioning of Sam's life forever. Bethany listened intently, nodding when appropriate. When Sam was finished, Bethany continued to stare at her.

"Sam, I had no idea." Her expression was pleading.

"How could you know? Is there another way to help you find peace?"

Bethany dropped her gaze, a frown tugging at her lips. "I don't know. Lauren is all I can think about. My family...sure, they're grieving, however, Lauren is the one I keep coming back to." She lifted her head. "I can't leave her."

"She's going to be here any minute, and I don't want her thinking I'm crazy because I'm talking to myself," Sam said gently. Bethany nodded, taking the hint.

"Just..." Bethany sighed, her face disconcerted. "Never mind. I'll be back," she said and turned, disappearing through the front door. Sam chuckled, shaking her head, dumbfounded at the display of the impossible.

Chapter Fourteen

LAUREN GRINNED WHEN Sam opened her door after the fourth knock. "I brought some food," she said, holding up the bags from the Chinese restaurant she'd gone to before driving over to Sam's apartment. Sam's face broke into a genuine smile and Lauren felt lighter as she walked into the small living room.

"I seriously appreciate you bringing something. I could've cooked or ordered in, you know," Sam said sheepishly, relieving Lauren of the bags and placing them on the kitchen counter.

"No, I figured cooking would be the last thing on your mind after your first week back at work. There's a few different things, so I hope you like one of them." Lauren touched the small of Sam's back

"I eat far too much takeout, to begin with, but I'm not complaining about free food."

After they ate, Sam suggested a movie, and the two snuggled on the couch under a heavy blanket. Lauren wrapped her arms around Sam, resting her head against her shoulder, breathing in the aroma of her cologne and a hint of sandalwood, coalescing into Sam's unique scent Lauren couldn't get enough of. She sighed, content to cuddle with her girlfriend, feeling safe and cherished as Sam's arm tightened around her back. The loss of Bethany hurt, the pain revolving around her own guilt of pushing the woman away time after time without allowing her to apologize for her past transgressions. She was too young to be gone forever and the realization of how quickly life was snuffed out frightened Lauren. Only a few weeks prior had Sam nearly become a life cut short, and Lauren shivered at the thought. "Are you cold?" Sam murmured, pressing her lips to Lauren's head.

"I'm okay." Lauren closed her eyes, allowing herself to take solace in Sam's warmth and presence. "Thank you for giving me space this week."

Although the movie had begun, Sam brought her full attention to Lauren, running her fingers through Lauren's hair. "Of course. I know you two had a bad ending, but I also know how much you cared about her." *Holy crap, how is she this sweet?* Lauren wondered.

"You're amazing," Lauren proclaimed. They fell into a mutual silence, watching the movie. Lauren closed her eyes, permitting herself to be swept up in her ardor for Sam, to admit her feelings were far from platonic and hadn't been for a while. With a contented sigh, Lauren fell asleep.

SAM'S PHONE RANG, the shrill noise cutting into the quiet living room. They both jumped awake and Sam fished through the couch cushions for the device. Lauren's heart fluttered at the sleepy look on Sam's face, her eyes half-lidded, lips pouty as she found her buzzing phone.

"Crap," Sam muttered.

"What's wrong?"

A flush crept up Sam's neck as she said, "Work stuff."

Red flag. Lauren sat up on the couch, waking fully with alarm. First, Sam worked for the post office, and second, according to the ticking clock on the wall, it was two o'clock in the morning. "Work stuff on a Friday night?" Well, technically early Saturday morning. She fought the battle to reign in her calm when every instinct within her was screaming not to trust Sam. The guilty frown on her face wasn't making things any easier. "Sam, what's going on?"

Letting out a long sigh, Sam shifted herself. "I don't know how to explain this." She ran a hand through her hair, fingers visibly trembling.

Swallowing back her fear, Lauren whispered, "Try me."

"I'm like a Grim Reaper's assistant and I have to help spirits cross over," Sam blurted without prelude.

"What? Is this some kind of joke?" Lauren asked, desperately hoping she was wrong.

"When I was in that surfing accident, I almost didn't come back. The only reason I'm here is because...this is going to sound insane. I shouldn't even be telling you because I'm already in deep shit." Another shaky sigh. "I drowned. I saw myself on the beach lying in the sand as the paramedics tried to bring me back. This woman, Margo, she's kind of like a Grim Reaper." Lauren laughed without humor, shaking her head as this had to be a joke.

"Sam, stop kidding around."

Sam's jaw tightened as she met Lauren's gaze. "I'm not, I wish I were. I was dead. I saw my body, I was gone, and she offered me a deal."

"This isn't funny." Her voice shook, her thoughts going to Bethany's passing. Why would Sam play these games with her when such an event had just transpired? The behavior wasn't Sam. After standing from the couch, Lauren moved through the living room without conscious effort while Sam continued her strange tirade.

"Wait, please hear me out. I'm not being facetious. Let me finish…please. Katie doesn't even know, and no one can know, but I trust you, Lauren," Sam pleaded. She seemed flustered, her nose crinkled, eyes narrowed but behind this, she looked terrified.

Lauren paused her movements as Sam joined her in the kitchen. "Fine."

Moving closer to her, Sam reached her hand out, gripping the edge of the counter beside Lauren. "I wish I could say this was a joke, but I'd be lying. What I'm telling you is the truth. The thing is, because Margo brought me back, I've got to help her bring spirits closure, to aid them to the other side, so to speak."

Oh, my God, she's crazy. Lauren pinched the bridge of her nose. "Okay. Are you sure you didn't wake up from a weird dream just now? I mean, this is really creative but—"

"Please, hear me out," Sam cut her off. Brows knitted, hazel gaze searching Lauren's face with uncertainty, hand shaking, she said, "My most recent charge is…is Bethany."

Enough was enough. Pushing off the counter, Lauren rushed past Sam, snatching her coat and purse from the desk chair beside Sam's bookshelf. "I'm not going to stand around and let you mess with me, Sam. I don't know what you're going on about, but I can't do this." Her back was turned as she shrugged into her coat, her eyes thankfully dry. Where was all of this coming from? Why was Sam hurting her?

"Do you remember the night Bethany rented out that house in Cape May?" Sam's soft voice was close, filled with trepidation. Lauren froze, her fingers halting their buttoning.

"This is ridiculous," she whispered, closing her eyes.

Floorboards creaked behind her, yet Lauren kept still, as if the silence would remain as long as she kept quiet. Sam wouldn't continue bringing up the night she had no business knowing about. "Bethany rented a seaside cottage down on the Cape. You guys rode the ferry over to Delaware and you had dinner, went shopping. She found you this beautiful emerald necklace she said matched your eyes. Afterward, you two went back to the little cottage."

Lauren bit her lower lip to cease the trembling, and she squeezed her eyes shut tighter, willing the tears not to fall.

"She brought your favorite wine; you two watched the stars come up that night." Sam paused, her breath uneven. "You told Bethany you loved her. She stared at you and said nothing for the longest time. She saw you start to cry and couldn't stop thinking about how gorgeous you were, how much your new necklace matched your eyes. She was so scared when you said those words, so scared she got up, went inside, and left you by yourself on the balcony."

"Sam, stop!" Lauren's eyes stung from the onslaught of tears. She whipped around to face Sam, her hands in clenched fists at her sides. There was no way Sam knew about the night. No way she could know about the stupid necklace Bethany bought her with such detail, the same necklace she threw out days after she discovered Bethany's unfaithful action. "What is wrong with you?" She couldn't know. She couldn't have possibly known the events of that evening. Jackie didn't even know about the necklace.

"I'm not trying to hurt you, Lauren. I only want you to believe me. Bethany's unfinished business is you. She was so scared of losing you, she feared if she let herself love you, she'd inevitably lose you."

"Stop!" Lauren repeated in a sob. Gaze pleading, Sam tentatively reached for her but Lauren stepped backward. No words came to mind. No plausible explanation. Instead of examining the possible merit behind Sam's explanation, Lauren feigned her distrust. "I'm not going to stand here and listen to this garbage. There's something seriously wrong with you," Lauren concluded. "I can't... I don't want to see you again, Sam."

Her words were cruel. Nonetheless, Lauren wouldn't consider the prospect of Sam's discourse being true. The only way for Sam to know of the evening was if Bethany told her, alive or dead. Since they held a mutual dislike for each other, the only possibility was the latter. Scoffing at her own intrusive thoughts, Lauren gave Sam one last glance as her fingers clasped around the doorknob. There was no such thing as ghosts, no afterlife. "If you really believe all that, you need to go to the doctor. This isn't normal." She slipped out into the night, the sound of the door closing echoing along with her receding footfalls down the wooden stairs.

Chapter Fifteen

THE SOUND OF Lauren's car pulling away diminished, rapidly replaced with the sheets of rain hitting the porch behind the closed door. Sam stared at the door, teeth on her lower lip. "I told you," she mumbled. Clenching her fists at her sides, Sam cursed under her breath, furious she'd let a goddamn ghost talk her into ruining her relationship.

"Things could've gone better," Bethany agreed. Her arrival shortly after Margo's text was eerie, and Sam had to hold in her frustration once the ghost started berating her for being dishonest to Lauren when she inquired about her late-night text message. Hypocrite.

"No, shit. Things would've gone better if I'd kept my mouth shut. Now, not only are you going to continue with your unfinished business, I lost my chance with an amazing person because she thinks I'm fucking nuts." Sam fell back onto the couch and put her head in her hands. Her phone buzzed in her pocket and she yanked it out, half hoping it was Lauren. Nope.

Be there in ten.

Margo's curt text said. "Fuck this," Sam muttered. "I'm going for a walk." The last thing she wanted to do was help Margo force a soul to cross over. She hadn't kept her end of the deal with getting Bethany to move on, so she could handle one on her own.

When she lifted her gaze, Bethany was gone. Sam grabbed a hoodie and headed out the front door. A storm had rolled in, thick, rain-laden clouds obscuring the moonlight and coating the city in a layer of moisture. Lauren's pained face flashed in her mind, tears streaking her freckled cheeks, green irises vibrant against the reddened white of her eyes. Shoving her hands in her pockets, Sam breathed in the scent of fresh, damp earth, willing the aroma to clear her mind.

Rain pelted Sam's head as she bounded down the stairs and turned left on the concrete in the direction of the boardwalk. Water pooled over the roadway and in the cracks in the cement. What the hell did she expect when she'd told Lauren about Margo and Bethany? Of course, she'd think Sam was crazy. Sam had to convince herself daily she wasn't nuts. The bewilderment on Lauren's face when Sam mentioned the memory Bethany had relayed to her was undeniable. For the briefest of moments, Sam thought Lauren believed her, especially when she brought up the necklace Bethany described with pristine detail.

Sam tilted her head toward the sky, relishing in the cold stream of raindrops splattering her face. Thunder rumbled, the weather concurrent with her state of mind. What the hell was she going to do now? Bethany wasn't going to move on without Lauren accepting her apology, and the probability of Lauren speaking to Sam ever again was slim. Not to mention the ever-looming threat she'd be taken out by the leaders of the Grim. A horn honked loudly in the sleepy neighborhood, and Sam dropped her gaze from above. Margo's powder-blue MINI Cooper sat idling by the curb. The passenger window rolled down, and Margo cut the music. "Get in the car."

"Why?" Sam snapped. She didn't have time for the cryptic nonsense that Margo surely had in store for her.

"We've got a job, why else?" Margo asked. Sam flipped Margo her middle finger and took a few more steps. "I'm feeling the love, Sam. Get in the fucking car. Not only do we have a job, but we have a meeting with the board of directors in a few hours."

This piqued Sam's interest and her stomach flopped. "We?" Sam asked. Margo nodded, her eyes narrowing and jaw tight.

"Yeah, *we*," Margo said. Grumbling, Sam hopped into the car. Droplets of water trickled over her face, a flash of lightning illuminating the dark car. Margo stared at her as her brows knit in confusion. "What the hell is up with you?"

"You texted me, Lauren was suspicious and rightfully so—she hasn't had the easiest dating history—and I told her the truth."

Margo's jaw literally dropped, and her hands flopped from the steering wheel into her lap. "You what?" she hissed through gritted teeth.

"I told Lauren about everything. She thinks I'm crazy, and now I doubt Bethany will ever move on." Sam turned. "What the hell is going to happen if I can't get her to move on?"

Shaking her head in disbelief, Margo put the car in drive, slamming on the gas before Sam could prepare herself. "Her moving on is the least of your worries. I can't believe you told your girlfriend."

"What was I supposed to do, with Bethany badgering me, and Lauren wanting to know what kind of work-related shit I had at two in the morning?"

"Lie?" Margo suggested.

Sam threw her hands up. "Oh, yeah. Let me just screw the situation a little more by lying to her." She glowered at Margo and sighed, recalling the suspicious statement regarding a meeting. "What kind of meeting do we have?" Fear threatened to break the surface of her anger as Sam noted Margo's tension.

"They found out about you, so now we get to have a jolly old meeting with the board of directors before they decide what to do with you."

As blood over a fresh wound, Sam's fear budded, spilling over her in a torrent. "Great."

"But we have a job to do first," Margo reiterated.

THEY ARRIVED AT the hospital roughly twenty minutes later, the visitor parking lot deserted save a handful of cars. As she exited the vehicle, Sam gazed up at the massive five-story building, zipping her hoodie up and wrapping her arms around herself. "What are we doing here?" The hospital was the same one Katie worked at, but lucky for Sam, Katie was off that weekend.

"The way things work in this field is kind of funny," Margo began, cupping her hand around the cigarette in her mouth. "Think of the system as sections or divisions. I'm responsible for souls who are restless: can't move on without meeting a goal. Usually, they've been hanging around for a little while by the time I get to them. This is after the first line is unable to help them move on shortly after death." Margo blew smoke through her nose, pulling a slip of paper from her pocket. "This is what we get once a week. In case those psychopaths at corporate are willing to give you a chance, I figured I'd show you what to expect."

Sam's gaze scanned the sheet as Margo handed it to her. Basic demographics. A name, age at time of death, death date, general vicinity. "You get a stack of these every week?" According to the information, Richard Mank had passed on four months prior in the Somers Point area at the age of eighty-five.

"Sometimes there's more information, but this is enough. I've already found the guy, and he has very specific wishes before he'll move on. This will be an easy job for you."

"I know I've asked this before, but you really don't know where they go?" Sam asked. If Bethany ever passed on, Sam wanted to know where she would go—where she herself would've gone if Margo hadn't intervened in her death.

"I have a rough understanding of where they go. There are no pearly gates, no gaping black hole to hell. It's all cosmic, in the sense that their karma dictates where they go and for how long, before they move on to their next life." She held the lit cigarette between pinched fingers and blew the smoke upward. The clouds moved rapidly above, a sharp wind swiftly tugging them across the sky, clearing away the rain. A sprinkling of stars was visible between the passing tufts of darkness, and the smoke twirled against the backdrop of night.

"Like reincarnation?"

"Right. Eventually, they'll be reborn down the line. I don't know when it takes place or how long they stay in limbo before they do." Margo started toward the entrance, kneeling to stub her cigarette on the ground. A man stood beside the main lobby doors, hands limp at his sides, navy-blue jacket billowing in the wind coming off the bay past the parking lot.

"You're back," the old man said, pointing at Margo from his spot beside the lobby doors. A glare from the streetlamps shined off the automatic glass doors leading into the facility, reflecting directly into Sam's eyes as they approached. The man, whose name Sam knew was Richard, according to the paper Margo had given her, towered over her and Margo. His back was hunched, but he still appeared to be about six feet tall.

"Yeah so we can head up now," Margo said without stopping. The man's snowy white hair fluttered in the breeze, his wrinkled face breaking into a smile as the two women passed him. The doors opened, and Margo strode through them, bypassing the registration desk, making a sharp turn toward a darkened hall. Sam followed close behind, wondering whether the man sitting behind the desk had even seen her pass. When she turned to track the location of their newest charge, Sam noticed he was gone.

Margo opened a door and led Sam into a narrow service stairwell, climbing the stairs two by two. "Now, sometimes our sections intertwine, and we have to help each other out in one way or another."

"If your section is the restless, what about the first person you showed me—the old lady? She had just passed away. Why did you help her?" If Margo was responsible solely for the restless spirits with unfinished business who were reluctant to leave, how did she come about finding Sam shortly after her drowning?

Margo didn't pause as she answered. "As I said, sometimes we help each other out. I helped her cross over for a friend."

"Brent?" Sam asked, assuming he was the only other psychopomp in the area she had met. Margo laughed as she stopped moving forward, grabbing the railing, turning to face Sam.

"Brent is not a friend; he's a business associate. No, I was helping a buddy of mine who is helping us sneak in here in return this time around. Now, come on."

Sam was grateful for the late hour, as she knew if one of Katie's coworkers saw her, no excuse would suffice for her presence in the hospital. "Where are we going?" Sam muttered as they bounded up the concrete stairs. Instead of answering her, Margo halted on the third landing, quietly opening a door. A long hall lay on the other side, a nurse's station at the far end. "Come on," Margo whispered, ushering Sam through. Their footfalls were silent on the tile flooring, the eerie sounds of snores echoing into the halls mixing with the incessant beeping of medical equipment.

As they approached the nurse's station, Sam noticed only one nurse sitting behind the counter, dressed in dark blue scrubs, brows scrunched, a glow from a monitor illuminating his tanned face.

Margo cleared her throat, and when the man didn't look up, she whispered, "Luis."

He lifted his gaze, smiling broadly at her voice. "I didn't think you were coming," he said, standing from the wheeled chair before rounding the counter. He glanced at Sam, nodding his head in greeting then turning back to Margo. He was roughly the same height as Sam, causing him to tilt his head upward slightly to look at Margo. "Is this the one you've told me so much about?" he asked, a light humor tingeing his tone.

"Yeah. I planned on showing her the ropes a bit more before we go meet with the board." Margo rubbed her hands together. "So, where's the room?"

"She's through here," Luis said, gesturing they follow him. He led them through a door, the room darkened and silent aside from the soft beeping of a heart monitor. Another hospital worker stood beside the bed, scribbling notes on a clipboard.

The worker glanced over and smiled before saying, "I thought all of Mrs. Mank's family members were deceased?"

"Sorry we're late," Margo began, her tone softer than Sam had ever heard it. "We're her sister's brother-in-law's nieces."

Internally, Sam chuckled at the vague pretend familial connection but soon sobered when she noticed the spirit of Richard, leaning by the bedside, a hand gripping the arm rail. "Oh, wonderful. I hate to see anyone pass alone. I'll leave you two here. Let us know if you need anything," the nurse said kindly before stepping around them to exit the small hospital room.

"I'm Luis by the way," the first nurse said, offering Sam his hand. "Margo's told me all about you."

"Sam." Like Margo, there was nothing otherworldly about his appearance. Black gauges hooped in his earlobes, warmth in his dark gaze as he smiled at her, and a light stubble on his chin.

A dinging noise in the halls pulled Luis's attention, and he let go of her hand, nodding at Sam and turning to Margo. "The patient isn't going to hold on for much longer now that he's here," he said, sadness in his tone as he gestured to Richard. "You guys let me know if you need anything." He left the room, pulling the door closed behind him.

The room seemed smaller than Sam noticed at first with the bed positioned directly in the middle, a small television set off to the side, three folding chairs stacked a few feet from the bed. A window adorned the wall opposite the door to the hall, showcasing the bay. Margo grabbed two folding chairs, opening them before plopping in one. "Take a load off, this could take a while."

Lying in the bed was a frail old woman, her eyes closed, cheeks holding a distinct pallor. Richard leaned forward, his voice a whisper as he spoke to the woman. She smiled, sparking confusion in Sam. "Margo, can she hear him?" she whispered.

Margo nodded. "There's a strange shift in the brain before death that also happens when you're about to fall asleep. Right before you slip into REM, you're open to things, like, hearing ghosts talk to you."

"How weird," Sam muttered as she sat next to her.

What was Lauren doing? Sam hoped she hadn't inadvertently ruined their relationship by giving Lauren the knowledge of what she truly was becoming. This wasn't the life Sam wanted, but it was better than no life at all, she reminded herself. If Margo hadn't interfered, Sam would be one of the many spirits who crossed over to the other side each day, spirits she soon would be equally responsible for if everything went well during the meeting.

"You can go introduce yourself to him," Margo said, her head bent over her phone.

Sam nodded although Margo probably couldn't see her movement. Standing from the uncomfortable folding chair, Sam cautiously approached the ghost.

"Hello, Richard," Sam said. He regarded her with a tip of his head.

"You must be the trainee this young lady was talking about." He jutted his thumb in Margo's direction.

"Yes. I'm here to help you move on to the other side."

"Getting old is for the birds," the old man digressed with a shake of his head. Sam noticed the deep wrinkles on his face. Maybe this one wouldn't be as bad as she anticipated. Sam wasn't opposed to helping spirits cross over, but the process became unbearable when the individual was a young person, such as the little boy and the homeless man. She was almost one of them. Sam turned her attention back to her latest charge.

"I've never heard that saying before, but I have heard getting old isn't for the weak."

"I wholeheartedly agree." He grinned at Sam. "Ah, you're just like your friend over there. Nice gal." Sam glanced over at Margo who had her head bent over her cell phone, splashes of light coloring her face in the dim room.

Richard sighed, a frown replacing his smile as he gazed at the woman in the bed. "Poor Gwen. She didn't recognize me before I passed."

"How come?"

"Late stage dementia. Things have been rough since I had to move her over to the convalescent home. She'd been telling me for years she'd end up in a home, and I brushed her off every time." He clicked his tongue. "Until she couldn't take care of herself anymore and nor could I."

"I'm sorry," Sam offered. He waved his hand and shook his head.

"No need for apologies. We had a good life together until she lost herself. I do miss her, but I know we'll be together again soon enough. You don't fret yourself, dear. I'll be okay until it's time."

Sam wandered over to the seat beside Margo, feeling dismissed. The plastic chair squeaked as she sat.

"You really know how to listen to people. I wish I would've been as good as you are when I first started," Margo admitted.

"How did you find out what you were?" Sam picked at the laces of her shoes while she waited for her companion to answer, forcing herself not to check her phone. There wouldn't be a text message from Lauren, and she wanted to save herself from the disappointment. A few minutes passed before Margo cleared her throat.

"Luis and I," she scoffed, "We were a bad mixture. He was transferred from the foster care system in Camden over to Philly, and we were placed in the same group home together as teens. Fuck, we got into some serious trouble," she said, chuckling as she reminisced. Even though the time spent with Luis was brief, the mild-mannered nurse didn't seem as if he'd keep company with the likes of Margo. But Sam had learned in the last two months that looks could be quite deceiving. "Anyway, angry at everyone, we found kinship in each other when we figured out we both saw the weird shit of the world. Up until then, I believed what everyone told me—I was fucking crazy. There is nothing normal about seeing the things we see. Luis and I were both seventeen, with a foot in the door to jail for the shit we got ourselves into. That's when we met Brent." She reached for her pack of cigarettes before stopping herself, seeming to remember where they were.

"What kind of idiot comes up on a couple of punks in the middle of the worst part of town wearing Prada and Armani with a gold Rolex around his wrist? I told the nosy fucker to back off, but he was persistent. Eventually, a question sparked both our interest. He asked us, 'Haven't either of you ever wondered why you're able to see the macabre of the world when no one else can?' Of course, I wanted to know; we both did. I'd been seeing shit my whole life."

"He wanted us to go with him and eventually we did because curiosity took over. Both of us had been told our whole lives we were fucking crazy, taken to doctor after doctor."

"Margo, that sounds pretty—"

"I don't want your pity. I want your understanding. This isn't the life I expected but I deal with reaping souls because I was born to do it. You were forced into the situation you're in, and I'm sorry. But if you were given the same option with all the shit you know now, would you take the deal again?"

The question had floated around Sam's mind numerous times since she'd made the deal. Although Katie had been her initial thought when she'd agreed to work for Margo in lieu of dying, Sam realized she never would've been given a chance with Lauren if she hadn't taken Margo's deal. They hadn't been a couple for longer than two months, but she started falling head over heels for Lauren well over a year before. "I would, and I don't think I ever thanked you properly."

"I'd do it again," Margo said before breaking their eye contact.

Sam checked her phone, debating if she should send a message to Lauren to ensure she arrived home safely. To ask if she believed her, or if she truly didn't want to see her again. Her phone was dead, the battery having run out sometime in the last few hours. To Sam, this was a sign of a cosmic favor, saving her from potentially making things worse between herself and Lauren.

The rhythmic beeping of the woman's heart monitor ceased, replaced with an alarm. The nurse who had been in the room previously entered, silencing the noise coming from the monitor. "I'm so sorry for your loss," they said to Margo and Sam. Margo stood, Sam following her lead as she crossed the small space to the bed.

"Thanks," Margo said.

The nurse smiled sadly, turning off the rest of the machinery beside the bed. "We'll give you a few minutes," they said. When the nurse left the room, Margo shut the door before turning to Sam.

The shimmering had already begun in Margo's hands, and Sam could feel the sensation building within herself. When she glanced at Richard, he had his arms around the spirit of the woman who had passed, both smiling widely. With his attention back on Margo and Sam, he nodded his head. "Thank you both so much for your patience. I couldn't think of leaving without Gwen." Margo positioned her hand toward the door to the room, the glittery iridescence forming, the colorful hues bouncing off the white walls. Letting the energy flow through her, Sam mirrored Margo's actions, basking in the power. The two spirits stepped forward, hand in hand toward the door the Grims created, the light shining over their faces. When they walked the few feet necessary, they disappeared, engulfed by the ethereal colors.

Sam doubled over, grasping her knees as nausea hit her and the room spun, the energy dissipating rapidly. "You're all right," Margo murmured, placing her hand on Sam's back tentatively. As the feeling subsided, Sam lifted her head just as Luis stepped into the room, asking if Sam was okay. "Yeah, you remember that feeling, don't you?" Margo asked him.

Luis chuckled, folding his arms over his chest. "Worst feeling in the world. Thanks for the help—she knew he wasn't around, and she was holding on for him," he said, referring to the spirit of the old woman.

Sam wiped her clammy palms over her jeans, shaking her head. "How do you get used to that?"

"You don't, but the feeling will die down eventually. The more you help cross over, the less it happens," Margo explained. Sam hoped she was right, but as their time at the hospital was nearing a close, she worried the meeting following their visit would eliminate her chances of ever finding out.

The three exited the room into the darkened hallway. Luis stopped and faced the two women, his expression apprehensive.

"Good luck," he said, clasping Margo on the shoulder. "I hope to see you back at the apartment later. It's your day to take out the trash." Sam was certain the flippant comment meant more, the look of concern etched across Luis's face as he turned, heading toward the nurse's station. Margo linked arms with Sam and dragged her in the opposite direction to another service stairwell.

"He's my roomie, if you didn't notice by his sarcasm," she said as they trekked down the stairs. "Now, let's go meet the shitheads who want to kill you."

Chapter Sixteen

THE RAIN CEASED, droplets of water sliding down the siding of the house as Lauren cracked open the back door to let her cat inside. Boo meowed, her little head poised upward, whiskers tickling Lauren's bare feet as she did figure eights around her ankles. Her damp feet left little wet paw prints on the linoleum floor in the kitchen and Lauren let out a ragged sigh. What the hell happened? Pouring herself a glass of wine, Lauren headed to the living room.

Bethany's unfinished business is you. What did those words even mean? Sam spoke with such conviction, such candor, Lauren had to question her own assumptions of the afterlife. What would Sam get out of lying to her? Their friendship didn't lead Lauren to believe Sam would say things simply to be cruel. She was too kind, too sensitive herself to behave in such a manner.

Lauren turned on the television and landed hard on the loveseat, causing droplets of wine to splatter her blouse. A mindless adult cartoon was playing, the colorful flashes from the screen splaying across the room. Lauren tried to lose herself in the idiocy of the show, desperate to take her thoughts off the bizarre night she'd endured. The distraction didn't last long.

How had Sam known about the evening between Bethany and Lauren with such detail? She and Bethany weren't friends and there didn't seem to be any plausible explanations behind her knowing other than...no, Bethany wasn't a ghost lingering around Sam. Lauren shook the notion from her head and downed the rest of her wine. Placing the empty glass on the coffee table, Lauren closed her eyes resigned to ponder the uncanny happenings in her life. Even in the off chance that Jackie told Sam of the night in Cape May, how would she have known about the necklace? As stupid as the little accessory was, no one other than herself and Bethany would recall such a mundane item in the grand scheme of that night. Sleep was rapidly ascending upon her anyway, her thoughts jumbled, sporadic and untethered.

"Lauren," a voice called into the room. Lauren's eyelids fluttered but didn't open. She was warm, comfortable, and almost asleep when the voice spoke, and she wanted nothing more than to slip into a dreamless slumber.

"Hm?" Lauren heard herself sigh in answer. A featherlight touch caressed her cheek, and she smiled as she recognized the delicate fingers.

"I always loved watching you sleep, though that sounds really creepy out loud."

Lauren knew the voice as well as the humor. "That is creepy."

"You can hear me?" the voice chuckled in disbelief.

"Yeah, I can, and what are you doing here, Bethany? You're dead," Lauren murmured. She couldn't possibly be speaking to her dead ex-girlfriend. Bethany's brother told her she'd been cremated shortly after the car accident. She was gone.

A cold breeze brushed past her face as the sound of laughter filled her ears. "You've got a point there. I shouldn't be here, but I couldn't leave without telling you how sorry I am."

Lauren couldn't open her eyes and couldn't move her body. The term sleep paralysis was in the forefront of her foggy mind as she recalled reading an article on the subject years prior. "Why are you sorry?"

Another chill fluttered the fine strands at her hairline as Bethany sighed. "I hurt you and I didn't mean to. I didn't know what the hell I was doing... I was scared, and we both paid the price for my shitty decision."

"Why did you cheat on me? I loved you, Bethany."

A cool caress touched her face. "I'm sorry for walking away from you. I do love you, and I should've told you then, but I was so damn scared of what admitting my feelings meant. I was terrified of potentially opening myself to getting hurt, to the possibility of you leaving me. I screwed us up on purpose, Lauren, and I'm so sorry for hurting you."

"I forgive you," Lauren said without preamble. She'd forgiven Bethany a few short weeks after she'd been unfaithful when she realized there was never a point in keeping a grudge. "You don't need to stick around here—you've got bigger, better places to be, don't you?" she asked.

"I really don't know what comes after this. I have an idea of what it might be like, but I won't know until I'm ready to go." Bethany's tone was quiet and bleak.

"What do you think will happen?" A pang of guilt filled Lauren at her dreary outlook on the afterlife, or lack thereof. To Lauren, consciousness was akin to a flickering candle. When the wick ran out, there was no longer a light. They'd had the debate a handful of times during their relationship, as Bethany was raised with strong beliefs. Bethany said nothing for a few moments, leading Lauren to believe perhaps her dream had passed or switched to something different. She took a long breath and settled under the blanket.

"Do you love her, Lauren?"

"Who?"

Bethany cleared her throat, her voice sounding farther away when she spoke again. "Samantha."

The image materialized in Lauren's mind, Sam's lips curled in a crooked smile, the rich sound of her laughter lifting in the air. The swell of emotion associated with her searching hazel gaze. "I think I could easily fall in love with her and that scares me," Lauren whispered.

Fingers threaded through Lauren's hair and she shivered. "Don't let fear hold you back. She's a good person," Bethany said.

"She is." Lauren ineffectively tried to open her eyes again, to catch a glimpse of Bethany but failed again. "Is she really trying to help you move on?"

Bethany chuckled warmly again. "It's ironic, isn't it? I was such a horrible person to her in high school, and she was always so nice, so sure of herself. Now, she's responsible for bringing me closure. The least I can do is make sure you believe her and give her a rightful chance. She isn't lying to you."

"But this isn't possible," Lauren murmured as she tried again to stir her body and failed a second time, her limbs leaden.

"Lauren, there isn't always a definitive way to explain things. You believe in quantum mechanics and there's not one way to fully understand that. We can't explain why things happen—they just do."

"Like you dying." Lauren sighed woefully. "Oh, Bethany, I'm so sorry you're gone. It's not fair you died so young." Another chilling graze across her face.

"Don't be sad for me. Like you said, I've got bigger, better things ahead of me. Maybe we'll meet again when I come back. For now, don't shut Sam out. She cares about you more than you know."

"She does?" Lauren whispered. Her own feelings for Sam were stronger than she could've imagined in the short span of their relationship. Why did she tell Sam she never wanted to see her again?

"Yes," Bethany said, her voice close, a frigid gust fluttering the hair by Lauren's ear. "I have to go now."

A boisterous commercial blared from the television, causing Lauren to jolt awake, her heart racing as her head whipped around. Her living room was empty and cloaked in darkness, the only light coming from the screen, flashing over the room in an eerie display of blues and whites. "Bethany?" Lauren whispered, heart thudding in her chest. There was no reply.

THE CITY SKYLINE was visible outside of the tall floor-to-ceiling windows facing the water that stretched out for miles. Sam rubbed her palms on the knees of her jeans in a poor attempt to assuage the nervousness threatening to send her into a full-blown panic. The sky was lightening on the horizon, and the faint call of a flock of seagulls was audible through the thick glass. Her fear began on their drive over to Atlantic City, where the closest corporate office was located, cresting when they walked through the lobby doors and were escorted to a large conference room. Perspiration prickled at the nape of her neck and her foot bounced off the floor repeatedly, her loose laces hitting the hard marble with a soft ticking each time. Margo tapped her fingers impatiently on the table, the thump of each strike on the wooden surface resounding in the otherwise empty room.

Letting out a shaky breath, Sam ran her trembling fingers through her hair. Since her phone's battery had died while they were at the hospital, she was left without the option to busy herself with mindless games until the meeting began. Margo nudged her arm. "Be cool, dude," she whispered. "We'll sail through this, and everything will be fine." Sam couldn't place when Margo had gone from dismal pessimist to Pollyanna in the last few hours, but the switch was disconcerting. Sam blamed Margo's behavioral shift on the lack of sleep and dawn's approach.

Finally, the tall oak doors opened, and a trio of sharply dressed individuals entered the room. The arrival of the board of directors did nothing to hinder Sam's anxiety. Two women flanked either side of a tall man as they all took their seats at the far end of the long table. One of the women appeared to be the oldest among the board members, her white hair in a tight bun at the back of her head, face weathered and blue eyes watery.

To Sam's horror, Margo lit a cigarette and a tuft of smoke rose to the ceiling. The first to speak was the tall man, his black hair combed back and his dark eyes beady, voice heavily accented as he began without any perfunctory introductions. "Margot Petrov, this meeting is due to a recent discovery regarding your initiation of an apprentice during a routine quality assurance survey. It has come to our attention you were not fulfilling your requirements as a member of the Grim and may require disciplinary action. Is this the apprentice in question?"

"Okay, for starters, the T is silent, dumbass. Second, yes, and she has a name." The man reacted as if Margo had spit on his five-thousand-dollar shoes and she might as well have. Sam sank into the chair, wishing she could vanish into the floor as Margo took a long drag off her cigarette and blew the smoke toward the three board members. "Sam here makes a fine assistant, and she's doing a damn good job, so give her some credit."

"Be that as it may, your inability to assist in the appropriate passing of recently deceased spirits does not warrant the creation of an apprentice," the older woman said. Her face remained rigid as she spoke, the deep wrinkles resting in the corners of her eyes unmoving. If Sam hadn't been close enough to see her lips move, she wouldn't have known she was the one who'd spoken.

"Bullshit. You guys dump on an extra load, because you can't find a replacement for Roz, and then you rag on me for finding a helper?" Margo growled. Ash littered the glossy surface of the table as she leaned on her elbows, her face contemptuous.

"Your crude language is unnecessary, Ms. Petrov. The problem you've presented us isn't one to take lightly. Although I believe each individual should be given a fair chance to plead their case for inclusion, my colleagues voiced their dissent," Alfonso said.

"The resolution I offer is complete exclusion, which in my understanding, is a definitive route to remove any issues before they can arise. There is no alternative to reverse the effects of the blood bond," the younger woman said assertively.

Sam feared by the time the decision was made, the inside of her lip would be raw. At that point, she knew it would be the least of her worries.

"I disagree, Sybil. The condition is not reversible; however, in time, we may learn from the situation. Think of this as an opportunity to collect a wealth of knowledge and perhaps a chance to eliminate some ambiguity surrounding Cur," Alfonso countered.

The woman in the middle, Cynthia, crinkled her nose. "Absolutely not. I fear the possible scientific properties presenting themselves to you aren't worth the risk. What befalls the corporation if a mistake is made?" Her pen tapped the table as she waited for a reply.

Sam's fate teetered before her, in the form of bickering corporate bigheads. Sweat prickled the skin of her back and settled between her shoulder blades. A warm hand gripped Sam's beneath the table, offering her a tight squeeze. She knew the gesture portrayed Margo's support, but her trepidation didn't abate.

"Cynthia, are you honestly denying the potential behind this?" Alfonso's brows disappeared beneath his dark bangs. The three board members began to bicker viciously, the superfluous words pouring from each of them dripping with venom.

Sam tasted blood in her mouth, her teeth puncturing her lip.

"He does propose a valid point," the one named Sybil voiced as her resolve seemed to diminish. "The issue—"

"Would you please stop referring to Sam as the issue or the problem?" Margo shouted, stumping her second cigarette out on the table in front of her.

Cynthia scoffed, her thin lips curling in disgust. "To continue with this absurd discussion is futile and a waste of valuable company time.

"Perhaps we should conduct our deliberation elsewhere," Sybil said.

"I agree," Alfonso said, his voice resounding over the room. He and Sybil stood simultaneously, making the decision for the trio. Margo grumbled, folding her arms over her chest as the two walked out the door.

Cynthia stared pointedly at Sam, her face full of malice as she rose. "The decision to allow a Cur to exist among the Grim is a rarity. Do not believe yourself an exception." The oldest member from the board of directors left the room last, pulling the heavy door behind herself.

The door closed with a reverberating boom, a lock clicking into place. "Did they...did they just lock us in here?" Sam panicked, shooting up so fast her chair fell to the floor with a loud clatter.

"Yeah, they did. We'll be in here until they decide to keep us or kill us, so calm your tits."

Chapter Seventeen

LAUREN LEISURELY ASCENDED the stairs to Jackie's loft, her mind still reeling from the events of the previous night. Had Bethany truly visited her while she slept? No, ghosts didn't exist. Bethany was dead. Letting herself inside, Lauren found Jackie sitting atop the oak table, legs folded beneath herself. Jackie scraped a tiny knife over the wooden block in her hands, nodding upon Lauren's entrance. "Hey." Surprisingly, no music poured from Jackie's speakers, the silence in the loft eerie.

"I've got coffee," Lauren sang, feigning her joy. She placed the coffees she purchased on the way over in front of Jackie, steam billowing from the paper cups.

"Thanks. Let me finish this commission." The gentle grating sound of Jackie's carving filled the void. Oak shards littered the table, Jackie scrunching her brows briefly in concentration. The peace exuding from Jackie as she worked, back hunched over the wood in her hands, face relaxing in serenity, made Lauren wonder how she achieved such calm, and she longed for the tranquility her friend possessed so effortlessly. Jackie transformed the chunky piece of wood into a delicate sparrow in a matter of ten minutes. "So," she finally said, dusting the shavings from the bird in her hands. "What's going on with you?"

"I went over to Sam's last night—"

"Ooh la la," Jackie interrupted, smirking.

"Jackie, she told me some weird things. The night got really strange."

"What do you mean by 'weird things?'" Jackie asked.

Where was she supposed to start? Lauren brought her coffee cup to her mouth as a diversion to give her more time to consider her explanation of Sam's bizarre rambling. Not to mention the lucid dream her outburst sparked. The tepid liquid tasted terrible and she put the cup back on the table. "She told me she's talked to Bethany."

Jackie pulled her brows together in a dramatic display. "Like when you and Bethany were dating?"

Lauren shook her head. "No, like recently." She sucked in a deep breath and rolled her eyes. "She said Bethany's ghost can't move on because she was never able to apologize to me properly." Lauren left out the part about Sam knowing detailed information she shouldn't have known.

"Interesting," Jackie said, head bent over the table, swiping the wood shavings into the palm of her hand.

"I wouldn't call it interesting, more like disturbing." The memory of Bethany's cold caress sent a shiver between her shoulder blades. "Jackie, she told me she sees ghosts, talks to them, has to help them pass on, not to mention she said she died in her surfing accident last month but was brought back by a Grim Reaper," Lauren said, laughing without humor.

Her friend was very still. "What do you think?"

Lauren snorted. "About what Sam said? I think she's crazy. God, I feel like *I'm* crazy. After I left her apartment, I had the weirdest dream about Bethany. I know it had to have been sparked by what Sam said." She paused, chewing nervously on her lip as she recalled the details of the night with Bethany. "Did you ever tell Sam about the night in Cape May?"

Jackie shook her head without lifting her gaze from the pile of wood shavings in her hand.

"She must've been friends with Bethany. Sam told me about this necklace... There's no way she could've know about it unless she talked to Bethany." Shaking her head, Lauren tried to force her uncertainty away. "The dream I had was Bethany asking for me to forgive her for cheating on me. Sam told me the crazy story, and I just know that's why my brain went there."

"Not necessarily. She could've visited you," Jackie muttered.

"Maybe I should've let you use the cards of creepy, so I could've avoided all of this. Two cheaters and then a crazy person." Lauren paused, swearing she hadn't heard Jackie correctly. "Wait, what'd you say?"

Her head rose, and she fixed her gaze on Lauren. "I know Sam can see them, and she's not crazy. Rather than it being all a dream, Bethany could've visited you."

Letting out a crude laugh, Lauren pushed back from the table, shaking her head. "Are you two in on this messed-up joke?" Although she knew Jackie believed in such things as seeing the dead, even speaking to them, she couldn't believe Sam actually helped them cross over. Surely, her best friend wouldn't be out to make her feel crazy, nor would she band together with the girl she was dating, simply to mess with her. This assumption seemed better than admitting the possibility of the situation being real, and Lauren was grasping at anything adding value to her belief.

"No, Lauren, all of this is way more complicated than that." Jackie wrung her hands on the tabletop, worry lines etching her forehead. Lauren had never seen her carefree friend so distraught before, and her own heart began to race at the possible implications.

"Tell me what's going on, please."

"This isn't how I wanted to tell you," Jackie began, dropping her eye contact with Lauren. Butters hopped onto the table, ramming his face against Jackie's as if sensing her distress. "I'm, well, not normal. I...uh."

"What?"

"Lauren, there's no easy way to explain," Jackie snapped.

"Come on, just tell me!"

"I'm basically a vampire," Jackie mumbled.

"What the *hell*?" Lauren scoffed, stomping away from Jackie and the table. She'd had enough. She turned, and ran out the front door, bounding down the stairs. The cool air pushing off the ocean was tinged with a salty mist, dampening Lauren's hair as she trotted off toward the boardwalk. The warmth of the autumn sun fell upon her back, casting a dark shadow in front of her as she continued to the stairs. There was no way this was her reality. Sam couldn't see ghosts. Jackie wasn't a monster. Vampires weren't real. Ghosts didn't wander around the world, haunting the living. Perhaps Jackie and Lauren stumbled into the same psychosis, and Lauren was the unlucky friend who endured the crazy fantasies.

"Lauren, wait!" Jackie called, running up behind her. Lauren was halfway up the stairs when she twisted, glaring at her best friend.

"If you're a vampire, how are you not burning up into flames in the sun?" she sneered. She instantly regretted her venom when she noted the dejected frown upon Jackie's face. "I'm sorry. This is crazy. How do you expect me to believe what you're trying to tell me?"

"I said *basically* a vampire because I'm an Empusa, however, the two aren't synonymous. I know there's a lot to take in right now, but you need to give me the chance to explain. You've known me for six years. Sure, we fuck with each other, but would I lie or tease you on this scale?" Jackie approached slowly, reaching the same step as Lauren, her face full of concern.

Lauren knew she wouldn't. She also knew she was behaving like a child. "I'm sorry. I don't know how to process any of this."

Jackie gestured to the bench a few feet from where they stood, and they climbed the rest of the stairs before sitting. Lauren stared at the ground where tiny black ants threaded over the uneven terrain of the boardwalk, disappearing in the gap between the wooden planks.

Jackie cleared her throat, and Lauren peered up at her. "Okay, let me try to explain this without slaughtering your understanding to hell and back." Jackie took a deep breath and pinched the bridge of her nose. "Think of this like an autoimmune disorder. The hemoglobin in my blood sucks so, if I want to keep living, I have to drink blood to keep up what my body destroys on its own. I don't have to drink blood all the time but frequently enough to become an issue."

Lauren blinked. Blinked again. Folded her leg under herself and leaned toward her friend, hanging onto Jackie's last words. "Wow." Her reply wasn't a very articulate response, but it was the best thing Lauren could muster. "How long have you dealt with this?"

"Forever," Jackie muttered. Lauren widened her eyes and her friend chuckled. "No, not in the immortal sense of forever but since I was born. We aren't the stereotypes portrayed, which is most times the case with any otherworldly beings, like the Grim. Sam isn't a skeleton wearing a black robe and wielding a scythe, is she?"

The mention of her name caused Lauren a wave of grief. If what Jackie spoke was true, then Lauren had to apologize to Sam and hope she could forgive her for being so uncouth. "No. Do you always have to drink blood?"

"Nah, not all the time. A friend of mine is an ethnobotanist; he gives me an elixir that helps me cope so I don't have to all the time and it limits my need to about once or twice a month."

"Wow," Lauren repeated, shaking her head in disbelief. Jackie looked the same; her smile warm but cautious. Nothing changed about her with the new revelation. "Why didn't you tell me before?" At first, her feelings were hurt but the more she allowed herself to accept, the more she realized she wouldn't have believed her if Sam hadn't divulged her new identity beforehand.

"Because," Jackie sighed, leaning forward, elbows on her knees. "You would've told me to get the hell away from you." Would Lauren have shooed her best friend away at such a reveal? She'd like to think she wouldn't have.

"I'm sorry, Jackie. I'm sorry I've been such a jerk about your beliefs." Her thoughts went to the deck of tarot cards, to Jackie's assortment of crystals and the deities she swore by, her holidays surrounding the seasons. Although Jackie played along with Lauren's playful jesting around the subject, Lauren felt awful for behaving so childishly.

Jackie shrugged, straightening as she met Lauren's gaze. "I want you to know Sam's telling you the truth."

"So, Sam really died during her surfing accident?" Lauren whispered, a lump forming in her throat at the thought of Sam's demise. Sam wasn't dead, though. Lauren saw her the night before, touched her, kissed her.

"Yeah." Jackie glanced up at the autumn sky. "She really did die and a mediocre Grim brought her back, accidentally turning her into one of them during a blood bond—the blood bond that saved Sam's life. Margo and I have had our differences, but I can't say I'm mad she did what she did. If she hadn't, Sam wouldn't be here."

Lauren brought her hands to her face, shaking her head. "I can't believe this. Did the blood bond...did it change her?"

"Well, yeah. She's a Grim now but it doesn't change who she is." This made sense to Lauren as Sam didn't seem different. She was the same kind, compassionate person she knew before the accident.

"I can't believe I was so mean to her. God, Jackie, I told her she was crazy, and I never wanted to see her again. What do I do?"

"Sorry is always a good starting point."

TRYING TO GET ahold of Sam proved futile as her phone continued to go straight to voicemail. Jackie suggested they check out her apartment. The door was unlocked, striking fear within Lauren as the two women walked into the quiet space. After checking every room and determining Sam was not present in the apartment, Lauren dragged Jackie to another neighborhood a few blocks over. If Sam wasn't at her own apartment, perhaps she was with her sister.

She took the stairs two at a time, the old wood creaking with each stride, until she stood in front of the door. Taking a deep breath, she knocked softly, absently hoping Sam's sister, Katie, didn't think she was crazy for coming to her home in search of Sam. Katie answered on the third knock, her voice loud as she said, "When do you ever knock, Sam? You usually waltz right into this place like you…" Katie paused, blinking rapidly as she turned to Lauren. "Hi, there. I thought you were Sam. Lauren, right?"

Lauren nodded. "Yes. I'm sorry to bug you but I'm actually looking for Sam. Have you seen her today?"

Katie rested her hand on the doorframe as she shook her head. "No, she was supposed to be here for lunch today but was a no-show and isn't answering my calls. I figured she's probably sleeping the day away, maybe had a few too many drinks with Josh at the bar," Katie laughed.

For a moment, Lauren contemplated whether to tell Katie she'd already been to Sam's and she wasn't there. Oh, how Lauren wished she were. How could she think normally when things were anything but? *Katie doesn't even know. No one can know, but I trust you, Lauren.* The words echoed in Lauren's head, forcing her to be mindful of Sam's trust. Her sister didn't know what she was, nor did Lauren want to tell her. There wasn't a way for Lauren to explain the situation without potentially exposing Sam's secret—a secret that seemed far too important to be thrown around.

"Maybe I'll pop in and be her wake-up call," Lauren said with faux humor. A small voice shouted from deep in the condo and Katie turned.

"No, honey, it isn't Auntie Sam." She faced Lauren again with a warm smile. "If you do, let her know she missed our lunch date and her nephew is grumbling."

"I sure will," Lauren chuckled.

As she began to descend the stairs, Katie called out her name. "In case she hasn't told you already because I know she can be a little bashful, she really enjoys your company." Lauren grinned and with a slight wave, continued to the sidewalk.

When she reached the car, Jackie stared at her expectantly from the passenger seat. "So?"

Sighing, Lauren started the car. "She's not here either. Her sister said she was supposed to come for lunch but was a no-show, and her calls are going straight to voicemail too."

"Shit."

"What?" Lauren asked. Jackie wasn't staring at her anymore; her face was poised over her phone, typing away on her screen. She looked up at Lauren.

"We may have a problem. You know the friend I was telling you about?"

Lauren nodded.

"He knows where Sam is and she's in trouble."

Chapter Eighteen

THE INCESSANT TICKING of the clock filled the room, and the heating unit rumbled to life above their heads. Sam paced the conference room, pausing as Margo climbed onto the long table in the middle of the room. "What? I'm going to take a nap while these assholes figure out what they want to do. It's been what, two hours already?" Without waiting for an answer from Sam, Margo settled back, folding her arms under her head and kicking her feet out to lay flat. Sam pulled her phone from her pocket and cursed when she remembered the battery had died at the hospital hours before.

She peered up at the annoying clock. Only two hours had passed since the board members unceremoniously locked them in the conference room, the ominous warning from Cynthia at the forefront of Sam's mind. There didn't seem to be a chance in hell they'd allow her to live, let alone continue reaping souls alongside Margo. She was frustrated with the turn of events. Sam kicked the door. Kicked it again. Rattled the doorknob. Kicked a third time. "Would you stop already?" Margo snapped from her position on the table.

Sam threw her a sidelong glance and started to brood. Her behavior was verging on childish, but Sam didn't give a shit. The four walls surrounding them were closing in, with the prospect of spending the last few hours of her second shot at life stuck in that room, and the woman she loved at home thinking she was batshit crazy. Maybe she was. Maybe the events leading to this moment were a vivid and long-lasting hallucination. "Fuck," Sam muttered, slapping the wall.

Margo lifted her head, glaring at Sam. "Pacing around and wallowing in your own self-pity will get us nowhere. They shouldn't take much longer to make the decision. Hell, maybe they'll surprise us and let you live." Again, with the cynicism.

"I'm pretty sure they made their decision clear before they locked us in here. What they're doing is a goddamn formality," Sam said. She met Margo with a steady gaze. "The question is, will they let you walk away from this?"

Margo swallowed and dropped her head. "I don't know. It wouldn't be fair if they killed you and let me off the hook. You didn't ask for this."

Sam shook her head as she pushed off the wall and moved to the corner, sliding to the floor. She was right; Sam hadn't asked for this. Lauren lost Bethany two separate times in two different ways. Now, she was going to lose Sam because she believed she was crazy. Poor Lauren would be left with two dead exes in the span of two fucking weeks. Things wouldn't have progressed to the level they were at if Sam hadn't agreed to Margo's deal.

Katie wouldn't have any idea where Sam had gone, no closure, possibly spending the rest of her life trying to find Sam, without a clue she was killed by supernatural forces. All of this could've been avoided if Margo hadn't saved Sam. "Maybe you should've let me die the first time," Sam muttered, folding her arms around herself as she sank into the corner of the room in lieu of taking a chair.

"Don't you dare get all grim and mopey on me. You know damn well I would do it all over again even if they decide to can my ass. You're not allowed to have an existential crisis until they snuff you out," Margo growled, sitting up. If they canned her ass, Sam knew it meant they'd remove her the same way they intended to remove Sam.

"Lauren was cheated on, hooked up with me, her ex-girlfriend died, she figures I'm nuts because I told her about you, and now I'm going to die. You saved my life for it to be ended again. What kind of shit is this, Margo? Is this fate?" Sam questioned as she stood from her spot on the floor, irritated she couldn't articulate her words. Emotions flooded her conscious thought. "Was I supposed to die, and you messed with my destiny by bringing me back?"

Silence expanded through the room, the only sound reaching Sam's ears the humming of the ventilation system above their heads. Letting out a frustrated sigh, she wiped her face free of the tears that had the audacity to trickle down her cheeks. Margo's gaze was downcast as she hunched over the table, her fingers fumbling with the laces of her boots.

"Why did the chicken cross the road?" Margo asked.

Sam sighed obnoxiously. "Seriously, Margo?" Margo smirked, lifting her head as she waggled her brows at her. "Fine, why did the chicken cross the road?"

"To see if it came before the egg. Did I mess with fate by saving you, or was I supposed to save you from dying?" The analogy was fitting, although an odd question. Was there a possibility Margo was destined to save Sam from her watery death rather than having disrupted destiny doing such an act? "I've got to get something off my chest, Sam," Margo said gravely.

"Okay," Sam said.

"I never needed an assistant."

"What?"

Margo dangled her legs over the side of the table and looked up. "The day you drowned, I was in the middle of helping a spirit move on. Her family spread her ashes on the beach, which I thought was illegal in New Jersey, but whatever. I saw you struggling in the water, heard your friend screaming. Just when he was ready to jump into the water to save your ass, the ambulance arrived, and a couple lifeguards helped wrangle you out and started working on you right there. I saw you, your spirit. You were still there, still with your body but dead. They wouldn't have been able to bring you back."

Sam swallowed the lump in her throat as she listened to Margo's recollection, recalling the very same image of herself lying in the sand, dead.

"I see death every day. When I saw you with a tiny glimmer of life in you, I couldn't stand by and be idle. I knew exactly what I was doing when I saved you. Was saving you with a blood bond wrong? Fuck yeah, but I couldn't let you slip away when there was a chance I could save you. I watch good people die every single day. I thought if I could save just one, maybe this existence of mine wouldn't be so bad." Margo shifted off the end of the table, hopping down to kneel beside Sam.

"How'd you know I was a good person? I could've been a sociopath or a serial killer," Sam said, sniffling.

Margo whacked her arm. "I'm a good judge of character, and I don't make mistakes."

"I want to argue with you, but I don't have enough energy," Sam chuckled. Margo smiled warmly at her as she squeezed her shoulder. Without another word, Margo rose and climbed back onto the table, her legs dangling over the side once again as she lit a cigarette. She blew the smoke upward, her gaze following the tendrils of smoke. Sam sighed, yanking her hood over her head and closing her eyes, hoping for a dreamless rest.

SAM WAS JARRED awake by the large door opening abruptly. Sitting up, she tried to rub the sleep from her eyes as the members of the board filed into the room, taking the same seats they had their previous visit. Margo had moved from her perch on the table to a chair, ash falling from the cigarette between her fingers.

"We apologize for the wait," Alfonso said with a slight bow of his head. Cynthia scowled, pursing her lips as if in protest of his apology.

"During our careful deliberation, we've considered this an opportunity to pivot from our original direction," Sybil added.

"English, please," Margo blurted.

"We've decided to offer Ms. Diaz a position among the Grim, beginning with a sixty-day probationary period that will be conducted by another member other than yourself. An individual whom we consider to be reliable and seasoned," Sybil announced.

Sam gasped, and Margo grabbed her arm. "What happens to Margo?" Sam inquired, elated she wasn't going to die.

"She'll be closely monitored for the same length of time, and we will reconvene at a later date if another problem arises," Cynthia said with malice.

"What does this mean?" Margo asked, stubbing her cigarette on the table.

"You two are free to go. Ms. Diaz, if you would be so kind as to pick up your welcome packet on the way out at the main lobby, it would be much appreciated. The date, time, and location you are due with your mentor will be within this packet, as well as your stipend amount," Alfonso said.

Sam laughed, unable to contain her jubilation and the ludicrousness of picking up a welcome packet. "Okay, sure, I will."

Alfonso nodded as he stood. "This concludes our meeting. Have a wonderful day, ladies."

"SHIT, MY PHONE'S dead," Margo grumbled as they climbed into her car after leaving the bizarre closure of their meeting.

Sam thumbed through the large folder she picked up from the receptionist on the way out the front door, flabbergasted at the similarities to when she began at the post office. The pages the folder contained were formal, bland, and full of regulations. An employee handbook was also included in the packet, and Sam chuckled as she flipped through it. "This is rich," she laughed, turning the dress code page over to Margo. Her companion wasn't amused. "Do you get a stipend?" Margo nodded, brows furrowed as she pulled out onto the highway. Sam always wondered how Margo afforded her vehicle as well as her smoking habit without a day job.

"I can't believe they didn't kill us," Margo said in astonishment.

"I can't believe they run this like you're working for Walmart or something." She finally found the page with the information about her new mentor, however, she was surprised to recognize the name. "Brent? Brent is my mentor?"

"Big surprise. He's their golden boy, but they have no idea he moonlights as an ethnobotanist, selling potions and shit to anyone who's willing to pay." A thought dawned on Sam—Brent was the one who supplied Jackie with her elixir, which made sense to her. He didn't seem like a bad guy, but Margo obviously held animosity toward him.

"So, where are we going?" Sam asked as they drove south.

"To your apartment. I don't have any beer at my place, and I need one after that shit show."

The rest of the drive back to Sam's apartment was silent and the quiet didn't bother Sam. What in the fuck even happened? She wanted to talk to Margo more about the situation but couldn't bring herself, either because her mind was too weary from the cluster fuck of the last twenty-four hours or because she knew Margo likely didn't have an answer. Margo pulled her car up to the curb in front of Sam's place and, without a word to each other, they got out of the car and climbed up the stairs. Her door was unlocked, as it had been the night she took off in the rain after Lauren left. *Lauren.* Sam's chest hurt when she thought of her. Would she ever speak to Sam again?

What she would do to be able to have that woman in her arms again. She gasped when she opened the door to find Lauren and Jackie sitting in her small living room. "Sam! Oh my God, Sam," Lauren yelled as she hurried toward her, slamming her body into Sam's. Lauren wrapped her arms around her in a crushing hug, and Sam let out a chuckle, the sound coming out more like a wretched cry than laughter.

"What are you doing here?" Sam managed, breathing in the scent of Lauren's hair, cherishing her closeness.

"I thought I was going to lose you. Jackie told me everything, about the Grim, Margo turning you into one. I'm so sorry I didn't believe you," Lauren rambled. The rest of her words were muffled as she put her head to Sam's chest, tears dampening the material of her hoodie.

"How'd you know about the meeting?" Margo asked Jackie.

"Brent," Jackie answered, rising from the couch. "Why don't I make some tea? Come on, Margo." Much to Sam's surprise, Margo followed her, leaving her and Lauren alone in the living room.

"Let's sit," Sam offered. The two found their way to the couch, Lauren gripping tight to Sam's hand.

Drawing a deep breath, Lauren met Sam's gaze as they sat. "I am so sorry I called you crazy, and I told you I never wanted to see you again."

Sam smiled, bringing Lauren's hand to her lips, kissing her knuckles. She never thought she'd see this woman again, whether due to the Grim killing her or due to Lauren wanting nothing to do with her. "You don't have to apologize. This is all crazy and I don't know if I believe everything all the time."

"I went to Jackie's house this morning to tell her what happened because I wanted to believe you, truly, I did. She told me about herself, and I was such a jerk at first. Eventually, I let myself accept the unexplainable."

"I'm glad you did," Sam whispered.

"I tried to call you, I came here and then I went to your sister's place. She told me she hadn't heard from you and you were supposed to have lunch with her today. I didn't tell her anything but when I got back in the car, Jackie told me you were in trouble."

"I was. I still don't know how Margo and I got out of there unscathed."

"I pulled some favors," Jackie said from the doorway to the kitchen, holding two mugs. Margo was beside her with two more, and they joined the other women in the living room.

"What kind of favors?" Sam asked, confused.

Jackie shook her head, placing two steaming cups on the coffee table in front of Sam and Lauren. "Doesn't matter. You're being given a real chance here Sam, so don't mess it up. Brent is a good guy and knows what he's doing."

"How'd you know..." Sam trailed off when Margo gave her a pointed stare. Ah, Brent pulled some favors. Now Sam understood. "Thank you," she said to Jackie.

"No problem," Jackie said.

Lauren lifted her head, the steam from her mug of tea wafting over her face when her gaze met Sam's. "Are you sure you're okay with all of this?" Sam asked her.

"I found out my best friend of six years has to drink human blood to survive, my current girlfriend is a Grim Reaper who is trying to help my dead ex-girlfriend move on, plus the added weight of the leaders of the Grim wanting to kill my girlfriend because of how she became what she is." Sam laughed at Lauren's seriousness. "Despite all of that, I still want to be friends with Jackie. I still want to be with you," Lauren said. Sam kissed her softly, the warmth of her lips spreading to Sam's core. Margo clicked her tongue.

"Yuck, you guys are disgustingly cute. I need to get the hell out of here," she said.

"Can I hitch a ride home with you?" Jackie asked as they both stood. Sam grinned at them, pulling away from Lauren. "We have stuff to talk about, remember?"

Rolling her eyes, Margo nodded. "Whatever. Catch you later, kid," she said to Sam. Turning, the two women headed to the door, Margo shrugging into her jacket.

"Margo," Sam called and the Grim threw her a glance. "Thanks for everything." Shooting her a thumbs-up, Margo shook her head and walked out the front door. Jackie trailed her, closing the door behind them. No thank you would suffice in expressing Sam's gratitude for Margo's selfless act. Undoubtedly, she risked her life to save Sam's, regardless of how she tried to tell the tale.

THE CLOCK READ shortly after three in the morning when Sam's blurry gaze took in the red numbers. Throat parched, Sam disentangled herself from Lauren. Her heart ached as she gingerly climbed out of bed, Lauren's prone form beneath the tousled blankets, cheeks holding a tinge from the hot shower she'd taken before they had gone to bed. Her love for Lauren was undeniable and Sam sighed, taking a moment to appreciate the sight before her. She'd come close to dying a second time, and all she could think about was Lauren.

Sam wandered to the kitchen, her bare feet thumping on the tile floor. Turning the light on, she gasped, taking a step back as she noticed the figure standing in her kitchen.

"Holy shit, don't do that to me," Sam hissed. Bethany chuckled, leaning against the counter, her jacket hung over her arm.

"You scare far too easily," she mused. She seemed different somehow, lighter perhaps. "I'm glad to see you're not dead."

"Thanks?" Sam couldn't discern if Bethany's statement was candid or made in jest.

"I was worried for a minute there," Bethany said.

"Yeah, me too." Sam snatched a glass from the cabinet and filled it from the tap, sipping the water as she waited for Bethany to speak again.

Sighing loudly, Bethany folded her arms over her chest. "I think I'm ready."

"You are?"

Bethany nodded. "I don't have anything to worry about, nothing tying me to this place anymore. I just want to move on."

"You're sure? What about Lauren?"

"I guess you could say we talked things through in the only way we could, and she forgave me," Bethany explained.

A flickering sensation poured through Sam, scorching a path to her arm. Light shimmered between her fingers, the energy wavering as she lifted her hands in the air. A melancholy smile graced Bethany's lips as she stepped toward the dancing display of color as the portal formed. "Take care of her, Sam. Love her like I couldn't." Her gaze was far off, poised at the door beginning to open.

"I will," Sam whispered, tears stinging her eyes.

Bethany turned, shooting Sam one last glance. "I know." Taking a step forward, Bethany dissipated, the fuzzy image of her gleaming as the door shuddered closed. Sam wiped her face, sniffling softly as she turned away from the empty space of her living room. Her stomach clenched, and she stood frozen, holding herself up with her palms on the walls of the hallway as she heaved. Sweat trailed down her back, dampening her T-shirt, causing the fabric to stick to her skin. The walls wobbled, her head pounding. With a shaky breath, Sam straightened, thankful the unpleasant sensation lasted far less than the last time. Maybe Margo was right; maybe each time would get easier.

"Are you okay?" a voice whispered from behind her. Sam whipped around to find Lauren approaching her.

"Yeah, I'm okay." Sam stepped over to the kitchen, grabbing her water from the counter and taking a heaping sip. Swallowing, Sam decided to tell Lauren the truth. "Bethany moved on."

Lauren bit her lower lip and closed the distance between them. "She did?"

"She did just a few minutes ago."

Touching the countertop, Lauren leaned in, placing her head against Sam's chest. Sam put the glass on the counter and pulled Lauren into a tight hug. "I'm glad," Lauren whispered. "She didn't need to stick around here anymore." She moved back, her gaze meeting Sam's. "Where did she go?"

"I don't know for sure. All I know is, just like life, death is a journey and eventually, she'll be reincarnated."

The sheets were warm as they clambered back into the bed, Lauren immediately shimmying up to Sam. Sam took her into her arms, kissing her head. Perhaps Sam would know more once she began with Brent, hoping he would shed more light on the afterlife than Margo did. Margo was responsible in aiding her to dodge death the first time, but Brent was clearly the one who helped her cheat it a second time. Soft snores came from Lauren, and Sam chuckled as she thought about the last two months. She'd gone from surfing mail carrier to Grim Reaper in the matter of a few weeks.

Eyes awash with fresh tears, Sam tightened her hold of the woman in her arms, dumbfounded by the events preceding to this moment. "Oh, my god, I love you," Sam whispered into Lauren's hair. Lauren stretched with a loud yawn, clutching Sam, her eyes still closed.

Burying her face against Sam's chest as she let out a hefty sigh, Lauren murmured in a voice rasped with sleep, "I love you more."

Acknowledgements

Firstly, I'd like to thank my awesome editor, BJ, for loving my characters as much as I do and for giving this book a chance. You rock! A huge thank you to my close friend, Eddie, who has been my sounding board for *Tales from the Grim* and has helped tremendously to bring my characters to life.

To my amazing and supportive spouse, Leslie, for supplying me with so much caffeine, we've practically taken out stock in Costco coffee, and for keeping the littles at bay while I write, and ensuring there isn't any peanut butter smeared on the keyboard. Thank you to Dave for letting me complain about falling into plot holes, and to Jane and Alex, for reading early versions, and offering me irreplaceable advice.

About the Author

Jodi Hutchins is a healthcare professional by day and fanatical writer by night. They are also an avid reader, coffee connoisseur, helpless romantic, amateur artist, enthusiastic maker-upper of things, spouse, and parent. The frequent rain of western Washington doesn't stop Jodi and their wife from gallivanting through the next trailhead with their two children.

Email: itsatimemachinething@gmail.com

Twitter:@HutchinsJodi

Other books by this author

Yule Love Her

Also Available from NineStar Press

Connect with NineStar Press

www.ninestarpress.com

www.facebook.com/ninestarpress

www.facebook.com/groups/NineStarNiche

www.twitter.com/ninestarpress

www.tumblr.com/blog/ninestarpress